PRIMAL RITES

The girl Tina watched as Ruben made love to Ingrid. He was amazed to find that his climax was swift and complete. But, as the door softly closed and Ingrid disengaged herself to lie beside him, and as Martin Ruben rose on tottering legs to go to the bathroom, he heard the sound again.

It was the sound of someone in pain. He was sure he was imagining it.

But then came a primal scream that ripped through his brain—that he couldn't have imagined. It was the sound of a woman screaming in tortured agony, animal-like, desperate.

For the first time he was afraid. Who was Tina and why had she watched them? Ingrid knew the girl had been there. But did Ingrid hear the scream?

It was a bizarre nightmare and he was afraid. What in God's name was going on here?

Also by J. N. Williamson:

THE TULPA (LB 799)
THE HOUNGAN (LB 744)
THE RITUAL (LB 673)

We will send you a free catalog on request. Any titles not in your local book store can be purchased by mail. Send the price of the book plus 50¢ shipping charge to Leisure Books, P.O. Box 270, Norwalk, Connecticut 06852.

Titles currently in print are available for industrial and sales promotion at reduced rates. Address inquiries to Nordon Publications, Inc., Two Park Avenue, New York, New York 10016, Attention: Premium Sales Department.

PREMONITION

J. N. Williamson

LEISURE BOOKS ❧ NEW YORK CITY

This book is for my wife, **Mary,** *and my literary agent and friend,* **Ray Puechner.** *It doesn't take ESP to know that they're the absolute tops.*

A LEISURE BOOK

Published by

Nordon Publications, Inc.
Two Park Avenue
New York, N.Y. 10016

Copyright © 1981 by J.N. Williamson

All rights reserved
Printed in the United States

Prologue

The naked, old white man sitting expressionlessly in the corner of his room was both completely bare and indescribably old. He seemed propped there and left, idly, the way someone might lean a dilapidated umbrella against the wall, forgotten until one just had to use it again. His corded sinews and veins, products of a long life spent in ceaseless labor, appeared to be the ribs of the umbrella, his nearly emaciated body the shaft. Strangely, the features of nudity and great age—generally unacceptable in many regions of modern life—combined to give him a certain aura of the commonplace. At a glance, Sorib the Elder gave the impression of an oversized and harmless infant to whom some thoughtless fool had attached a flowing, false white beard.

But for the ambitious people who had brought him here to Nommos Island, with a contractual pledge that knowledge gained would be shared, Sorib was anything except commonplace. To them he was a delicacy for the scientific connoisseur, a *pâté de fois gras*, which one placed beneath a microscope. In his aged genes or perhaps his traditional memories, they felt, resided secrets to prolonged life for which countless millions of men and women might kill. Happily for old Sorib, it wouldn't be necessary for them to murder him. The Director asserted it would be possible to extract his precious secrets while yet he breathed.

It was that feat—breathing—which made him valuable to them. They did not care that he was considered a man of honor in Georgia, an ambulatory filing cabinet of the village moral values and traditions, nor even that his fellows handpicked him for this extraordinary removal from his homeland. It was only that Sorib went right on breathing at an age reliably reported to be in excess of 120 years. That fact kept him alive.

So far.

It wouldn't be precisely accurate to say that Sorib was lonely for two reasons: first, he had never experienced such an emotion before, and his people had no word or symbol for it; second, Sorib was a man of honor and he had come here voluntarily when Drakovich asked him. To complain now would be unmanly. "You will be revered by your sons and brothers, a noble representative of them in all that you do," the man from Moscow had assured him as they stood on the rocky ground and the Moscovite perspired heavily. Sorib remembered thinking that the Americans could not seem stranger to him than this stolid, dark-suited official with his sleekly trimmed black hair and uncalloused palms. "They will surely build a statue for you. You shall carry their wishes in your memory anytime you feel an urge to come home. In a manner of speaking, comrade, you are taking your whole village with you!"

It seemed clear duty to Sorib, then; and duty was all that mattered. He had been surprised to learn that people elsewhere in the world did not live so long as his fellow Abkhasians, that they often died in their sixtieth year. *Kronye djet*, he'd taken women *twice* after that age! So if the foreigners might live longer just by examining his scrawny old body, it was obviously right that they have their chance!

All those charitable feelings he'd had, when he boarded the airplane-thing a few months ago, were hard to believe now. Americans were even stranger than Drakovich. It was as if he had been mesmerized by one of the bright, sparkling lights in the sky and miraculously taken there. He sighed, rolled himself forward like a ball till he was on his feet. Then he peered myopically out the window of his room, shivering, though the weather was hot.

It was all so hopelessly alien to him. The walls of this wonderful room, this window ledge, were made of some strange substance the old man had never seen. There was the new feeling of being embarrassed when strangers gaped at his naked form. He'd even volunteered to wear their clothes but they'd said, no, you must live as you do at home. Beneath Sorib's feet, the smooth wood floor felt chill, impersonal; his long, curling prehensile toes longed for dirt and its insinuated proximity to life.

Not that they mistreated him. No, not at all! He wanted to be fair about that, as about all things. While they kept him on a low-fat diet, eating very little the way he'd always had to dine, there was more to eat than he'd ever seen before. They gave him the chance to sleep in the wondrous main building but the rooms were feminine; air was somehow piped into them until one could scarcely know what *real* weather was like, outside. He smiled wryly in the forest of his tangled white beard. They even gave him little chores to do, when he insisted, so that he could keep steadily busy when they weren't prodding or listening to his shrunken carcass. But he knew the chores were only busy work, wholly unimportant to these fabulously rich foreigners.

Not a matter of loved ones literally living, or dying, the way it had been most of the time during his century of industry.

Worst of all, when Sorib peered out this odd window he saw nothing even faintly reminiscent of his beloved Georgia, that hard, demanding land which rose like a blister between the Caucasus mountain range and the depthless Black Sea. Instead of unbroken stretches of land, partly cultivated and partly sparse with little sign of life, Sorib saw mostly buildings: huge, functional structures two- and three-stories high. There were dozens of glassed-in windows through which he sometimes made out serious, studious doctors and their assistants. It was like peering into enormous eyes and seeing other beings dwelling in the skull.

It was hard for a simple man—an Abkhasian man, at any rate—to believe he was still on the same plain planet.

"Your people's chance of exceeding ninety years of age is more than *six times better* than that of our people," the bald, mean-eyed doctor told him. Sorib had come to despise that boy privately; he couldn't have been more than seventy, yet he behaved like a chieftain in every word, every motion. "There must be a scientifically verifiable fact to explain such fantastic good health. With your full cooperation, Sorib, we may discover it in you. But we shall surely find it."

Words, the old man thought now, moving slowly to the door of the island work shack and opening it. These people, *pah*, they talked constantly, used hundreds of sounds he'd never even attempted—as if life itself required a complex language! As if life were something more than arising to hard labor, doing it with a willing spirit, dining with one's family, seeing that they adhered to Abkhasian values, making love to one's woman, and sleeping. Why could these aliens not perceive that they made life too complicated, too *important*, really? It was no mystery to Sorib why the foreigners didn't live longer than they did!

Smiling faint derision, he followed the others this time, toward the great mound that lay at the center of Nommos Island. Possibly twenty or thirty adults preceded him—a small fraction of the persons who were here, he knew—and Sorib saw, with his nearsighted gaze, that many of these men and women were also from different lands than America. He grinned, amused to feel a sense of kinship with overdressed Spanish, black Africans in loincloths, an Arab with a robe that swept the earth up in little volcanic bursts. And these *children*! Sorib thought, marveling; they're *everywhere*! They, too, were not American only; he observed with ignorant astonishment a small boy with skin nearly golden in hue and eyes that squinted as if he looked too long at the sun.

Did *all* these people foreign to America live long lives like Abkhasians or were they invited here for a different reason?

They stopped walking, and Sorib stopped, staring. The mound before them looked almost like a burial grave of the kind in which his own grandfather was buried, mused Sorib. Only larger. It was more than twenty-five feet long, a dozen wide. A rope had been brought about the mound, squaring it, keeping everyone at a discreet distance. The mound was the only thing here that did not seem made recently; somehow it gave Sorib an impression of great age and, because of that, it compelled his attention. What could be the purpose behind it? Was it perhaps the grave of the Director's father? Surely it had special significance to those who were in charge of the Solomon Studies.

For a long while the aged man was part of the crowd, just beyond the rope, sensing mild camaraderie. He noticed that no one prayed, which he recalled his grandparents—who were allowed to believe in a chief spirit—doing sometimes. As a matter of fact, this crowd did not one thing. Most of them looked bored, restive; as if they had been *told* to come here, but had no clear reason for it.

Yet when the others in the crowd began to drift away, Sorib felt an odd sensation shivering through his ancient body; he remained where he stood. Vaguely curious, he scratched beneath an arm and tried to recognize his sensation. Heat, excessive heat, was part of it; but more—there was something *more*.

When the old man was starting to turn away, strangely disturbed and uneasy, he found that he could not quite do so. It was as if the mound had control over him, almost as if it desired to—to *communicate with* him. He felt bound to the spot.

Just when panic was welling up and Sorib was concluding that there was something unnaturally evil about this chunk of raised dirt, he found himself able easily to turn from it and begin moving back toward the buildings.

His mind sought its customary stressless condition once more; it felt like his own again, even though that odd heat continued moving through his body, stirring his aged blood, slowly but surely galvanizing him to action.

Sorib had no idea what action he sought until, twenty minutes later, when he saw her.

She stood in the shadows of something flat, large, and circular with funny animal-like things mounted on it. The bald doctor had told Sorib, he remembered, that this was left behind by the people who once owned Nommos; he couldn't recall what it was called except that it was for children.

And now he didn't care because he was held in the grip of a hideous, entirely foreign passion and found himself walking directly toward the girl, as if he knew precisely what he intended to say, or do. But he didn't; his mind was no longer stressless but clouded with conflicting instructions. *Wrong*, a voice said in his head; *not her*.

Before he was a dozen feet from the girl, she sensed him coming and her glance dropped down his nude form and then back up again to his face, frightened. It would have been beyond the Abkhasian's mentality and experience to understand that this young Italian woman, barely twenty years old, could see more clearly what jumbled thoughts formed in his head than Sorib himself could see. Psychic, keenly telepathic and there on Nommos because of it, the girl became the first person under the auspices of prestigious Solomon Studies to learn that the island itself contained terrible secrets. But she would never be able to tell anyone.

Sorib's aged hands were upon her with a strength he had not summoned in nearly half a century, and never against womankind. He tore the clothes from her sweet young figure and drove her to the ground, the hands pawing, cupping, prodding everywhere. A part of his mind was astonished by the desire that rose up from his engorged member, the steam-hot desire suffusing both his mind and body, clouding his knowledge. He knew that he must take this female, now—even while he sensed a terrible *misdirection*, even while something tried to reach his control center and send him elsewhere —and he took her. Rackingly. Explosively.

Never had it been this way before. Never had he lost all function of his pragmatic, flinty little brain. Never had he enjoined his work-hardened hands to express such a fury of need.

Trembling involuntarily and abruptly so cold he thought he might well freeze to death, it was like Siberia, old Sorib lifted himself from the still female body and knelt beside it in awful embarrassment. The entire lower portion of his body, his legs, was stained by semen, as if she could not contain it all. *Nyet*, he muttered into the dark, shaking his head; that was not the way to take a woman. Among Abkhasians, women had possessed the right to be asked, even possibly to decline, since Sorib only reached his father's shoulder. Now he was almost himself again and truly ashamed of what he had done.

But the part that wasn't—*quite*—himself felt much, much more—

Because Sorib the Elder remained impossibly, maddeningly frustrated even after the most violently explosive sexual release of his life. Impossibly, he *craved* sex with a lust he knew was lunatic.

When his hot eyes discovered that he had been so brutal in attempting to satisfy himself that he had broken the girl's spine—that she was, in point of terrible fact, irremediably dead, eyes staring in sightless terror— Sorib began to cry.

He remembered all the good in his 120 years, saw how he had dishonored and ruined it, leaned on his bare haunches and wailed at the careless moon. Tears washed down his caved-in cheeks, flowed into his tangled beard; but they would not, could not, purify him.

And so he stopped crying and got to his feet. That was when he realized for the first time, the message that had been striving to reach him. And for a blazing instant a new kind of passion thrilled his heart, enthralled him. The sensation was so shocking that, though he remembered it, he regained control of himself and stared imploringly at the sky.

In despair the old man tugged at the few scraggy remnants of white hair as he accepted the awful truth. And he realized, in the way that his earthbound family of man always accepted unavoidable truths, that his acts were those of a man who had gone quite mad.

He sobered, accepted it, nodded. Madness in the small Georgian community was always, for centuries, and aside from leprosy, the worst disease a man might contract. It permeated everything, everyone; it would not pass, like a woman's labor. Like leprosy itself, madness was simply unacceptable to Abkhasians.

Sorib found the long knife in the laboratory building when a technician's back was turned and then went back outside, alone in the alien night, and took a deep breath. Even wind itself seemed strange, harshly tainted with exotic hints of a civilization Sorib would never know. Worse than that, he sensed in some chambers of intelligence devised by a good man who lives many years, that he had become trapped between civilizations: one quite new, one much older even than that of his native land; one so old, so impure and pervaded by evil, that he suddenly wanted to turn to the godly chieftains of his grandfather's lost faith.

Instead, he went where he knew he must go. Once there, he arranged himself in the only way with which he might convey the agonizing secret he had learned from the ancient mound—the one that meant he was mad—and placed the point of the huge knife against his naked abdomen. "Grandfather," he said in Georgian, and plunged forward, impaling himself.

But the people who were in charge of Solomon Studies knew nothing of Abkhasian morality or tradition. After they found the dead Italian girl and then discovered Sorib, they did not understand that he was telling them with all the fervor of his ancient heart that he dearly *loved* this impossible plot of ground, that he *craved* this earthen mound like no man had ever wanted mere woman. And that he had raped and murdered an innocent human girl only because his adoration of the mound could not yet be consummated, except with death, yet that release from his impossible rutting urge had been mandatory.

All those who operated Nommos Island saw in the rising sun of a mad spring morning was an amazingly old man, spread-eagled face down atop the rising mound, his blood flowing freely and darkly into its implacable brown breast, his ancient mouth filled to overflowing with dirt from the mound.

Almost as if Sorib had parted his lips for a lover's last kiss.

PART ONE

One

It had been a theory of Ruben's for quite a while now that he would stop having these fiendish nightmares if he could acquire a working relationship with a woman. Preferably an attractive, bright, knowledgeable woman who didn't make a fetish of holding out.

Ruben's definition of a "working" relationship, despite his elevated status as the ranking psychologist on the faculty at Badler University, wasn't an iota different from any other man's. He differed only in not thinking of intercouse in crude, inelegant terms, just as he rarely thought of *anything* in such a way. That was too simplistic and, besides, applying rude labels to things one liked only reduced the pleasure one could take from them.

It wasn't that Dr. Martin Ruben, scarcely forty at this midpoint of the Seventies, lacked the requisite charm to bed an eligible damsel from time to time. He was tall, at six-two and militarily erect; outwardly athletic in a slender, quicksilver way (in point of fact, Martin hated doing any exercise at all and thought the new joggers were out of their minds); well-mannered and frequently witty. His rather dramatic profile, with the shrewd brown eyes, slender nose, somewhat sensual lips, and black hair that combed straight back, may not have been Barrymorish or even Redfordish but it was certainly Basil Rathbonish. Since reaching manhood, a day scarcely passed that someone didn't call him "Sherlock" or "Mr. Holmes," although the resemblance was actually to the late star of Baker Street cinema. Consequently, he had made an obsessive study of the Holmes tales and enjoyed quoting the Canon, as he called it, whenever he could.

Part of the reason Ruben didn't have a frequent working relationship lay in the fact that he drew the line at making it with college girls, and the women on the Badler faculty might have been doing a collective tryout for Lady Macbeth. Part of the problem was that he seldom went anywhere except Badler or to someone in need of an amateur parapsychologist, and women who were in terror over poltergeists or demonic possession seldom were romantic. And the rest of the problem involved Martin Ruben's acute observational gifts and primary preoccupation with the supernatural. Combined, they tended to be offputting for Indianapolis women.

To his credit, Ruben knew this and lived with it. How could an eligible woman fall in love with a man given to deducing everything she'd done that day? And how could a charming lady tumble into bed with a man who felt that studying spirits at a seance, or putting her into hypnotic age regression, was more fun than Monday Night Football, bar hopping, or visiting Mama?

Truth is, Ruben sometimes thought with wry philosophy, he always managed to wind up either boring women or taking command of them. He had no wish to play either Svengali or Professor Henry Higgins but he *did* want his women to know some of the things that interested him. Once they did, with women's lib well under way, they were off in pursuit of a simple businessman, assembly worker, or basketball coach—

sometimes it seemed every fifth job in Indiana was in basketball—whom *they* could dominate and mold.

A week ago, from out of the blue, it got worse. For reasons he could not fathom, Martin Ruben felt a growing need for sex, and it troubled him. Additionally, his usual neurotic tendency toward bloodcurdling nightmares made a subtle shift. Quite without consulting the proprietor of Ruben's brain, the nightmares changed tactics and began sending up warnings. Warnings that might, he realized for the first time this morning, prove to be premonitions. Prophecies of future events.

Ruben's father, who was a carpet cleaner, had the dirtiest rugs in town. Police who are suspended for gambling are always surprised to learn it was wrong. Doctors are always the last people to discover that they're ill. And Martin Ruben suddenly found that he didn't know if he believed in premonitions.

It didn't matter that he'd worked with clairvoyants, indeed with psychics of all kinds, a thousand times. Few parapsychologists in the entire Midwest had more varied experience than Ruben. But finding the rational, judgmental, observant, intellectual Martin Ruben in such a state seemed intolerable and certainly erroneous.

He sat on the edge of his bed that morning, the sheets he hadn't washed for nearly a month crumpled like used tissues at the foot, lighting his first Camel of the day. Absently, he tried to make the burnt match sit atop a week's towering collection of butts and matches growing like a latent volcano from an old Campbell's soup can. Like it or not, he was still shaking a little from the nightmare—he *wouldn't* call it a premonition, dammit, not yet!—and it stuck to his keen mind like Elmer's glue.

Ruben's anxious gaze passed across the bachelor wall, ignoring the Normal Rockwell print left there by the apartment manager, reached the table piled with terrifying statements from a dozen creditors, and nervously bounced back until it dropped down his long, naked legs to his immense bare feet. They looked like two ugly white rabbits, he thought, in mild self-disgust.

Sighing, Ruben ran a hand with slim, lengthy fingers through his dark hair and told himself firmly that it was the bills causing his nightmares. Although he hadn't been a practicing Jew in years, he'd even flirted with Christianity when he thought his family wasn't noticing, Martin had considered it his duty to take over the debts left by his dying father. All his work with the paranormal taught him there was a hereafter—several of them, in fact—and he wanted Max Ruben to enter his Hebrew paradise with clean hands.

Trouble was, the bills added up to several thousand dollars and his stipend from Badler wasn't nearly enough to clear the debts away for years. Ruben knew it was absurd but he kept thinking of lovable old Max, his father, sitting like a schmuck on one side of the wall and a bearded Moses, sternly shaking his head, safely on the other side. If only Badler would do what they kept promising and allow him to head up a parapsychology department, it would mean not only that he could spend all his time at his favorite work but the salary, too, of a department head.

Again, unsought, pictures from deep inside his head flashed past his mind's eye like silent films: People of several races dying under horrifying conditions, a plot of ground like that of a new grave, and, most important, somehow, the *woman*. Perched on the edge of his mattress, Ruben couldn't quite see her features now. He knew she was blond and beautiful—a gorgeous creature, actually. And he knew that if he ever saw her in real life, he'd know her in a moment.

Which was how childish and neurotic a bachelor could get, he told himself, getting back on his feet and reaching into his closet for a suit that was threadbare but clean. Even when he was dealing with people who had genuine intimations of the future they scarcely ever "saw" anyone except public faces, celebrities, in real life. The unknown faces lived only in their unconscious minds; possibly they were faces known in a prior life, an earlier incarnation. But they didn't belong to living people in *this* day and age, not as a rule.

For breakfast Ruben had his customary glass of iced tea, his one vice being the consumption of six ounces of Nestea a week, and a boiled egg. The latter turned out so runny, so anemic, that he had to swallow it down with cold toast left over from yesterday's breakfast.

It had dawned on Ruben that he had an appointment this morning and had to get out to the airport as quickly as possible. One of the dearest friends he'd ever had in this life was flying in: Dr. Jacques Coquelion, a Belgian who was once an exchange student and fellow pupil at Badler, Indiana University, and Harvard. Jacques liked American life so much that he became a citizen and soon worked his way upward in psychological circles until, today, he would be the most influential visiting lecturer whom Ruben had brought to Badler. He felt that his students would love the man.

Whether it was American life in general that made Jacques stay, Martin mused with a smile as he got into his old Granada and edged his way onto I-70, it was difficult to say. Jacques had spoken mostly of how much he liked the way American women responded to his accent.

"To them, Marteen," he had said many times, smiling, "I am not Belgian, but French. All they hear ees my accent and I would not lose eet if I remained in your fair nation the rest of my life!"

Jacques had underestimated his charms, if anything, thought Ruben as he drove through the early summer morning. The Belgian had a kind of debonair lifestyle that would keep him young for years. He had worn a mop of hair so blond it was bright yellow; he had even affected a walkingstick. While Jacques never had been remotely proper, when they were in school, he had calculatedly developed a Gallic courtesy that appeared natural to him even when he was bowing low to kiss a damsel's hand. The two young men had become friends because of their shared fascination for parapsychology, the study of phenomena that cannot be quickly attributed to normal causes. At that time, such an interest had to be whispered, private, and circumspect. Probably, Martin thought now, it was the very clandestine nature of their mutual avocation that kept them corresponding and telephoning each other over the years.

But as he was thinking how much fun it would be to talk with Jacques once more, Ruben winced. The tattered remnants of his persistent nightmare flashed once more in his mind. For a moment he lost sight of the road; his gaze turned inward; then the bellowing yowl of a semi behind him brought the Granada back between the white lines, Ruben's hands trembling slightly on the wheel.

The truth of the perhaps-premonition Martin had experienced simply wouldn't leave him now: The entire internal experience had been tainted with a heavy aura of some lurking, ancient evil, of some gross monstrosities that, whether he ignored it or not, were meant to assume actual form in the near future.

Ruben's imminent future.

Nonsense, he told himself firmly, perspiring slightly

in the July heat and dangling his long arm out the window until the knuckles tapped against the door. *You've never been psychic in your whole life.*

But dear Dr. Ruben, his alter ego argued persuasively with him, *what about medical doctors who suddenly become addicted to their own drugs; what about actors who take direction so many years they absolutely must become directors?*

He made himself think again about Jacques, hoped that his old colleague had watched a tendency to drink too much, wondered about Jacques' latest sexual exploits. The man was too gallant to commit his indiscretions to paper, but over a glass of Grand Cru Bourgros his recollections could be hilarious.

Indianapolis International Airport is set far back from the weaving, busy road, not enough so that drivers on the road fail to have the impression that planes which are landing or taking off will inevitably land on I-70. Happily, they never do. There was a time when the Hoosier capital was so inconsequential on a national scale that the airport was little more than a picture. Sarcastic residents took their offspring out to the airport on the west side of town so they might have a close look at a real plane.

Now, Ruben mused appreciatively, the city was growing so fast and becoming so modern that few midwestern airports, other than O'Hare in neighboring Chicago, did more thriving business. It was hard to find a decent place to park in the vast lot and Ruben's walk to the multiple doors, indicating different airlines, was tedious in the gathering summer heat.

You've been warned, came the thought, not another voice but his own alert mind speaking, *warned about the most basic concerns of life and death. Even your own.*

Vastly annoyed with himself, he broke off the persistent thoughts by beginning to trot through the lengthy corridors of the airport, feeling like a pallid O. J. Simpson.

Jacques' American Airlines flight was just taxiing in for a landing as Ruben stepped into the visitors' lounge and peered through the immense windows. Already the long tunnel used for boarding and dispersing passengers was being slowly run out to greet the plane.

Martin found that he was smiling with an anticipation which was nearly boyish. Jacques Coquelion was a living reminder of a past that seemed so much simpler, full of so much more joy and, for that matter, challenge. If things aren't interesting enough when you're young, he decided, you *make* them that way. And that's precisely the ability you lose with the years. His eyes bright, his palms moist, Ruben became conscious of the way his pulse was racing.

Then a shadow crossed the psychologist's face.

He almost didn't recognize Coquelion when the Belgian, briefcase tucked under his arm, came striding out of the tunnel with an ear-to-ear smile.

Jacques Coquelion had gone totally gray. He wore an absurd little white goatee. He looked to have lost twenty pounds or more, and his face was lined, even at the decreasing distance. While he didn't really appear unwell, exactly, Jacques did look like a man under considerable strain.

But it wasn't just Jacques himself who froze Ruben to the spot, his lips parted. Someone was accompanying his old friend. A stunningly beautiful blond woman—dressed in the height of fashion with her light hair spun sleekly back to accent a high forehead and deep cheekbones, her face perfectly poised and very nearly amused

—had her slender arm linked in Jacques'.

It was the mysterious woman of Martin Ruben's terrible premonition.

Two

She was introduced to Ruben simply as "Ingrid Solomon," with no further explanation offered. He thought for an instant that there was something in his friend's tone to indicate that the name should be sufficient, but he wasn't sure. There wasn't time, after collecting the luggage and striding toward the distant exit, to do much more than a quick appraisal of the woman.

But Ruben's first impression was simple and direct enough: Ingrid Solomon was the most beautiful woman he'd ever seen. More, she had the most self-possessed, disquietingly confident air in Ruben's experience. He began putting the facts together in his customary deductive fashion.

Outside the building, he offered to fetch the Granada, but Ingrid gave Jacques a quick, inquiring glance and then they were walking together across the enormous lot. *Interesting glimpse, that*, Ruben observed to himself. *Usually the man looks questioningly to the woman. But there was nothing obsequious about it. It was only . . . deferential. Mildly so.*

"I can't possibly tell you how happy I am to see you, old friend," said the Belgian, pausing to let a car out of its slot. Sun glinted on his almost-white sideburns, and Ruben again thought how under stress he seemed. "You haven't changed a whit."

"*Au contraire*, Coquelion," Ruben murmured, "but thank you for saying that." He looked fleetingly at Jacques, gave him a smile. "And you, sir, have become extraordinarily distinguished. Even important. You remind me of that professor at Harvard; what was his name?"

Jacques looked impish. "George Bankfield?"

"Good God, no!" Martin exploded with laughter. "Bankfield must have been two hundred years old," he explained to Ingrid Solomon, noticing that, despite his height, he didn't have to look down at her much. "He was a socialist who honestly believed that most mental problems could be cleared away simply by sharing the wealth."

Her violet eyes studied him for a moment as they reached the car. "I don't suppose it would hurt."

"But it might mean *more* aberrations for the man whose money they shared," Ruben remarked with a smile. He unlocked the passenger door. "After you, Ms. Solomon."

There was a flash of long, silken leg in a slitted skirt as she stooped to get in, and then Jacques was obliterating the view, taking the bucket seat beside the driver. Ruben went with a sigh around the rear of the car to his own door.

He caught a glimpse of Ingrid in his rearview as he was starting the motor. She was looking out the window, one slim hand raised against the sun; her demeanor—cool, detached, in control despite unfamiliar territory—made him feel chaufferlike for an infuriating moment.

"Have you enjoyed teaching at Badler?" Jacques inquired.

"Very much," said Ruben, pulling into the lane leading back to I-70. "But it has its limitations, I fear."

"Yes, I recall a letter of yours in which you said that they have no intention of seeking an endowment for a parapsychology department." While Jacques seemed much older, his charm was very much in place. When he spoke, there was an unfailing gleam of snowy, perfect teeth and his eyes danced with humor as if he found it necessary to throttle a dozen hilarious comments. "The same weary nonsense about the subject being scientifically suspect?"

Ruben glanced at his friend, nodded. "This city of Indianapolis is outwardly middleclass in mentality and trying to improve itself. One could easily take it for granted, but that would be a mistake. There are people who are so cosmopolitan, so brilliant and creative, so sophisticated in the best sense of the word that could fit into any society. There is an equal portion, at least, of men and women who honestly believe agriculture is still the most important thing in the world and who resent anything that's happened since nineteen ten. The tension between them is growing and there'll be trouble except that the cosmopolitans won't come out and remark upon their plans to change every iota of the town and the farm types don't realize it's already changing." He paused. "Jacques, you finally lost your accent."

The Belgian shrugged. "I haven't visited my native country in twelve years. It seemed about time to allow myself to become absorbed by American culture."

Ruben looked at the quiet beauty in the back seat and wondered if he should say what occurred to him. He modified it. "I remember when you swore you'd never lose it because of its . . . uhm . . . social value."

"Times change," Coquelion replied with a slight sigh. "I've come to have a little more respect for the truth than I had once. Which does not mean," he added with a flashing smile and quick jab of his index finger, "that you and I won't have time to reminisce about our madcap youth."

"We have a limited amount of time to spend in this city," Ingrid Solomon said from the back seat. "I understand the urge to friendship and I endorse it. But don't lose sight of our objectives."

Objectives? Ruben wondered. *Our* objectives? He met her gaze in the rear-view mirror. "Tell me, Ms. Solomon," he began, pleasantly, slipping easily into a faint British accent that went both with his Rathbone-resemblance and autocratic teaching manner. "Did you select the Salon on Fifth Avenue or the one on Third? Your hair is so lovely I'm certain you made the best choice."

He was rewarded by her eyebrows raising in surprise. "How could you know that I had my hair done?" she demanded, leaning forward slightly.

Jacques answered with a boyish grin. "That's an old trick of Martin's," he explained. "Since everyone thinks he looks like Sherlock Holmes, he worked very hard to develop his deductive prowess."

"And I never explain my little ventures," Ruben put in. "Whenever Holmes did, Watson immediately concluded it was easy."

Now her breath, perfumed and hot, was on the back of his neck. "What else can you tell me about myself, dear Doctor?"

"Other than the obvious facts that you came here from New York but your residence is elsewhere, that you have been married in the recent past, that you chose yellow in your dress because of its sunlike vitality, and that you are studying me intently for reasons that completely escape me, I cannot tell you a thing."

"Wonderful, wonderful!" she applauded in delight,

29

the first time she had openly smiled. "But I think there *is* something else you can tell about me."

"There is?" Now it was Ruben's turn to be surprised. "And what, pray tell, might that be?"

"While you were startled to see me with Jacques at the airport, you recognized me somehow. And it hasn't been entirely pleasant for you." She paused, frowned prettily. "But I'm not photographed that frequently, so I can't complete my little deduction."

"But you've been quite observant," Ruben praised her without explaining his predictive nightmare. "And there *is* something more I can say about you: You are extraordinarily bright—I'd estimate a genius intelligence quotient—and self-employed in some eminent organization. Am I not right?"

"You are," she said with a nod. Then she looked toward Jacques, who was turned from the front seat to her. "You're probably right about this man, Jacques darling. He may prove to be ideal."

Ruben turned right into a northside exit from the road. "I don't wish to appear ungrateful that you're here, or that you think I am ideal," he remarked affably, "but exactly *why* have you come with Jacques?"

Her expression was alluring, almost suggestive. "To *examine* you, Doctor Ruben. To watch you at work and appraise it."

The psychologist's brows curved. "For what earthly reason?"

"If I approve of what I see," Ingrid replied candidly, "there is a strong likelihood that I will offer you a position with us. Doctor Coquelion, as I'm certain you know, is a psychiatrist with experience in biology. You—if I am not mistaken—are a psychologist and we are in need of a parapsychologist to head up our teaching department. That is your specialty." She spread her hands with a slight smile. "That explains why we are here."

"What about research?" Ruben managed to ask.

"That wouldn't be a duty, but our labs and libraries would be open to you. Fundamentally, we want someone dynamic who deals well with young people— young people who are already gifted in areas of the paranormal. Expand their horizons even while helping us learn the secrets of their current capabilities." She looked at him, albeit through the rear-view mirror, directly in the eye. "I'm in a position to fulfill all your dearest dreams in parapsychology. You see, I'm the Founder and Director of Solomon Studies."

Flabbergasted, Ruben struck the center of the steering wheel with his open palm. "Of course! I should have known the name at once. In the two years it's been in existence, Solomon Studies has become a rather enigmatic attraction for everybody interested in psychology or parapsychology. Although, I must confess, I have no clear idea what you're doing there."

"That's intentional, Doctor," Ms. Solomon retorted. "Outsiders aren't intended to know what we're doing."

"Why?" Ruben asked pointedly.

"First, the entire field is highly competitive. All the faculty and staff of my organization are contracted; they pledge total secrecy." She was ticking her reasons off on her fingers in a businesslike fashion. "Second, that which is mysterious in this open, often outrageous nation of ours makes everyone so intrigued that when facts come out—as they will, when I choose the time— they will have far greater impact. Third, I do not like being raided, especially when I've handpicked every professional on Nommos Island. The wining and dining of competent people is probably more ferociously frequent in science than business. And—there are other reasons."

Ruben smiled into his mirror. "Is the location of Solomon Studies a secret, too? That's the first time I've even heard Nommos Island mentioned. In fact, I never heard of the place before."

"You were quite right about us coming from New York but being based elsewhere," Jacques put in, pinching his trouser crease and recrossing his tailored legs. "Several months ago Director Solomon purchased the entire island of Nommos, north of Indianapolis and south of South Bend. In Lake Triton."

"Only a few miles from here, and I haven't heard of it?" Ruben asked.

"Well, around a hundred miles. This is the first time the island had been given its ancient title for nearly a century. In reality, it's the oldest plot of land in the state—and by the way, Martin, you *have* heard of it." Jacques smiled. "It was most recently known as a site for a children's amusement park, a sort of poor man's Disneyland."

"Of course!" Ruben exclaimed. "Boysangurls Place. I heard it had been closed and sold, but I had no idea why or when it happened." He had turned off I-70 and was driving west toward Badler University.

"The proprietors of the park were delighted to get rid of it," Ingrid said from behind him, her scarlet-tipped fingers touching the back rest at his neck. "They had a strange series of unfortunate accidents. Children who attended Boysangurls became ill, some fell off rides and, finally, a little girl was killed. That's when the owners were persuaded to sell. For our purposes, Nommos Island is easily isolated from the mainland and provides us with the privacy we wish for our experimentation. It's working beautifully."

Ahead, several low, brown buildings appeared on the horizon and Ruben slowed the car. "Was Solomon Studies named for you, Ms. Solomon?"

"It was. I was proud to have my name on it because I've arranged for the most advanced parapsychological testing and experimenting in the world to be done there. By the time we're through, we'll know exactly how and why people use ESP. We'll know if it can be taught to others. And, in the process, we believe we may learn more about mankind's final frontier—the human mind—than anyone has known before."

"I'm deeply impressed," Ruben said sincerely, "and pleased to be considered. I've heard the rumor that Solomon Studies is looking into every paranormal possibility, however insignificant, excluding nothing."

Jacques raised his head with pride. "The rumor is true. We even schedule our daily routines by the more time-tested elements of the paranormal. We have an immense, growing library of reports, from the present reaching back to ancient Greek, Babylonian, and Egyptian papers on mythology. We have unearthed data on alchemy and early medicine in the hope that our discoveries will benefit mankind in other areas. Rather than scoffing, we're studying—testing, experimenting, recording—to determine what has a kernel of truth and what hasn't."

"We want to learn what phenomena are repeatable under clinical conditions," Ingrid picked up the thread, "and which may be transferred, not only to individuals but to groups."

"We plan," said Jacques, "to learn the *how* and the *why* of the occult. Information of this kind, with the exception of its cousin religion, is the oldest subject matter on the globe. And when ten years of intensive effort has passed, I believe we can say, to everyone's satisfaction, *this* realm of ESP is neurotic fraud, *that* realm is the way to a better future."

"We?" Ruben inquired. "You're already working for Solomon Studies, then?"

Jacques bobbed his handsome head in agreement. "You recall the time, almost a year ago, when I wrote you that I'd been granted an interview? Well, my life has changed drastically since then because I was accepted." He paused, took a deep breath. "For the first time in my life I see no reason to chase women, to drink too much, to spend every night in a different bar or hotel room. Solomon Studies has given my life a sense of purpose and a great deal more, my dear Martin, which I dare not discuss at this time."

Ruben parked the car in his slot in the Badler faculty section of the university parking lot, and hung back a moment as the other two headed toward the east entrance to Rice Hall.

Dizzying news, they brought him heady, dizzying news. He realized with a thrill that his career might be on the verge of its greatest plunge forward.

And as he trailed after the sleek back of the beautiful Ingrid Solomon, he wondered why, when his dearest friend, Jacques Coquelion, said he didn't dare discuss what *else* he had acquired from Solomon Studies, a vision from his premonition invaded his consciousness: The picture of a plot of ground, perhaps a natural mound, that seemed for all the world like the downshaft to Hell.

Three

The enormous lecture hall into which Martin Ruben showed his guests always reminded him of an old-fashioned medical theater, with steep rows of seats rising from a relatively small platform and a glassed-in section at the top which was a part of the third floor.

Someday, he had told himself before, I will be eighty-five years old when I come here to lecture and break my idiotic neck descending this mountain-range flight of steps.

Now it occurred to him that this might be one of his last lectures at Badler if cool, ambitious Ingrid Solomon liked what she heard. He was filled with mixed feelings when he stepped up to the lectern.

Instantly, all those students who had listened to Ruben before fell silent and those who were new were elbowed into indignant quiet.

"Ladies, gentlemen," he began, speaking in his normally somewhat strident tones, in full awareness of the public address system and Rice Hall's wonderful acoustics. "My remarks today won't be extensive and you needn't take notes unless you want to." He paused, pleased to see that the notebooks already opened stayed that way. "I am more anxious that you hear our guest speaker, a parapsychologist whose study of the human brain is more biologically focused than my own and whose insights, in my opinion, are second to none in our profession."

Jacques Coquelion, seated with Ingrid Solomon at a table a few feet from Ruben, was wearing his Professor Face. Martin saw that his usual smiles had made way for Pontification.

Ruben lifted his head to enhance his height and his impressive hawk's beak of a nose. "If I have concentrated on one subject of the paranormal more than any other, students," he began, "it is surely astrology. There are several excellent reasons for that. For one, it is the oldest organized discipline in the world, the father of astronomy, which took the name from what we now call astrology.

"How old is astrology?" he continued, rhetorically. "While most anthropologists and historians would dispute it, Hindu legend dates astrology from *two hundred thousand* years ago. Some say 'Preposterous, for man himself was barely striding on two legs.' But I will remind you that, every two or three years, discoveries and carbon datings continue to shove farther back into time the age of this planet and the moment when Man first set foot on it. Apparently astrology was taught by the Manu, who was in command of the fourth rootrace."

Ruben stopped to allow his startling information to penetrate. Then he continued: "Whether we wish to accept these premises or not, our subject is surely lost, as they say, in antiquity. Recently archeologists have found a bone some thirty thousand years old which bears marks clearly indicating the phases of the moon. Over five thousand years ago, Babylon's astrologer-priests were identifying and naming stars. In a very real sense, then, astrology was the first scientific effort, the first recorded science, the first technical language in its system of useful symbols. There was a literal school of astrology taught by Babylonians on the Greek island of Cos about three hundred years before Christ." He took a breath. "Remember this: Anytime you hear about 'ancient astronomy,' anytime you are told about Stonehenge or the markings on Egyptian tombs and pyramids, anytime you study the Mayas and their great sun wheel, you are learning of astrological traces which reach back to the dawn of Man."

A student was on his feet, waving his hand. Powerfully built, his face was pink, unlined and seemed inappropriate on a man's body. "Barry Caldwell, Prof," he announced with casual disrespect. "A freshman in this dump. Look, because something is old doesn't make it correct or accurate. Right? I mean, about the same time your Babylonian weirdos were drawing circles and dividing them into twelve equal parts, Babylonian *female* weirdos were dividing up the men for fun and profit. You said there were other reasons you talked so often about astrology, and I wondered what they were."

He'd ended on a challenging note and Martin Ruben repressed a smile. Ah yes, Barry Caldwell, the sharpest mind in all the psych classes already—but as big and restive as a linebacker. He'd been to Ruben's apartment twice, with other students, quarreling about UFOs even while his smart, blue eyes widened with every reported sighting. Something in Barry craved facts at the earliest possible opportunity and virtually dared a speaker to produce them. If the boy ever decided to concentrate his efforts in a single area, and shut up long enough to do a little hard work, he might prove to be the smartest student at Badler U.

"My dear Caldwell," Ruben said in his snidest, most superior tone, "your impatience is exceeded only by your incomparably bad manners. A challenger looks much better when the person he's challenging can't produce the facts."

"I haven't heard any yet," Caldwell called, and smiled when his friends near him winced at his daring. "Not a one."

"Possibly your behavior is so execrable because you're preoccupied with personal problems," Ruben continued. "I strongly advise you to ask for the return of your class pin this evening at the latest. The moon is quite adverse to you tomorrow."

Barry still hadn't taken his seat. He gaped at his professor, still irascible. "How d'you know about my pin? And how in the hell can you know the moon is adverse for me tomorrow when you don't even know when I was born?"

"You *are* a Cancer native with the moon in direct, investigative Scorpio, are you not?" asked Ruben, quite softly. Every eye in the hall turned to Caldwell who could only nod weakly. "As for your pin, sir, I fear that I have added to my astrological practice a simple deduction. To quote Sherlock Holmes, my dear Caldwell, 'You see, but you do not observe.' Otherwise you wouldn't need to pose such absurd queries."

"I still don't see how you knew I was a Cancer what's-it," Barry muttered stubbornly, finally sitting.

"Native; the term you seek is native." Ruben gave him a cool smile. "I am merely attempting to answer your earlier question, my boy. You wished to know why I frequently speak on the subject of astrology and now I have demonstrated the answer: Because—at least in terms of character, of personality—*it works.*"

There was a smattering of applause and Barry Caldwell reddened. Ruben bowed slightly at the waist.

He spoke a few minutes longer, introduced Dr.

Jacques Coquelion, and took his seat beside Ingrid Solomon.

"I enjoyed that," the director of Solomon Studies said in a swift whisper. She had leaned forward and a waft of delicious perfume mingled with delicious Ingrid. "You must have a sixth sense, doctor, to have spoken today of astrology."

He smiled. "I could say that I realized, if you were deep in the study of the ancient sciences, you surely would be drawn to the oldest subject of all. But this was merely what I had planned to cover today."

Then he leaned back in his chair at the table so that Ms. Solomon, closer to the lectern, was also in front of him. His shrewd eyes examined her microscopically. Intellectually, he felt, she was first-rate. He recognized a decisiveness about her that he knew would make her decide about *him*, and Solomon Studies, before the day was out. He liked that—*wanted* to like that—in a woman. There was nothing but her autocratic manner, her aloof air, that kept her from being the kind of woman who was constantly on the verge of getting either a proposal, a proposition, or an attack. Her hair was such a light, shimmering blond that Ruben felt it must be natural. In profile, Ingrid's face was perfectly proportioned along classical lines; her violet eyes, as she listened to Jacques' lecture, became almost smoky with sensuality. But he did not think it was his friend, in particular, who captivated her. This, he told himself, was a beautiful woman in her thirties who liked and experimented with men. He also concluded that part of the expression in her eyes arose from myopia and a vain refusal to wear glasses.

It was difficult for Martin to judge her figure adequately, since she was wearing an expensive yellow suit over a puffy white blouse which protruded deliciously in a myriad of feminine frills. How much was Ms. Solomon and how much outer frills he couldn't determine. Her legs, crossed but yet slightly apart in a curious tension he found exotic, were long enough to give her height but not to seem fashion-model frail. Indeed, the thighs were somewhat generous and he thought them to be utterly alluring. I was right the first time, Martin Ruben decided at last, closing his eyes with a sigh. She *is* the most lovely woman I've ever seen.

Jacques Coquelion had chosen as his topic a speculative discussion of the afterlife experienced by those who had passed on. His audience was fascinated. He began with a scientifically acceptable rattling off of facts and figures concerning those who had reported actual death, and had then left their bodies in astral form. "Momentarily," he said, "they raised the veil to paradise and peeped in." The number of such reports was growing, Jacques continued, but whether that meant more and more people were temporarily enabled to see into the world beyond or that more people merely felt comfortable about admitting to it, he could not say.

Jacques did, however, observe the close parallels among all the reported visits to an afterlife: The presence of an intense, vivid light which did not blind but beckoned, instead; a welcoming either by beloved faces of the past who had long ago died or by religious figures, frequently Jesus Christ.

So far, Ruben thought, so good. But then, to his amazement, the Belgian began his speculations. It was almost as if Jacques were thinking aloud. Instead of producing facts, or citing valuable professional opinion, then identifying it as such, the handsome Jacques ventured into regions of absolute guesswork. For a moment Ruben was embarrassed at asking him, since he had so instilled scientific principles in his students' minds; then he realized Jacques was, at least, *admitting these were his own views and speculations.*

"What, we may well wonder, is the nature of the afterlife, whether we call it heaven, paradise, Valhalla, or anything else?" The Belgian's face was oddly intent and a line of perspiration formed across his forehead. "Is it a question of time being merged so that a spirit exists in the past, present, and future simultaneously— or is it, as I have thought might be true, a matter of time being hastened, speeded up? The common housefly lives for perhaps twenty-four hours, but who is to say that it does not cram into that period sixty or seventy of our human years? I have even toyed with efforts at establishing ratio; a minute of our time representing, perhaps, a year of spiritual existence.

"When we say quickly, 'There are no ghosts' or with equal alacrity, 'Ghosts exist,'" Jacques pressed on, "we must be willing to suspend our own physical laws and extrapolate those that may obtain beyond death's curtain. The answer to the ancient question, 'How many angels can dance on the head of a pin?' may not be as absurd as we anticipate it to be. But it is my conviction that the answer *is* subject to some laws, somewhere, and is therefore ascertainable by the living. For if temporal laws have no basis in a spiritual world, *spatial* laws, too, may be different. And to adjudge the possibility of their otherworldly existence on terms with which *we* are familiar is to ignore completely the obvious facts of sharp distinction between the living and the dead."

From where Martin Ruben sat he could see young Barry Caldwell's face filling again with his yearning for data, could sense Barry's hand about to shoot up. But he could also see that Jacques was so involved in his remarks that he would not even notice Caldwell, unless the boy dashed to the platform and waved his arm beneath Jacques' nose. Which, Ruben thought with amusement, was not an impossibility.

"No, my friends," continued the imperturbable Coquelion, "what we require is some workable and finite starting point—some clearcut, established fact on which we may build. We find ourselves presently in the midst of a childish dot-to-dot puzzle, or maze, without knowing where to begin or what we shall find when we reach the big picture in the center. But we must have a fact that is *always* repeated, that is *consistent* in the world of what might be called the 'post-living.' Once we have such a fact in our grasp, I believe we can begin to learn the secrets of that nebulous, presumably adjacent and mysterious dimension; and perhaps we can succeed in doing what Thomas Alva Edison once strove to do: Begin a dialogue with the dead.

"And when we reach that moment," Jacques drew near his close, eyes hot, "we may also begin, at last, to know the answers to some of the questions raised—largely inadvertently—by those who are religious among us. *Do* God and his counterpart exist? *Is* there such a thing as genuine good; and *is* there such a thing as absolute evil? *Does* the human concept of right and wrong have any factual meaning and, if it does, must it be modified by what occurs elsewhere? *Is* nature both for the living and the dead—and *is* it intrinsically fair, coherent and cohesive, rational and understandable? Our future lies not, my friends, in outer space—" now Jacques straightened, seeming for a moment the sleek sophisticate of Ruben's youth—"until we have conquered *inner* space. The space not only between our two human ears, but as well between the nonexistent or not-here-at-all and the newborn, the just-arrived. For in the final analysis, it is not the world immediately *after* our deaths that should interest the scientific among us the most, but the instant *before* we are born. What, and where, are we, then?"

The applause that greeted Jacques when he finished was a strange mixture, Ruben felt, of warm appreciation—from the more emotional students, perhaps, or those who had lost loved ones and longed now to believe in a hereafter—and cold, resentful astonishment at being subjected to such a speech.

Martin suggested that they have refreshments at the nearby Campus Clubbe and, after the class had filed out, more animated than usual, Ruben, Ingrid, and Jacques left Rice Hall and trekked across a well-worn path to the nearby cafeteria. Somewhat to Ruben's surprise, Ms. Solomon took his arm as they walked and he could feel a certain tension electrifying his elbow and bicep.

Here at the Campus Clubbe more than a few students, over the past thirty years, had learned more about bridge, gin rummy, euchre, and pinochle than the courses offered by Badler. Ruben and Coquelion themselves had dallied here from time to time; the Belgian smiled nostalgically as they entered.

"The only thing that's changed," he said softly, smiling, "is the fashions."

Ruben seated Ingrid in a booth beneath a wall mural of cartoon figures doing outrageous collegiate nonsense and glanced up at Jacques. "And, of course, the ex-students," he added.

The two men got in line at the cafeteria counter. Two or three of the students waiting had been in Ruben's class and buzzed about him and, as he overheard it, "that weird Frog." Suddenly Ruben turned to his friend, frowning.

"What in the world possessed you to present such a speculative lecture?" he demanded, overstepping good manners as the privilege of longstanding friendship. "I've spent weeks telling them you were the most scientific man in psychology, certainly the most in *para*psychology!"

"I'll explain it to you in a few moments," Jacques replied with an elegant yawn. "The immediate question is how impressed with you was Ms. Solomon?"

"I put on no show for the lady," Ruben commented in a tight whisper. "I have managed to live forty years without the lady or Solomon Studies and I can make it a few additional years."

Jacques studied Martin closely. "Methinks the gentleman doth protest too much," he said at last, as they turned to the waiting countergirl. "That woman can give you paradise on earth, old friend, simply by deciding she likes you."

They carried sandwiches, cokes, and iced tea back to the booth and spread them carefully on the table.

"You're an able speaker, Doctor Ruben," Ingrid murmured. "They listened to you with rapt attention."

"Not, I fear, to the same degree as Doctor Coquelion," Ruben replied without looking at Jacques. He took a bite of his ham-salad sandwich and wondered how many of them he'd consumed here in the past. "They found Jacques fascinating."

"Jacques was riding his hobbyhorse," the blonde said, "and it's always intriguing to watch a grown man playing with his toys. Doctor, I want you with us at Solomon Studies and I shan't take 'no' for an answer." She paused, her violet eyes studying his face. "My offer is fifty thousand dollars per annum, your contract calling for raises at a ten percent increment each subsequent year. You retain, of course, the right to write papers of scholarly journals at your own discretion."

In the years to come Martin Ruben would think that he had never surpassed the acting ability that he exercised at that instant. Although he had deduced the fact that she would make him an offer today, the amount she mentioned sounded like a fortune.

"You will be the professor in charge of the teaching end of the Parapsychology Department," Ingrid continued when he did not reply, "with access to whatever materials you may require. The budget will be open-ended."

In his excitement, Ruben stuffed his mouth so full of ham salad and toast that he couldn't immediately reply. Trying not to be offensive, he worked the food forward toward the front of his mouth and the protruding lips suggested reflection as well as hesitation.

Ingrid Solomon shrugged, picked up her coke and sucked on the straw. "Very well, let's not quibble," she said around the straw. "I'll make it one hundred thousand a year with incremental raises of ten thousand each quarter, indefinitely. Is that acceptable?"

Ruben swallowed hard. It hurt. His mind raced with excitement. "I'm astounded by how well funded you are," he managed.

"The funding is entirely my affair, Doctor," the blonde snapped, "because it's *my* money. The group I've handpicked and assembled on Nommos Island is *mine*. There is no other money and there is no interference from outsiders. I have received and I seek no governmental grants. We do not waste our time on commercial R and D activities that appeal either to government or business. At Solomon Studies, sir, we are engaged in parapsychological research, study, and instruction. We are, putting it in the vernacular, working our asses off!" Her gaze at him was both bemused and challenging. "Don't concern yourself with crass money matters, Doctor. I'm almost indecently well endowed."

This time Ruben returned her cool gaze and, though it did not drop below her full lips, he knew that he conveyed his message. "No gentleman could argue with that point," he observed.

"Perhaps," she said pointedly, openly smiling now, "perhaps I'll let you—examine the books one day."

Ruben broke their mutual gaze reluctantly and sighed. "Your offer is certainly more than fair, and I am honored. Please permit me time to consider it."

"I must have your answer by morning," she told him flatly. "Afer that, the offer is canceled."

"You were about to tell me," Ruben said to Jacques, turning his lean body in the booth, "why you chose that particular topic for your lecture? I really am curious!"

Jacques' sandwich and tea had not been touched. The Belgian was twisting the straw in his glass and didn't answer for a moment. When he did, his expression was bold and frank.

"Let's put it this way, old friend," he said. "I'm under a death sentence and I've grown curious about what my neighbors will be like. When I—move to the other side."

Four

"They come," she said, not aloud.

"I know," he replied. "Same way you know."

Others of the children seemed also to know. All the multicolored little people had begun turning to the west, toward the buildings, to stare.

At nothing.

They stood, most of them, on the silent merry-go-round which had been left behind in the owners' urgent need to leave Nommos Island for good. The circular plaything's elaborate carvings were tarnished now, but a tiny Japanese boy had done his telekinetic best to make the animals move, once again. The golden horses and overfed brown bears and dignified tawny lions stayed still, frozen as if themselves haunted by what was near. An acne-cursed Indian girl with a caste mark harsh above hirsute brow and knowing black eyes almost managed to persuade them that they heard music when it was only the lyric of youth humming in her head.

All had stopped when the vibrations were picked up, vagrant foregoings absorbed like the scent of animals, telling them—one by one—that the adults approached.

And soon it was possible to make them out, coming in a businesslike manner to the great mound, circling it and continuing to come. Two American men in white medical uniforms. One was a giant to the children, middle-aged and thick with clumps of steely hair rising spiderlike from the sweaty open top of his shirt. The other was the real attendant in charge, a wiry elf of a young man, his face wreathed—as it always was, tirelessly—in smiles. Each man wore sandals; their feet pummeled the earth, kicking filthy weapons (each child secretly felt), though neither man had ever kicked any of them.

It is doubtful that either noticed the way they backed away, edged oh-so-cautiously, trying hard to blend brown and yellow and reddish faces into a human sea that was predominantly whitecaps.

"You, Pietro," the young, small man said, beaming his facial beatitudes upon them as he pointed. The little Italian lad flinched as if the finger had been loaded. "And you, Katrina." Another gesture. Another flinch, this time by a child with the color of saved cotton and a doll-like face. "*You're* the lucky ones today!"

Neither Pietro nor Katrina moved an inch. At the rear of the massing of children—there might have been thirty or more gathered at the dead merry-go-round, a fraction of their population—several tiny forms bunched themselves into hopeful invisibility and ran as only children can run.

"We isn't gone have more trouble, is we?" This from the burly giant. He didn't even bother to smile.

"When will they be satisfied that I can levitate but do not know how I do it?" It was Pietro speaking in perfect English. There were tears in his liquid eyes. "I have done it for them many times. I have lost much sleep. I am losing weight from the tests, and some of them hurt my head."

"C'mon, kid," the giant ordered, reaching.

For a moment they thought Pietro would float away from the men. But he knew he could not float from this island to Italy. Ducking the outstretched arm by normal means, Pietro began walking obediently toward the central laboratory without waiting for the men. Then white-haired Katrina followed him, her head lifted and her doll's face radiant.

But at the last, she paused to look back at the elfin young man: "Must I be seen by the Professor today?" she asked softly as he turned. "Must it be—him?"

"Sure, sweetie," replied the youth with an awful dummy-smile. "He's the *real* expert around here, y'know."

Her china-blue eyes glazed with fright, remembered and expected. "The Professor," she said simply, her Dutch accent precise. "He is full of hatred. He is full of violence. And—more."

But the young man laughed. His pat on her back started her after Pietro. Behind them, the other children watched the exodus, saw the two men, satisfied by completion of their task, trailing after the boy and girl.

The little brunette who had first sensed them spoke, this time with her voice. "What, exactly, do you think they do with them? When they come back, they blot it all out. They will not let us see."

Dhombola did not answer.

"Whether they refuse to show us from shame, or fright, I do not know."

Dhombola's gaze met the eyes of a Japanese boy and held while he replied to the girl. "Don't know. Can't see." He shrugged his small, ebon shoulders. "The vibrations, they're bad."

She considered for a moment. "Sometimes," she said at last, quietly, "they don't come back quite the same. I think it has been stolen from them, in part. And sometimes," her eyes were enormous, "they don't come back."

The African boy nodded his understanding.

Then she was close to Dhombola and the Japanese, her face urgent. "When d'you think th-they'll choose *us*?" she inquired, voicing her most important question.

"Maybe they get all they want from others," Dhombola answered as his eyes flicked across the distant mound. "Maybe our turn not come."

The Japanese boy, however, was peering into the future. His voice was soft and sinuous, yet jarred them with its adamant acceptance. "Oh you," he promised. Then, without a single alteration of expression: "Soon, I think. Very soon."

The atmosphere of the world was a hazy scarlet, thick enough with the red air to make it hard both to see and to breathe. Martin Ruben, who was the only one to see it, twisted his lanky body on the bed, trying to awaken from the dream, the vision. Sweat, clammy in the midsummer heat, trickled down his restless forehead to his jawline and throat. One arm reached into the air, sought to brush the premonition away.

Ingrid was there, Ingrid Solomon, the Director, waiting in the sumptuous office. He was just outside the door in this crimson haze and the old man with the balding head was doing a body count. "Fourteen, fifteen, sixteen," he counted in his precise tones, adding something that sounded like "Sin this way, doctor, sin this way," before resuming his count: "Seventeen, eighteen, nineteen . . ."

Ruben squinted to make out what the man was counting. Bodies, indeed, he saw. Bodies stacked like kindling in the corridor outside Ingrid's office, more than half of them quite young—children, in fact. Children of many races and colors. "Twenty-nine, thirty-one," the implacable voice progressed, as unmoved and remorseless as early death, "thirty-two, Sin-this-way, doctor, thirty-three . . ."

Then he was entering the office, pointing with passion though the words would not come out, perspiring in his vision, too, anguished by what he had seen.

"Does it really matter, Dr. Ruben?" the voice lifted from Ingrid's head, though her lips remained in a tight, businesslike smile. "Does it *really* matter, at *all*?"

Wake up, wake *up*, his own voice told him (*Fifty-six, fifty-seven, Sin this way, doctor*), have to *wake up*!

His heart nearly stopped beating when the premonition appeared to become utterly, completely *real*.

He knew that his eyes were wide open now and staring into his own apartment bedroom—

But there was Ingrid Solomon, in the flesh, at his bedside. ". . . Knocked several times but you didn't hear me," she was saying with a smile. "But it doesn't matter, does it?"

For another instant Ruben felt drugged, unable to detect the difference between the reality of his vision and the reality of this inexplicable moment; he stared speechlessly up at *her*, uncomprehending.

Then his shrewd mental responses assumed control, shifted gears, meshed. With a shock he realized that he was sitting in only his shorts while a very real Director of Solomon Studies, a woman who had offered him one hundred thousand dollars a year to do what he'd rather do more than anything else, was looking down at him. But even as he flushed and tried to apologize, her hand was gently pressing on his naked shoulder.

"Academics retire so early," she said softly, those violet eyes of hers drifting boldly down his slender body. "You're overregulated, Doctor, too 'structured' —isn't that what you psychologists call it?"

Maybe I am still asleep, Martin thought, blinking.

She was undressing, the yellow suit jacket already hung on a chair, the skirt soon joining it. Her ornate, frilly blouse was incongruous with the slip below but she rectified it quickly, hanging the blouse across the suit. The motion she made as she pulled the slip up from her knees and over her blond head was the sweet, slithering gesture he had longed, of late, to hear. Her hands went behind her back to the snap of the bra, released it. There was a faint reddish mark beneath her breasts as she stepped close to the bed, to Ruben, her lower body—still clad in panties—near his face. Near enough that he could see the telltale outline of her pubic hair.

"Please help me," she said softly.

His eyes went up the standing woman's body. Her breasts were neither excessively large nor high-placed but with a marked division that made him hunger to rest his face between them. The nipples, however, were high-positioned and generous, twin targets for his waiting lips. Eagerly Ruben tugged down her panties, staying put when, as she stepped out of them, her pubis brushed against his face. He'd been right; she was a natural blond. Before him was the scantiest sampling of pubic hair he'd seen on a woman; it was as if it had been shaved and now grew back in, reluctantly. It was like that of a young girl, that light-golden mound of hers; his fingers reached out to it wonderingly.

Then she was kneeling on the bed in front of him, her own fingers busily delving into the thrusting gap of his shorts, extricating. Ruben moaned at her touch, somehow contrived to withdraw from it in something like exquisite pain and to thrust further forward in eagerness.

Her palms were on his chest, pushing him back. He obeyed the touch, went prone—most of him. In a flurry of little movements that were a thousand kisses and caresses miraculously combined, Ingrid's lips touched him everywhere even as she moved above him, raised herself into the air, poised herself above his enthralled and uptilted face.

His own lips moved in a secret kiss.

"Yes, ah-h, yes," she said softly, seemingly from the sky.

In a moment she had drifted downward, still hovering-hipped above Ruben, and he could see the way her violet eyes were half-shut, her lips moist.

Then she was impaling herself on him in a sudden, piercing motion so accurate the man was astonished. The fitting was perfect; the sheath encased his sword in sinuous precision as his hands went out to her, closed around the wide-spaced breasts, and her head went back in a spasm of joy.

While he could yet think, at all, Ruben concluded in a fever that he'd never before encountered such a practiced, perfect bedmate. She was not only beautiful—more lovely than any female Martin had seen in his life. That telegenic, enraptured, pale face above him now would have brought any man soon to climax—had he allowed it—by looking into the incredible, passionate eyes. Even though her nearly white hair remained in its fashionable, slicked-back style, every other inch of Ingrid was open, available, wanton. She was the ideal.

But this was not the cool expertise of a prostitute, the detached efficiency of a salaried woman; oh, no. It was the absolute acceptance of mutual need and of mutual goal evident in one who has always sought to share fully the joy of her men, who has placed the objective, that sharing, uppermost—and emerged triumphant always. In the dismissal of her fierce work-a-day ego for this act of sex, Ingrid Solomon had captured and practiced something unique among the women Martin knew: absolute *comprehension* of what was needed each second and absolute *demand* of them both that it would be made manifest and real.

Now the Director of Solomon Studies rode his upthrust member with the acute timing of a circus aerialist. She was with him, with every movement. She brought him close to the draining climax a dozen, twenty times, till his head reeled and the universe contained nothing more than them. Even as he felt his own hips instinctively lift, masculinely demanding, she somehow resisted, deliciously; when his fingers involuntarily tightened on her now-sweaty breasts, slick-sweet globules with nipples taut and elongated, she darted forward rapidly to free them, her tongue searching between his lips and her own hips raised in anticipation he feared would drive him mad.

Lord, he thought then—she was *talking* to him: with strain, insistently: "A bundle of myrrh is my well-beloved unto me; he shall lie all night betwixt my breasts. *Arise*, my love, my fair one, and *come away*!"

He was stunned and she struck therefore when he least expected it. He'd felt this might last forever; when she uttered the words—familiar; they're so *familiar*!— he was frozen like an immobile stone in her.

Then she began a racking series of thrust-forward movements that shot his eyes wide open and spread his unclutching fingers on her breasts. *Now* he could see nothing but a cascading blaze of red and blue. She pumped and his lips shot apart in a silent scream. She was doing battle with him, shifting now to furious up-and-down motions: abandoned, frantic, knowing.

And Ruben cried out, beyond the ability to stop. His arms flayed the air, his hips seemed to leave the rest of his body as they shot up. The instant was timeless, it was all-time. Unlike other nights he'd known *this* was prolonged, enduring. And above him, to his great delight, he heard her, too, shriek in lyrical ecstasy.

And Ruben collapsed back on the bed, spent, the beautiful blonde above him, a sweet jouncy blanket of flesh.

Time began again, inevitably. Seconds that were smaller than before ticked away in Martin's mind. Inescapably, the life clock summoned him back.

He gasped. Ingrid lay now across his thighs. He saw her violet eyes down there, twin flowers gone mad in the noonday sun. And, "I rose *up* to open to my beloved," Ingrid intoned, reaching above her to release her bountiful blond hair at last. Her eyes did not, then, leave his. "My beloved is white and ruddy, the chiefest among ten thousand. His head is as the most fine gold; his locks are bushy, and black as a raven."

Madness, he had wandered into madness. But with her gaze holding his, as he started to stay this wondrous woman from a new and impossible quest, the words leaped to his mind and he uttered them, feeling oddly hypnotized: "Honey and milk are under *thy* tongue," he replied. "And the smell of thy garments is like the smell of Lebanon."

Yes. *Song of Solomon*. Ruben nodded as he realized. He'd loved it in the Bible years ago.

When again he looked down the length of his body he saw only the spreading marvel of her pale, golden hair. Her eyes looked elsewhere. Then he felt her, *there*.

Incredibly, impossibly he began to respond.

Moments later, lying atop as well as in her, slowly readying, all the lazy time of the boundless world in their grasp, time to explore a million tiny sensations he'd not known were available to mortals, Ruben raised himself enough to peer down at her. His eyes trailed down her slender, sloping abdomen, admiring the way they were joined. "How fair and how pleasant art thou, O love for delights!"

Ingrid nipped the side of his neck, lifting and grindingly writhing her hips. "Make haste, my beloved," she implored him, "and be thou like to a roe or to a young hart upon the mountain of spices."

When at last it again happened, it was like the drawn-out scream of a man and woman, hand-in-hand, vaulting joyously from the top of the earth's highest mountain. Red nails raked his back and hips; her call, Ruben thought, must have soared to the ears of Sheba herself.

Rest. Now, finally. Rest.

He gripped her against his sweat-soaked chest, his own hand languid, toying with her golden fur. "If this were an effort to convince me to come to Nommos Island," he began, making his tone as light as possible, "and work for Solomon Studies, it was the most remarkable salespitch in my experience."

She wriggled at his touch, smiled up at him. "Call it the—uhm—'fringe benefits' to which you're entitled. Martin, will you come?"

He sought to think but his mind had become soft, oozy mush. "I just don't know, I don't *know* what to do. It's such a total change in my life."

"You," she said with not-altogether imitation rancor, "are the most stubborn man I've ever known in my entire life. But I'll tell you something, Martin Ruben: What you have had this night is only a *sample* of the happiness that awaits you."

He shut his eyes from the command in hers. It occurred to him that she was not only intelligent but demanding.

"I swear to you it is true," she persisted. "I'm only a sample."

He opened his eyes. "D'you want to explain that fantastic remark?"

"No, I don't." She shook her head in lazy confidence. "You, my friend, will have to come there yourself to learn what I mean."

He stared at the way their nude bodies looked, side by side, her foot across his ankle, and liked it; he sighed. "Very well, then, I'll *visit* the island at least. To see the setup, to determine if I can fit into it properly."

She sat up, her shimmering hair a banner against her bare back, then went to the bathroom. In a moment he heard her calling him. "Martin?"

He was at once weightless and four hundred pounds of relaxed sloth, he thought grinning. Barefoot, he padded after her.

She was in the shower, water beating upon her upturned face and long, firm body. "Join me," she called. "Join me, Martin, in *all* ways, and I'll fulfill every desire you ever had. I will teach you things—feelings, sensations—you never believed existed."

He stepped into the tub with her, brought her close. "I warn you, Madame Director. I can be a slow learner."

She began soaping him, her fingers gently pressing. "That's just fine, Doctor. There is no rush at all." When she glanced back up at him Ruben knew that he was hearing more implied meaning than the words themselves conveyed. "*We have all the time in the world.*"

It was only later, when she finally allowed him to sleep, that he could wonder what Ingrid meant by that. And wondered, with a shiver of something like fear, if he would find the benefits of Nommos Island so great that he couldn't say no to anything.

Five

The beach was wider than it was deep, sun-kissed and lapped by the clear peaceful water of Lake Triton; it seemed larger than it had from the air, although finite distances could be absorbed by the eye. Ruben had come here with Ingrid Solomon and Jacques Coquelion in a commercial helicopter, knowing that he was committed to the visit for a period of at least one week. Only then would the helicopter return, bringing supplies and any new personnel or visitors. From what his friend Jacques had told him on the flight from South Bend, there would be precious few of the latter. "You're a notable exception, old friend," he informed Martin with a smile, "because we think we can make you a new associate."

A burly, expressionless fellow with thick chest hair protruding from his white uniform top took Martin's luggage as if it weighed nothing, then somehow added Jacques' and Ingrid's suitcases to his collection. Only toward the Director did he display any animation; to Ingrid he seemed deferential, even cautious. Then he started up a rise ahead of them like a man in a hurry bringing a small quantity of mail in from his rural mailbox.

In the distance Ruben could make out the famed golden dome of Notre Dame, in South Bend, a beautiful mark of civilization. There, in about four months, they would be playing championship football. The stands would be crammed with people.

But the well-known monument was unreal, here, nothing but a backdrop reminder of what had suddenly become Martin's past. He watched as the helicopter fluttered mechanical wings and slowly drifted until it was a rumbling star in the hot summer sky. When he lowered his gaze to peer around, shielding his eyes with a raised hand, he thought at first he was getting just what he'd anticipated: The feeling of being an adventurous castaway on a South Sea island, a sort of scientific Gaugin who threw away his cares to paint the psychic canvases of Solomon Studies.

From where he stood in the sand with the sun a flaming ball overhead, Ruben thought Nommos Island did appear well removed from all his other realities. For an idiotic instant he had an urge to kick off his shoes and run barefoot in the sand; or to make magnificent castles and wait until a bare-breasted native girl brought him huge quantities of thick rum.

But when he and his affable hosts had trudged over the small hill, Ruben realized that he had underestimated them. And for that matter, the whole scope of Solomon Studies.

It was rather like discovering a small but exceedingly modern city on an otherwise lifeless Martian landscape. To his left lay a series of small buildings—possibly ten or a dozen of them—built like a combination of bungalow and miniature dormitory. These, he learned, housed the psychic population itself. Ruben made a mental note to ask how they'd persuaded so many of these fascinating, often independent folk to come here.

To the psychologist's far right were more residential buildings, fewer in number but more elaborate and modern in style. The staff of Solomon Studies stayed there, Jacques explained with a nod. "There's a small but adequate cafeteria—the large one is in the main building—plus a huge swimming pool, sauna, exercise rooms, and all the rest. Everyone gets a color TV, of course."

Ruben, who rarely watched anything but public television on his set, nodded. "Of course," he agreed wryly.

He was studying the main building, as they approached, and he was immensely impressed. The structure might have been a three-story hospital with several hundred rooms except that the architect had designed it both to convey comfortable eye appeal and a hint of the scientific. One could just as easily consider it, Ruben thought, a university central hall.

"I like it," he said aloud, admiringly.

"You'll like the interior even more," Jacques assured him. "It houses not only laboratories of every kind and size but classrooms, even a first-rate library. There's a small motion-picture theater where we get first-run flicks, all manner of rec rooms, study halls, and the primary cafeteria where—if you'll pardon my obvious zeal—we have food that would do justice to the better restaurants."

"It's an amazing design," Martin murmured as they walked. "Who was the architect?"

Ingrid's gaze flicked toward him. "I was."

"You're a remarkably talented woman," he praised.

"Yes, but independence does it," she smiled frostily. "I always know precisely what it is I want, in all circumstances, and I settle for nothing less. I've found that most expertise in this silly world is badly overrated. Most of what anyone can do he's learned from others, without a smidgin of originality; and most of that is acquired by rote. If you know what you prefer, and if you have the gifts of communication to explain yourself lucidly to those who can put it on paper or blueprints, you can have anything you wish."

Ruben thought coolly, *if you also have the money to do it*, but didn't say it.

Now they were only fifty yards from the main doors and Ruben began seeing other surprising things.

He had the impression, for one, of hundreds of children walking here and there—children of every age, size, and color. Some of them appeared closely herded by adults and others seemed to be doing whatever they pleased. Toward the side-rear of the main building a number of them were sailing a Frisbee and chattering away.

To his right, just beyond that primary structure, lay an abandoned merry-go-round which he assumed was left behind by Boysangurls, the amusement park owners who had occupied Nommos in the past. Distorting mirrors were sprinkled about, some of them cracked. A funhouse waited hopelessly for customers, its doors boarded up and its boasts of "1001 Chills and Thrills" sadly proclaimed by faded signboards. Farther off, Ruben could see both an arcade and a small park area with shading trees and a small playground.

"We started to take the things from Boysangurls," Ingrid remarked, catching his stare, "and get rid of them. But then we saw that the kids might enjoy having them, even if things like the funhouse are unsafe and must be closed up."

Before Ruben could reply he saw another group of people—most of them children, but some of them dressed in the white uniforms of attendants or other staff members—loosely grouped around a sizeable earthen mound. It had been roped off; it was entirely unmarked so far as he could tell, and the people—wearing clothes from many nations—seemed aimless and bored.

"Everything in good time, Martin," Jaques assured him, clapping his back and guiding him through the sliding glass doors.

They proceeded through a large foyer with potted plants and reception desk to an elevator operated by a pert redhead who smiled welcomingly at Ruben. He smiled back. There was a hiss, a faint impression of motion, and the doors opened.

He had expected to be taken to Ingrid Solomon's office, but found himself stepping into a maze of laboratories. The director led them perhaps sixty feet down a luxuriously carpeted corridor to a glass door, knocked smartly on it, and walked in. Ruben and Jaques followed.

Suddenly Martin wished he had become a psychiatrist, as well as a psychologist, so he might now have an appreciation for the jungle of shining equipment he saw before him. There was nothing here, he could tell, of the "mad doctor's" beakers, sinister vials, or gigantic and quite phony lightning machine. At the center of the room a neatly humming IBM computer sang to itself and several data-processing people stood by, prepared to offer it a luncheon of software.

Those workers who bothered to look up from their obviously intense efforts recognized the Director at once, nodding or smiling at her, a few murmuring her name.

Then a single figure dissociated itself from a cluster of people near an interior door and bustled toward them. While he wore the white jacket of Solomon Studies, there were herringbone suit trousers beneath it and, instead of bare chest beneath the jacket at the neck,

Ruben made out a buttondown blue shirt with matching tie.

The man also wore a frigid smile of greeting that told them, as well as words would have done, that they were interrupting him. He was perhaps sixty years old, Ruben decided, tallish and erect with a balding head that retained a hedge of surprising black hair. His nose was huge, prominent and autocratic, his mouth wide with rubbery lips that immediately became a severe frown after their initial smile.

"I see you're back," he said curtly in a cultivated baritone. His hard brown eyes passed over Ruben's face without interest.

"Professor Sinoway, I'd like to present a guest who may agree to join the faculty," said Ingrid Solomon, gesturing. "Doctor Martin Ruben, this is Morley Sinoway."

"Oh?" the other man asked coldly. "And what is your discipline, sir?"

"Psychology," Ruben replied, extending his hand automatically. "But Ms. Solomon is primarily interested in me as a parapsychologist and instructor."

"I should have guessed as much," Sinoway declared, ready to turn away, already bored. He made a low humming sound, a nervous affectation.

"Why is that, Professor Sinoway?" Ruben asked, stopping the older man. "Is it psychologists or parapsychologists who have such idiosyncratic faces?"

Sinoway paused, appraised Ruben with a sneer. "I only meant that Ms. Solomon is generally more intrigued by supernatural mumbo-jumbo than by the sheer science of what we're attempting to do." He scanned Martin from head to toe, no longer than he needed. "Although it's possible that parapsychologists *do* have distinctive, uhm, faces."

Well, well, Ruben mused sardonically to himself. *If they don't see me as Sherlock Holmes, they spot me as a Jew. I think I've got me a bigot.*

"I should appreciate it, Professor Sinoway," Jacques put in, again stopping the bald man, "if you would explain some of our projects to Doctor Ruben."

He sighed. "Very well, if that's Ms. Solomon's wish." He frowned at Jacques, apparently dismissed him. "Geographically, Ruben, we have one hundred special laboratories set up on an individual, autonomous basis where we subject our—humm—subjects to the closest scrutiny. I'm sure you'll wish to watch the show personally during your stay." He gave the faintest emphasis to the word "show." "The effort entails completeness, you see. Our goal is to examine every reported extrasensory perceptional fear, every doctrainaire occult theory of long-standing, every myth of legend or alchemy. Hence, there is a constant turn-over of projects."

Ruben was fascinated despite the professor's manner. "You're testing reincarnation, then? With hypnotic regression therapy, I suppose?" He saw Sinoway nod. "Psychokinesis? Telepathy?" Further curt nods. "Out-of-body experiences?"

"Of *course*, Doctor!" Sinoway sighed. "But you're taking up considerable valuable time with these mild guesses. In addition to everything you can imagine—clairvoyance, PK, precognition, forecasting of all kinds, Psi in general—we have dolphins here with whom we're beginning to communicate quite famously. At Ms. Solomon's orders, we have initiated regular séances, utilizing the mediumistic skills of a number of people—always under the strictest laboratory conditions, of course. Altered states of consciousness, both through biofeedback and properly administered hallucinogenic drugs, are weighed; we are inspecting myths related to Satan as well as to Olympus, duplicating poltergeist phenomena, and attempting to create trance states akin to dying in order to test for an afterlife." His angry brown eyes sputtered at Jacques. "Doctor Coquelion's idea, that. In short, my dear Ruben, we have a massive amount of work to do and I am in charge of overseeing all such testing and experimentation. Please excuse me."

Before Sinoway could vanish, Martin raised his voice. "Professor, I'm not through; I have two more questions. I believe the Director asked you to speak with me."

"Yes, what are those questions?" Sinoway cocked a fierce eyebrow and waited.

"First, where did all the kids come from out there?" Ruben inquired. "I had the impression, on the way here, of perhaps one hundred people under twenty-one years of age."

The professor's manicured fingers ducked into the breast pocket of the suitcoat beneath his uniform top. He snapped up the lid of a notebook and glared farsightedly at it. "We have precisely one thousand forty-five children at the close of the latest census." He flipped a page. "There are two thousand, nine hundred and forty-four adults in residence on Nommos Island, in addition to the staff itself."

"Virtually a small town," Ruben noted with surprise. "Who *are* all those children?"

Sinoway glanced at the Director. Ingrid nodded. "They are orphans, Ruben. Orphans."

"Orphans?"

"The majority, yes. The unwanted, unwashed riffraff of the world. It was Ms. Solomon herself who found, before she purchased this island, that children who are left entirely to their own devices during their growing years are disinclined to put childish susceptibility to paranormal phenomena behind them. Instead, knowing no better, they cling to and develop psychic skills at a far greater rate than those respectable children who are properly reared by their parents. I'm absolutely delighted to say," Sinoway continued with a sneer, "that we have here a virtual United Nations of the world's principal undesirables."

"But those who were in orphanages," Ruben protested, "cutting all that red tape—"

"You do not understand, sir," the professor retorted without waiting for him to finish. "These brats were never in orphanages. They were never . . . *anywhere* . . . before. Except the streets, of course. Many of the children's population, especially the boys, earned a trivial living as miniature pickpockets and procurers. Pimps, I think the word is? Many of the girls, including some of the younger ones, existed as prostitutes. Both sexes produced their lamentable share of narcotic addicts and pushers."

"This is the first home they've had, Martin," Ingrid said to the astonished parapyschologist. "For the first time in their lives they're getting regular meals, a balanced diet, a comfortable and safe place to stay and to sleep. I—merely had them picked off the streets of the world. In addition to finding that they are often unusually gifted psychically, and exploring their abilities, I am providing them both with an education and proper standards and regulations."

Martin Ruben didn't know what to say. In a sense, of course, what Ingrid had ordered done was commendable. But in another sense, it was so cold, so functionally practical: Human beings yanked from their environments against their wills to be used as test subjects.

He approached a nearby window and looked out of it, hand trembling at the metal shade. A large number of people, mostly the kids, still stood at the mound and some of the younger ones held one another's hands. In the expressions of a few boys and girls, Ruben could detect strain, anxiety. They seemed to be keeping a safe distance from the ropes encircling the mound.

"You are looking at the scum-children of adult scumbags," Sinoway said from behind him. "Without their meager psychic skills and clever little tricks to advertise them, they would be fully worthless flotsam. Ms. Solomon is a dearly sentimental woman."

"My other question, Professor," Ruben began, turning and furious, "is very simple: If you don't like the brand of guinea pig you use—if you're so antagonistic to the paranormal—why in hell are you here?"

Jacques couldn't resist chuckling. He received an angry stare and fierce humming sound for his trouble.

"Whatever bias I may have toward ESP and the rest is quite beside the point," the professor snapped. "I bring to this work a detached and objective, dedicated, and trained scientific mind. There will be no wishful thinking in results *I* produce, no extension of neurotic hopes—" again he frowned at Coquelion—"into realms of total fantasy. I am, in addition, a bloody taskmaster, a whip-wielding overseer—at least in manner. Beyond those points, Doctor Rubenski, you will need to learn my qualifications from Ms. Solomon, since they are *none of your goddamned business!*"

He hadn't actually lifted his voice a whit, but Ruben felt the hair at the back of his own neck rising in fury.

Before he could speak, another man joined them, distracting him. He was a man in his early thirties, ruggedly handsome, the kind whom an idle glance might consign to the labor force but in whose bright eyes a fine intelligence shone.

"Ed Fribaron, Dr. Martin Ruben," Ingrid said briefly.

"Hi," Ed offered, shaking Ruben's hand with a smile. Martin tried to regain his equanimity.

"While you were having it out with the good professor," Ingrid explained, watching Sinoway's erect form stride off, "I took the opportunity of punching a button for Ed. I'd appreciate it, Ed, if you'd explain something of the engineering aspect of life on Nommos Island." She rested her fingertips on Martin's arm. "Fribaron is probably the most brilliant and versatile engineer on earth."

"Well, it takes more than engineering alone to make us self-sufficient," the amiable fellow said with a shrug. And Ruben thought *self-sufficient?* "Jeff Patterson out in Section Three on the west side of the island is in charge of agriculture, for example. Even has a nice little herd of cattle to keep us in sirloin. You should see, Doc, what Jeff can do with hydroponics too. It—"

"Simply explain your part of it, please," Ingrid directed him, glancing at her wristwatch.

"Right. Well, the island operates on solar energy stored in the wind, Doc, the wind energy in the water. It's pretty new and complicated as all-get-out. There's a system of underground cables with a number of hydroelectric generators." He scratched his crewcut head, got out a pipe and lit it. "All this involves a special plastic dielectric that allows direct-current and small-disaster aluminum cores to be tremendously charged. Pretty effective."

"Did I see a dam on my way in?" Ruben inquired.

"Uh-huh," Ed Fribaron nodded. "It uses turbine

generators, too, of course. The point is, Doctor Ruben, with what we got goin' for us here—the finest of equipment, innovation, the finest minds to run things, even improve 'em—well, we're autonomous as hell on Nommos." His ruddy face beamed with pride as he sucked on his pipe. "In a way, sir, I think this little ol' place could survive if every other goddamn part of the world went under!"

As they wended their way to Ingrid's office for more introductions, more discussions, Ruben saw again in his mind's eye a flicker from his dreaming premonitions. It occurred to him that Morley Sinoway could be the terrible old man of his visions except that Sinoway wasn't nearly so old, nor did he appear ill, as did the body counter of the premonition. But more to the point, after what he'd already seen and heard, it was almost as if brilliant, beautiful Ingrid Solomon were beginning her own community here. Even her own country.

As he was entering her office Ruben paused, fingers tightening on the door frame. It was actually more than that, he thought uneasily. *Secrets* lurked here, unaddressed and unspoken. It was really almost as if Ingrid were beginning . . . her own world.

Six

Ruben sank into a new, comfortable easychair beside his bed and lit a Camel with a feeling of relief. It had been an exceptionally long and fascinating day, and he finally had a chance both to relax and inspect his quarters. Much of what he'd heard drew his wholehearted endorsement. Ever since Martin had been a boy and acquired an embryonic interest in supernatural matters, only to discover later to separate the great welter of psychic claptrap from the hard and perplexing nucleus of data science could not account for.

Later, when Unidentified Flying Objects seemed to be on everybody's lips—except they were then called "flying saucers" or "discs"—it intrigued Martin enormously the way experts tended to "explain away" all but six or seven percent of reported sightings and be perfectly content that UFOs were a closed subject.

As a man of science himself, Ruben knew that the experts worked doubly hard on that fine residue. If they still could not explain six percent of sightings as representing hoax, weather balloons, swamp gas, weather inversions, planets or hubcaps, they represented a genuine hardcore of inexplicable fact. Fact he'd have given his eyeteeth to test.

On the one hand, consequently, he saw wild-eyed "believers" who accepted without a grain of salt everything from UFO to spirit phenomena to people who seemed to have been "banished," from bug-eyed little green men to Loch Ness monsters and Abominable Snowmen. On the other hand—and he thought it was much worse, since scientists are supposed to know better—the community of so-called "authorities" dismissed everything out of hand. Without examining a single report. In most cases neither side had witnessed arising phenomena, interviewed a single "contactee," or run even one small test.

Now, Solomon Studies was doing it right, at last. In a way Ruben even approved of the choice of Professor Morley Sinoway. Somehow the man had been trapped here, obliged to work regularly and exhaustively with data he despised. If such a fellow came up with conclusive evidence in a given project study, the facts he adduced would probably be widely accepted.

He had remarked to Ingrid Solomon his concern that Sinoway's abhorrence of the paranormal could have an adverse impact upon psychics who were tested, since the word often associated with them—"sensitives"—was an accurate term. "They may well sense his animosity and be unable to perform."

But Ingrid had given him one of her patented frosty smiles across the vast plains of her elaborate desk. "The reason Sinoway was glaring at Jacques the way he was involves the fact that your Belgian chum has *direct* contact with the experiments and test subjects. The Professor is what he said he is: a supervisor, an overseer. By the time Jacques has beamed on the Professor's 'guinea pigs' a dozen times, told jokes and shyly rubbed that silly goatee of his, they're ready to perform like they never have before."

It was as if Ingrid had thought of everything, as if she had taught herself the art of perfection as a human

72

being and, with her strange island in the middle of Hoosier Lake Triton, managed to detach herself from the errors of clumsy, ordinary mankind.

And that was what continued to trouble Ruben. He wasn't really sure if he could work beside anybody who was not only dedicated to a godlike perfection, but seemed to have *achieved* it!

And that, Marty m'boy, he told himself as he poked around quarters that proved to be typically comfortable yet ideally functional, attests to what a male chauvinist pig you probably are, at heart.

He found, to his delight, that the water faucets both in a superb little kitchenette and a tiled bathroom that would have made Conrad Hilton jealous, instantly produced either boiling hot or freezing cold water. There was a waterbed with just the right "pitch" to it, he decided, grinning and briefly rollicking across its surface. He not only had a color television set, but two, including one in the bedroom. And the living-room set was a gigantic wall contraption with the televised images nearly lifesize.

He was especially surprised and pleased to find a little study alcove outfitted with a typewriter, ream of paper, several choices of notebook, and a dozen good ballpoint pens. *Smart touch, that*, he thought; *these are quarters for the staff, and the more obsessive fellows will be able to get up and work in the middle of the night.*

But there was nothing on TV that he cared to watch, he'd already had dinner in the cafeteria—never would have expected a choice for entree between Peking duck and veal scallopine!—and he sank lazily back into his chair in the front room, musing.

It was good to be with people who shared his interests although some of the terms floating around, used casually by those whom he met, told him that he was rusty and needed to do his homework. Effectance motivation, PMIR, need-relevant object, cue utilization, theoretical variance, displacement, DT and GESP, preferential matching, microdynamic PK, screened-touch matching, remote viewing, and paradiagnosis were words used with the greatest of ease by people whom Ingrid wanted to be his colleagues. He heard names he hadn't heard used in years: Eisenbud, Matthews, Ehrenwald, Feathers, Krippner, Zinchenko, Roll, Ashby, Puthoff, Podmore, Garrett, and Dinwall.

And he heard his friend Jacques ticking off the major parameters, or "sensitivities": "We have taken, first, old friend, the categories accepted by most modern parapsychologists: telepathy, clairvoyance, dowsing, precognition or proscopy, psychokinesis, mental photography, and paramedicine. We have a fantastic middle-aged woman from Tibet, by the way, who excels in the latter—she's an incredible healer and she also promises to create a *tulpa* for us. Then we have expanded the usual realms of interest for psychotronics, bio-information and bio-introscopy. Although the more hidebound parapsychologists might resist the notion, we certainly include all methods of fortune telling, notably astrology, as well as yoga, age regression, alchemy, mythology, OOBE, astral projection, spiritualism, and much more."

"No," Ruben said quietly.

"What do you mean, 'No'?" Jacques scowled.

"You don't include *all* kinds of fortune telling. Heptascopy, for example," Ruben had pointed out with a smile. "I doubt that you let anyone attempt divination with the human liver."

And Jacques had laughed. "Around this place, *monsieur le doctair*, one cannot be absolutely certain! But the point is, what Sinoway told you is true: We're studying the whole range of the paranormal. Voodoo, elementals, demonology, the hynagogic state, witchcraft, the I Ching, pyramid power—everything!"

Then why, Ruben wondered now, tapping his long fingers on the chair arm, did I not get a complete tour of the facility? *Why* was one entire wing of the building ignored while Ingrid was explaining "the overall picture," as she put it?

There was a knock at the door. Ruben sat up straight, called "Come in."

The person who entered was a Eurasian girl who could not have been more than seventeen years old. She would be a fabulous brunette beauty one day, Ruben saw at a glance, rising. Her mane of jet-black hair trailed naturally behind her, reaching her round buttocks, and her bright-green eyes appraised him with the mature appearance of a much older woman. She wore a very American jeans-and-shirt combination.

"Hi," she said, "I'm Tina." She had a clipboard in one hand and a pencil in the other. Her smile tried to be businesslike but she seemed instantly drawn to him. "One of the things I have to do is go around getting info. When were you born?"

He told her, smiling but curious.

"Where, and do you know what the *exact* minute was that you were born?"

He cocked an eyebrow. "It sounds almost as if you're trying to erect an astrological horoscope," he remarked, perching on the arm of his chair.

"Oh, we *are*, Doctor Ruben!" she replied. Tina's shrewd little eyes continued to evaluate him and Martin felt disconcertingly like a test animal. "They tell me it's important for the—overall picture."

Her girlish impertinence, the manlike way she openly studied him, was both arousing and offputting. He studied her back, seeing that while she did not have a body built on the lush, even mammoth proportions favored by many of his American peers, she was very short, compact, and altogether adorable. When he finally noticed that she was barefoot he laughed inwardly, reminded of her youth.

"I suppose I can cooperate," he said.

"*Do*, Doctor," said another voice. "It's a must."

Ingrid Solomon appeared behind Tina, towering over the tiny Eurasian and patting the girl's shoulder as she entered.

"Humor us," she continued. "We like to know—*really* know—the people whom we ask here. Not that I anticipate any problems, of course."

"Well, then, I shall do better than humor you," Martin replied, again standing. "I'm Geminian, born May twenty-sixth as I indicated, with twenty-two degrees of Capricorn rising. That places my Sun, Mercury, and Venus in the Fifth House and—"

Tina interrupted him: "The Fifth House?" When her full lips smiled, a bright-red tongue crept out to moisten them. "That's very creative, Doctor. And also romantic."

"It's the source of my interest in things that are slightly more romantic than pragmatic science," he said, actually speaking to Ingrid. "I have poor tolerance for boredom, I fear. As most Geminians, I tend to be restless."

Tina had drawn near enough to him to touch. She did, a plump hand resting on his slender one. "And where is your Moon, Dr. Ruben?"

He chuckled. Clearly this child knew that the moon governed emotions, in astrological parlance. "I fear it's in Virgo, Tina," he told her. "So I have my private side, though its square to my Gemini sun."

To his astonishment her fingers tightened fleetingly on his wrist. "I'll just bet you do have your private side," she said in a husky voice.

Then she was shutting the door behind her.

"For the love of heaven, Ingrid!" he exclaimed, turning to see the blond Director. "That child seems to have a nearly abnormal, prurient interest in me!"

"Yes, I think she does," Ingrid replied, slipping out of her suit jacket. Today she wore a yellow sweater beneath it and it accented her widely spaced breasts. Beneath it, he saw, she wore no brassiere. "But I don't think it's abnormal in the least. You're a man who can be fascinating to an intelligent modern woman. And Tina's bright. She has an I.Q. in the one fifties."

"Well, after all, she's just a girl," he protested, putting his arms around her waist and kissing the end of her nose.

"Do you *want* her?"

"What?" he demanded, holding her at arm's length in surprise.

"We take an intentionally prurient interest in things around here, Martin. We advocate healthy, overt sexuality. You'll find many advantages to being on staff with Solomon Studies, just as I promised you. I asked: Do you *want* Tina?"

Something old-fashioned and moralistic in Ruben twisted uncomfortably and he released her completely, sat back in his chair with a mild feeling of repugnance. "My God, Ingrid, no! She's a child." It had also occurred to him with pique that he thought a relationship was beginning with Ingrid. What kind of games *were* these she played?

"Tina lost her virginity on the streets of Hong Kong years ago," Ingrid said matter-of-factly, slipping out of her skirt. Her violet eyes held Ruben's for a moment, then she removed her panties. The effect, with her yellow sweater still covering her from the waist up, was electrifying. "She was little more than a whore when I brought her to Nommos Island and I scarcely think that a romp in the hay with you will further tarnish her."

Ruben shook his head for several reasons. One was a rising conviction that much of what he saw, here, was a show, and that he was somehow being manipulated. "Do you mind changing the subject?" he asked with an irascible trace, trying not to look at her just then. "What does a doctrine of open sexuality have to do with parapsychology, with the study of myths and the occult?"

Now she stood before him, tempting inches away, simply standing. His fingers itched to reach for the faint golden fringe. "You forget your history, Doctor Ruben. Almost all mythology is inclined to involve sex and love or sexual prowess, one way or the other. Most of what the antipagan types have liked to call 'evil' is tied to sex, at least in their own minds. A large part of alchemy pertains not only to the search for a mysterious philosopher's stone, with which to transmute base metals to gold, but to aphrodisiacal potions or elixirs. Witchcraft is full of spells with which to attract and seduce the opposite sex; so is voodoo. Despite what our surly-tempered forbearers labored so damned hard to suppress, much of the progress of the ancient world was accounted for by sexual attractions between kings and their women, or kings and the sorcerers and magis who conjured marvelous things for them. Besides, Martin, it's more a question of what parapsychology has to do with . . . *special interests* of my organization than the other way around." Now she knelt between his knees and put her hands out, cupping. "You never know what silly little superstition, what little time-tested ritual, may have been based on fact. Unless you, uhm, examine it."

Dimly conscious that he was himself engaged in a game of resistance now, Ruben strove to concentrate despite the insistent press of her fingers. "While we're in the general area of the subject, Ingrid, what's the story behind that great mound of earth out there? It appears to be right in the center of Nommos."

He couldn't tell whether the expression that passed over her fair-skinned, lovely face was one of irritation or apprehension. But she drew back a moment before taking his wrists and firmly guiding his hands to her yellow sweater. "You are annoyingly observant, aren't you? Well, I'll take you there myself," she said, at last. "Probably tomorrow. You'll hear soon enough that one of our requirements is that everybody on the island go to the mound daily."

"Whatever for?" he asked. Now he was raising the sweater over her outflung arms, almost despite himself, but only for a moment. When she lifted her arms that way the curve of her legs where she sat with the big-girl pool of softness where her legs met, suggested a feminine frailty he rarely saw in her. "*Why*," he persisted, "does everyone go to the mound each day? To pray, or what?"

But she ignored him. Her own hands were insistent on his clothing, now, tugging him quickly out of his garments. "Just remember this, Martin," she began slowly, pulling his shorts to his ankles and watching the way he leapt to readiness. "Never go to that mound at night. I repeat: *Never go to the mound at night*." Nude, now, like Ruben, she still managed to summon her commanding authority. "And that, sir, is an order."

He frowned openly. "I'm not employed by Solomon Studies just yet. I must know why."

"The mound is the oldest artifact in this state," she

replied tightly. As if to punish him, she dropped her hands to the floor. "There are ancient legends about it. It would be inconsistent for an organization dedicated to the study of the paranormal to live contrary to the only aged artifact near us. Legend urges that all the natives—that's us—pay their respects daily, but never approach it at night."

"There's more, though, isn't there?" he demanded. "Something happened there. Someone was hurt, or even died. Right?"

She slipped away from him to undo her long, light-blond hair. She lay on her back on the sumptuous white carpeting, rolled like a kitten. Now she arched her back. "Could I possibly arouse your interest in other kinds of mounds?"

"You already have," he exclaimed, standing.

"Push number fifteen on the television set," she suggested with a smile full of unknown meaning.

He took his eyes from the beautiful woman on the rug with immense difficulty and did as she wished, bobbing as he moved.

On the wall screen before them, to his astonishment, came a full-color scene depicting two men and five women. It also portrayed such rich, inventive, and yet delectably tasteful sexuality that he could scarcely believe his eyes.

"That's only the Nineteen-eighties' version of background music, darling, music to you-know-what-to." Her hips began to writhe as he turned to peer hungrily down at her. Ingrid's hands cupped and gently lifted her breasts to him, as if offering baskets of rare, edible fruit. "Not the main attraction."

Unable to lay on his stomach, he reclined on his side for a moment, his mouth and tongue exploring. The combination of her sensual beauty and the incredible activity on the wall screen was heady. There were groans of joy, from the television set; then they came too from Ingrid Solomon. Once she raised her knees to enclose him, squeezing, and Martin thought he might happily die of suffocation.

But it was quite what, or all, that Ingrid wanted.

She wriggled away in a moment. He saw her pass, above him, looked up her tall bare body, a symphony of pink and gold. Then she bent, tasting him briefly, nerve responses flooding his brain. Then it was again the way it had been the first night—great heaven, Ruben thought, was it only *last night*!—as he lifted her soft underbody, then lowered it until his penis had entered it, eagerly.

". . . For there is a time there for every purpose and for every work," she intoned above him, her voice coming in quick gasps.

He looked up at her, startled anew. Her head was back; her fingers worked at her broad nipples. "Sh-h," he called softly, not wanting to talk, not wanting to quote *Song of Solomon*. He wearied quickly of that game.

But then he thought with his precise mind, *That's not from* Song of Solomon! *I don't know the source of that quotation.*

Was it his imagination or was this brilliant woman *still* teasing him, even now as she moved frantically to satisfy him? What was this new game? And why did she prefer sex *this* way? Most women did not, he knew. Was it something unique to Ingrid, perhaps to the way she was constructed; or was it only that she remained *dominant* this way—"on top," figuratively as well?

He was drawing near his climax when, to his dark and complete chagrin, he heard the door of his apartment open.

81

For a moment he couldn't see who it was. All the guilt of sex, all the moments of surreptitious pleasure he had stolen when he was a boy and very young man, froze him in breathless consternation. He squinted through the gloom of the night, sought to use the flickering light from the television screen.

It was Tina, the Eurasian girl, barely visible in the doorway.

He couldn't be certain but he thought she was naked. Most of her dark-skinned little body was dimly in evidence. Mostly, he could make out her green eyes sparkling as she stared openly at him and the Director of Solomon Studies—and a small, plump hand between her parted thighs.

Then he realized Ingrid knew, too. She had felt him stop, and freeze.

"The girl," he hissed in a tense, agonized whisper. "She's *watching*!"

"Yes, she is," Ingrid said in an almost normal tone of voice, her motion halted as she bowed her head to him and the long, pale-blond hair tickled his face and chest. "She certainly is."

"I can't finish now," he growled in frustration.

"Yes," Ingrid assured him, "you certainly can."

Instantly her lower body was a combination of sweet suction cup and perpetual motion machine. Somehow she succeeded almost in turning her body upon him; he knew that, when he reached up, it was to reach *around* her curving back and cup her breasts. When she turned back, again, she was ready herself and Martin became aware only of kaleidoscopic color flaming from the wall screen and of Ingrid's own sweet flashes of white, pink, and yellow—

And inescapably, two hot green eyes staring avidly at them from the doorway.

Unbelievably, in a moment, there were *three* gasps, a trio of relinquishing moans in Ruben's quarters—and none of them came from the TV.

He was amazed to find that his climax had been even better than before.

But as the door softly closed, without a word from the young Eurasian girl, and Ingrid disengaged herself to lie beside him in relaxation, and as Martin Ruben rose on tottering legs to go to the bathroom, he heard the *other* sound: It followed prior, smaller noises of someone distinctly in pain. He had felt he imagined them.

But he could not have imagined the primary sound, because it was that of a woman, somewhere in this giant modern building, screaming with a tortured agony that sounded animal-like as well as fatal.

It was the first time he felt this way.

Afraid, definitely afraid.

What in the *hell* was really going on here?

_____ **Seven**

The next morning Ruben awakened fairly well-rested but aware of a slight backache.

It's a wonder I can move at all, he thought, finding himself alone in bed and oddly grateful for it. While he showered, Martin gave some thought to this woman who apparently found him so attractive. Unquestionably, she was the best, the most absorbing and fulfilling bedmate he'd ever had. She was, as well, clearly the most brilliant woman he ever knew. Yet he had to confess wryly to himself that he wasn't terribly fond of Ingrid. We men, he sighed, are hard to please. A part of him still remembered with nostalgia and sweetness the first girl with whom he had gone to bed, many years ago. Inexperienced and clumsy, she had yet revealed a genuine interest in him and not just a part of his anatomy. Ingrid's warmth seemed limited to sexual acrobatics and an occasional wry joke. Whether there was, in the beautiful blonde, the slightest capacity to experience affection or love, he honestly couldn't say.

When she made love—actually, "made sex" was more accurate—it was as though another part of Ingrid remained constantly detached and watching. Possibly a vagrant strand of her thinking was always exclusively focused on her career goals. He smiled, toweling down. Probably it was a miracle that she even permitted a fraction of her mind to concentrate on sex. It was even possible, he thought, that Ingrid displayed the ranging imagination she did during sex play simply to advance some area of her work.

He'd known many people like that before, hating them all. Usually, they were men, mentally washed-out hunters of the almighty dollar who appraised even the pursuit of a rollicking good time in terms of whether they had successfully advanced their altogether-damned careers. If the tendency wasn't so common, Ruben thought, he'd be inclined to consider such attitudes wholly aberrant and linked to privately antisocial tendencies arising from roaring insecurities.

Yet such men were often the business geniuses of the world, toasted at luncheons from coast to coast, even appointed to Presidential committees. As his mother used to say to him, there was a thin dividing line between genius and insanity. And the line narrowed considerably when the expression of that genius lay either through business or science.

When he was cleanly dressed, he went out to the front room and found that Ingrid—or perhaps the Eurasian girl, Tina—had left him a blank form to fill out. It had been neatly thumbtacked to a corkboard beside the front door.

"You have to be kidding," he groaned aloud. "They have more questions to be answered than the IRS."

This new form demanded his preferences, in myriad departments. Familiar as he was with psychological profile testing, Martin couldn't quite perceive the intention behind either the queries or the form in general. He was asked to name his favorite colors, foods, fragrances, and all-time favorite movies as well as television programs. Some of these he could answer readily enough, remotely irked with himself that he really *did* prefer blue, and T-bone steak, that he couldn't imagine doing without his memories of *Treasure of the Sierra Madre* on film or "The Defenders" and "I Spy" on TV.

With his mood already soured by a realization that his honed critical faculties wasted time in rating and remembering such things, he began playing fast-and-loose with the damned form. He perched in mild ire on the edge of his sofa, reading and scribbling. To the question "What is your favorite song?" he answered, "Song of India." Asked to name his favorite novel of all time, he noted *Little Women*, scratched it off and stuck in "Linda Lovelace's autobiography."

Where it demanded his favorite sexual activities—somehow he *knew* they'd get around to that!—Ruben penned, very precisely, "I can't get off with just one woman; I require multiple sex partners, preferably female," and grinned evilly to himself. What was his favorite sex position? "I really prefer lying on my stomach in bed and being surprised by a bevy of beauties crawling toward me from nowhere." The next question read, "Do you consider yourself a political conservative, liberal, or moderate?" "All three," he scrawled, confusing them. The greatest President? Who else could a Hoosier name but Benjamin Harrison!

When he had completed filling out the form he took an elevator down to the second floor. Now that he'd expressed himself, Ruben felt good at nine o'clock in the morning for the first time in years. He felt, indeed, adventurous.

This was the correct floor for the countless suites of offices housing the business aspect of Solomon Studies, but it was necessary to walk some distance down the corridor until he passed from the residential area through double doors.

Immediately the impression was that of being in a high-rise, expensive office building. Typewriters tat-ratted, engines of many kinds groaned, air conditioners hummed; stray bodiless voices could also be heard, most human moods distantly familiar. It occurred to Ruben that it was the same area of the third floor which he really wanted to see, and wondered when they would invite him to inspect the entire Solomon Studies setup. And *if* they would.

He hesitated to scan the photograph of a tall, becalmed, thin-lipped gentleman with thick dark eyebrows, keen eyes beneath them, and a long Reagan-like upper lip. It wasn't named or titled, in any fashion; Martin remembered seeing the same shot in two other locations just the day before. He walked on, making a mental note to ask the identity of this man. Could it possibly be Ingrid's father?

At last he located Jacques Coquelion working with horoscope charts at a table next to a desk, so lost in thought that he jumped, startled, when the psychologist drew near. Jacques was wearing a white pullover and snowy shorts; with his tan, and despite the wan expression he had as a rule these days, he might have been preparing to trot out to the tennis courts. But he gave Ruben a cheery smile and healthy handshake.

"Well, my friend," he said at once, "everything is set up for you now. Of course, I must run it through Ye Olde Computer for matchups. I found your chart most interesting, *most* interesting, *mon ami*. Fascinating intelligence!"

Ruben took a seat at the desk. "*You're* the resident astrologer?" he inquired in surprise.

"Well, astrology permeates everything at S.S. Most of the staff can dabble effectively enough with it. But our approach is fairly mechanical, even pragmatic, except in the arrangement of each resident's schedule. That doesn't call for interpretation but precision."

Ruben tugged thoughtfully at his chin. "Jacques, what *is* all this about 'everything being set up' for me? *What* schedule?"

"I thought you knew." Jacques paused, ruminating. "I'm not sure Ingrid would want me to go into this yet, if she hasn't. She may prefer, uhm, to handle it herself."

"Handle *what*?" Ruben demanded, flushing. "Are you talking about a working schedule for me?"

"Not just that." Jacques' grin came close to apology. "Your *everything* schedule, Martin. We allow nothing to chance around here. Chance is *de trop* on Nommos Island. All activities, including those which are recreational, are finely planned and scheduled. Impulse is the mortal enemy of a dedicated scientist or researcher."

"That's ineffable rot and you know it," Ruben snapped. "Incessant scheduling inclines one to forming obsessions, to compulsiveness. A life that's overstructured is an ideal and fertile ground for neurosis."

"And *you* know, Marteen," Jacques pressed, lapsing into a French accent in his rising heat, "that the growing sentiment among psychologists is that the word 'neurosis' is inaccurate. Outgrown."

"Nonsense!" Ruben exclaimed, slamming the desk with his palm. "You still get hit by a charging bull or a falling meteor even if you never heard of either!"

"Marteen, you're wrong! *Sacre bleu!* I haven't—"

"Perhaps I can explain to the good doctor's satisfaction."

Both men looked around. They had been so absorbed in their dispute that they hadn't heard Ingrid Solomon enter the room. She lolled against the doorframe, not to appear sexy but with an air of propriety. Her complexion was marvelous this morning, Ruben observed: sex obviously agreed with her. But the subtly superior, aren't-you-little-boys-cute look in her bright violet eyes annoyed him.

"I'd like to have some answers, Madame Director," Ruben began, standing politely, "since I seem to have been inserted into some schedule of yours even before I've agreed to work here."

"Stop and think, Martin. How else can you know what our routines are *like*—how else can you judge your comfort in working within them—except by *sampling* them? By living a day or two in our regimen?"

He paused, unable to answer her. Finally he sighed. "You're right, of course. And as usual." He turned back to Jacques. "I'm sorry that I lost my temper."

Jacques grinned and pinched his little gray goatee with satisfaction. "So am I. All is forgiven. Look, as an astrologer, you're bound to appreciate our scheduling more than most people here. Several have grumbled about its occasional inconveniences, but I doubt that you will."

Ruben shook his head slightly in minor pique. "I dislike quibbling, but I am *not* an astrologer—let me get that straight. I *know* the subject, I often *use* it as a tool. But I had a good friend once who permitted it to rule every phase of his life. He got so that he couldn't eat lunch out if the stars didn't recommend it. I think astrology nearly drove him round the bend."

"Exception noted."

Ingrid glanced at Jacques, somewhat annoyed. "Not entirely. Everyone here *is* regulated by astrology."

"But it works well," said the Belgian, "because we're *all* doing it."

Now Martin Ruben laughed openly. "Do you realize —either of you—that I have no idea what you're talking about?"

And Ingrid smiled, warmly for once. "Pardon us, please. Well, Doctor, as you know, the year is astrologically divided into twelve segments—one for each zodiacal sign; Aries, Taurus, Gemini, and so forth."

"Of course," he nodded. "We needn't begin at the kindergarten level."

"I want to be thorough," she said firmly. "Now, for example, it is mid-July and we are in the Cancer sun-sign period. On July twenty-third, it becomes the Leo period. A month later, the Virgo, and so on." She lifted a palm at his impatience. "Most people know these things, but few realize that, during a given zodiacal period, *each* of the twelve signs *rises* on the eastern horizon each and every day. At dawn, during the present Cancer period, Cancer rises. Two hours later, approximately, Leo rises; around ten, Virgo; around noon, Libra; around two P.M. Scorpio. And so forth."

Ruben sighed his exasperation. "That's fundamental astrology: Stars one-oh-one."

Now Ingrid's gaze cooled, and held his. "What most people also don't realize, even those who try to live a given day 'attuned' to the solar and lunar influences of that day, is that the signs rising every two hours *also* have considerable influence." She glanced at Jacques, back to Ruben. "What we do here at Solomon Studies, then, is make sure that *all* staff members and *all* sensitives on the premises *live in absolute harmony with the planets*."

"It has never been done before, Martin, *anywhere*," Jacques commented. "Not on a regular basis with many people involved."

He nodded slowly, thoughtfully. "Very well, I can follow that. When Virgo is rising, one should study, right? When Capricorn does, one perseveres with business or ambition—correct?" They nodded. "One is extremely independent during the Aries ascending two-hour segment; lazy and calmly practical during Taurus? Right?"

"So far as you've gone, Doctor, yes." Ingrid lifted an eyebrow. "But it's rather more extensive than that."

Ruben tried to conceal his astonishment. "Well, I can readily see that it might keep us all more in tune with planetary influences."

"The computer helps beyond that, well beyond," said Jacques. "When your sun sign or 'birth sign' is afflicted—under influences that tend to be harmful to you—you can be in serious danger. The computer takes those factors into consideration and enables everyone here to live not only more sensibly and productively but more safely."

"A concept like that has much to recommend it," Martin agreed, meaning it, but unable to understand why the director would go to such lengths. "In other words *that's* the schedule you're preparing for me."

"Right! You'll know, at a glance, when to work, sleep, dine, *everything*. To your best advantage; always in tune with planetary influences and rising signs."

He looked from Jacques to Ingrid. "I assume this is your concept?"

"Entirely," she replied coolly, standing and drifting toward the door. "I can see that you're still wondering exactly *why* we're going to so much trouble. It's time for more of your tour, now. Afterward, I'll explain why we're so astrologically oriented."

Ingrid and Jacques Coquelion retraced by necessity, some of the territory Ruben had explored the day before, trying to be more comprehensive as well as responsive to his questions.

There was a chance for Ruben to ask his question

about the tall, poised man whose photograph was hung several places in the central building. They paused before it when Ruben dallied there, Ingrid frowning at his interruption of the tour. "Who *is* this old chap?" he inquired.

"His name," the Director retorted, "is Sir Francis Galton."

"I know that name but I can't quite place it," Ruben replied. "Had something to do with Darwin, didn't he?"

Ingrid looked into the steady eyes with admiration. "Sir Francis was Darwin's cousin, and the father of eugenics. The fact that his name is not on every pair of lips continues to infuriate me. He is—almost a patron saint around this place."

"Now I remember," Ruben said, snapping his fingers. "He was curious about why his own family tree was full of famous, contributory people, correct?"

"Galton was born in Birmingham, England, in eighteen-twenty-two, and educated at Cambridge," Jacques said with a nod. "He traveled extensively throughout Africa, writing a couple of books on his travels. But in eighteen-sixty-three—he was an author, anthropologist, and photographer by then—he became the first man to write a book on modern ways of mapping weather."

"At the age of two and one half," Ingrid murmured, almost dreamily, "Francis read fluently and was incredibly versatile. His research later established that all fingerprints are unique, so his contribution to law enforcement and justice was extraordinary."

"Eugenics," Ruben reminded her. It was coming back. "I believe he believed in what he called 'natural talents,' those that came naturally to a race."

"He was never a racist!" Ingrid insisted, coloring.

"He was simply—objective. He said, 'There is nothing either in history of domestic animals or in that of evolution to make us doubt that a race of sane men may be formed, who shall be as much superior mentally and morally to the modern Europeans, as the modern European is to the lowest of the Negro races.' "

"Shades of Hitler," Ruben whispered.

"Not at all!" Jacques replied hastily. "He was a scientist!"

"Who believed in the superiority of *certain* races!"

"He believed they were *possible*," Ingrid said again. "He wrote that 'it would be quite practical to produce a highly gifted race of men . . .' And it would!"

Ruben waited until she returned his gaze. "But what is he doing, in multiplicity, on the walls of Solomon Studies?"

"He's merely an early hero of the lady, Martin," said Jacques offhandedly, smiling. "Come, come, there's much to see."

That proved to be an understatement.

Ruben was introduced to a fifty-two-year-old, ordinary-looking woman named Maisie Plummer, who was blind. Yet she called to Ingrid and Jacques by name when they entered.

Jacques drew Ruben aside. "Maisie is much like Rosa Kuleshova of Russia, who lived in the Urals," he pointed out. "Like Rosa, Maisie has developed the gift of *reading* with her fingertips."

Martin was fascinated. "Yes, I recall Rosa. Russians called her talent 'biointroscopy,' Americans 'dermoptics,' implying some trick of the skin. But neither was more than a word. Such talents are truly inexplicable."

He watched, mesmerized, as Ingrid brought from a bookshelf a very old novel by Stowe. "We needn't blindfold Maisie any longer," she told Ruben in that pert, seemingly open way doctors use when discussing a patient in her presence. "Every physician on staff assures us that she can see nothing. Not even a glimmer of light."

But when Ingrid placed the book, opened at random, before Maisie Plummer's sightless eyes, her rather gnarled fingers shot to it and she began reading, aloud! Ruben noticed both that she was 'reading' words which her fingertips fully covered, and that her fingers seemed almost prehensile, separate from her.

When Maisie had finished a paragraph, Ruben put his hand gently on hers, peculiarly wishing to stop her; she looked up at the slender parapsychologist with a tender smile. She seemed almost to see him. "You're a decent man," she remarked. "I can tell."

Embarrassed, he patted her shoulder. "If you say so, my dear, I must be."

They moved on to another of the one hundred constantly busy compartments in the vast paranormal facility as Ingrid further elucidated: "Before Maisie goes home to Kentucky," she said, "we intend to know just *how* she does that. There's no retina in the fingertips. I'd swear to that. Or I would," she added wryly, "if I hadn't seen that display a dozen times myself."

Ruben was ruminative. "She reminds me of Mary Jane Fancher," he recalled, "only on a lesser scale."

"A *lesser* scale?" Jacques asked, startled.

"Mary Jane could do it all. She lived in Massachusetts about a hundred years ago. While she was totally blinded and paralyzed by an accident, with her right arm locked to the back of her head, Mary Jane also saw with her fingers. Part of her mystique was the way she didn't need to eat. A doctor reported, for official records, that from April fourth to October seventeenth, eighteen sixty-six, Mary Jane had no more to eat than four teaspoons of milk punch, one small section of banana, two spoons of wine, and a small amount of a single cracker." He looked at Jacques. "Her lips, you see, also were locked shut. She had to have them forced open in order to eat at all, and she didn't quite consider it worth the trouble."

Ingrid smiled easily, blind to Martin's somber tones. "No such problems with our Maisie. She eats like a horse."

"Mary Jane was extraordinary," Ruben continued, "predicting the future—always correctly—many times. She would jot down the name of a caller before he'd knocked at the front door downstairs. She lived, by the way, for over forty-five years in that room." He cleared his throat. "Mary Jane knew when her brother died, although it wasn't corroborated for twenty-four hours. She said she wasn't lonely because she could visit friends via astral travel." He stopped walking, raised his head. "I'm afraid I don't care for the way we normals make freaks of such people. We don't even know if these are additional skills, or as in Mary Jane's case, substitutes nature has given them for other lacks."

"What's your point, Doctor?" Ingrid demanded.

"I'd like to see us not only *learn* about these interesting people, but remember that they are human beings and *help* them. They are growing in numbers. If we do not help them, one day the freakshows of circuses will be full of them, rather than bearded ladies and illustrated men." He pulled his cigarettes from his shirt pocket, thoughtfully. "When Mary Jane Fancher was asked how she managed to inspire herself to all her skills, to remain active, she said something curious. At the time of her paralysis, Mary Jane admitted, she wanted to die. But eventually she realized—as she put it, boldly and without self-pity—'there was *nothing left of me to die.*' "

Later, Ruben sat in on a session involving psychokinesis, the art of moving things by the power of thought alone. The subject, a charming Brazilian boy named Carlos Adende, was able to duplicate the feats of the more-famous Uri Geller. He boasted, probably without a smidgin of truth, that Uri had imitated him. In addition to bending keys, spoons and forks, knives and rings simply by touching them as they lay in Jacques' palm, Adende grasped a vase of flowers in his brown hand and, as his generally sunny face settled into ominous, dark shadows, he caused the flowers to wither. Ruben found himself wondering about either Godly or Satanic influence but shook himself out of the mood. Carlos stopped Martin's watch for him, then got it going again, chattering boyishly all the while.

"The intriguing point here," Jacques began in a whisper, while young Carlos was occupied, "is that the lad was once involved with poltergeist activity. We want to learn if the unconscious force that once moved heavy objects around his parent's house, apparently without Carlos' knowledge, became the natural psychokinetic power he can command today."

"Did you have any trouble bringing him here?" Ruben inquired.

Jacques fingered his goatee. "His parents were glad to get rid of him."

To Martin Ruben's surprise, when he entered the hospital ward of Solomon Studies, he discovered perhaps three dozen infants, most of them in incubators and shielded by glass. Surely these babies were not psychic subjects!

He was introduced to a Dr. Julie Sarah Lyle, who, asked if she were a pediatrician, smiled shyly. "No, Dr.

Ruben, not principally; I'm a little more specialized than that. I'm a neonatologist."

He returned her smile, liking her. Julie Lyle was a sweet-faced, soft-eyed and soft-figured redhead who, rather than reflecting the fieriness traditional to those with auburn hair, seemed nearly timid, careful in what she said.

"And what, Doctor Lyle," Ruben pressed, "*is* a neonatologist?"

"A doctor who studies the newborns up to two months of age," she answered promptly. "I not only care for all their needs but chart areas of progress and I'm trained to notice subtle attributes a pediatrician might not observe."

"Where did all these kids come from?" Ruben asked, puzzled.

"They are babies of both staff members and our, ah, sensitive population." Julie paused, sought Ingrid Solomon's eyes. The Director nodded. "But a great number of them are merely children who were—unwanted. By anyone. Through arrangements with various agencies throughout the Midwest, we've succeeded in bringing to Nommos what are called 'doorstep babies.' Babies abandoned by the mother."

"Why?" Ruben asked. He felt that he towered over the tiny redhead and didn't want to dominate her, but he wanted the facts. "*Why* did you have them brought here?"

The neonatologist flushed. "To *care* for them, of course! We have one of the finest medical staffs in the nation here, Doctor Ruben. It's to Ms. Solomon's credit that she is flexible enough to want to help even those who *aren't* psychic!"

With that, piqued, Julie Lyle flounced back into the safety of the nursery and Ruben last saw her changing the diapers of a tiny creature with long, black hair. She ignored his gaze. The child was crying but all he could see was its angry, open mouth.

"My dear Ingrid, you never fail to astonish me!" Ruben told her, turning away from the window. He smiled. "Perhaps there's hope for you, after all!"

"I'm not quite as charitable as Doctor Lyle prefers to see me," Ingrid retorted, "and I'm no hypocrite." She pointed. "The children you see there, on the other side of the glass, will become the *first ones in history* to grow up in *absolute harmony* with the Cosmos! They will not only be examined for potential psychic gifts—those who have them won't be frightened by the discovery, the way sensitives usually are—but some will be taught the more communicable talents of ESP. And they will live every day, as they grow to adulthood, in fully charted unison with planetary influences."

They had paused at the end of the corridor, having spied Professor Morley Sinoway making his way toward them. Ruben was both impressed and puzzled by Ingrid's remarks about the infants. He looked to Jacques, then Ingrid.

"I believe I'm seeing signs that you are doing *more* than studying the paranormal here," he said slowly. "Somewhat like Sir Francis Galton, you're trying to find natural paranormal gifts and develop them. But that's just a *part* of it."

"Correct," Ingrid replied, nodding briskly. "You're quite perceptive."

"I'm quite aware that something *else* is going on at Solomon Studies," Ruben declared flatly. "*Why* are you going to so much trouble to schedule everyone, down to helpless babies, by astrological influences? What is the *far-reaching*, truly *ambitious* scheme you people have in mind?"

Now the Director's gaze crossed Jacques' face with a trace of sympathy. "Our friend Doctor Coquelion came here, Martin, hoping that this unique regimen might save his life, at least extend it. And it may. You see, Doctor, we are living our daily lives on Nommos Island by *every* cosmological or paranormal rule. Remember the mound which fascinated you so? No one here *believes* in its legends, but we propitiate it, anyway; we give it a *chance* to tell us its secrets."

Ruben sighed. "The question," he pressed, "remains the same. *Why* are you doing this?"

She looked him straight in the eye. "We actually have one primary, overriding purpose. One that simply includes the investigation of the occult." She drew herself to her full height. "We are pursuing, and we mean to have for ourselves—for everyone living on this island—*eternal life*!"

Eight

"That is the most remarkable thing I ever heard in my life," Ruben expostulated as Professor Sinoway drew within earshot, accompanied by two large attendants. It occurred to him that he had never seen Sinoway without them. "You honestly believe it's possible to *live forever* by doing it in tune with astrological influences?"

"Not that alone, Ruben," the professor replied as he joined them. "By following, hm-m, *all* the traditions of the supernatural."

"I wouldn't think it would get your endorsement, Professor," Ruben said. "It doesn't sound like the most scientific thing in the world to me. Not—" he paused to smile at Ingrid and Jacques, lifting his palms—"not that I'm saying it won't work."

Sinoway rubbed a hand over his bald head. "I prefer to think of it as just another Life Extension program. And we are scarcely the only scientists addressing the problem. There is, for example, the Gerontology Research Center of the United States National Institutes of Health, where they've been giving some eighty tests to more than six hundred healthy men, to detect the way aging begins. And who can really say what goes on beyond *any* closed laboratory doors?"

"Is the study of ways to keep men alive relatively new?" Ruben inquired.

"Scarcely," Sinoway barked. "You forget, hm-m, magic elixirs and the fountain of youth—all nonsense, of course."

"Don't be too sure, Morley," Jacques put in with a smile. "Some experts say there's a basis in fact for both."

Sinoway scowled. "Not for other ways man has tried to keep himself going—monkey gland surgery, pulverized bull testicles, European cell therapy. Wealthy people over there pay a fortune for a fluid based on cell extracts from unborn lambs to be shot in their rears. Other rich sons go to Rumania, where there's a spa that utilizes procaine hydrochloride—a drug called Gerovital." Sinoway sighed. "Alex Comfort, an English gerontologist, calls age a 'disease we have all got.' "

"But Comfort also says that by nineteen-ninety we'll have 'an experimentally tested way of slowing down age changes in man' that can mean a *twenty percent increase* in life span," Ingrid recalled. "It may not be as hard to achieve—advanced longevity—as we've been taught to think. The rate of aging was rather easily changed in laboratory animals, Comfort said, with 'simple manipulations.' "

Jacques looked eagerly at his old friend. "In California, the gerontologist named Bernard Strehlet claims that the average life expectancy by the turn of the century will be one hundred years, if enough money and talent are put into study. That's what we have going for us here, Martin! Plenty of money and talent!"

"Plus a unique theory whose roots are lost in antiquity," Ingrid declared. "Martin, it's *right* that we do this for ourselves and for humanity! Very few animals, including man, reach their ultimate potential age—that's a biological fact! Man should have a maximum of one hundred and twenty years, at *least*!"

Sinoway led them to a comfortable lounge where they could continue the discussion. His two henchmen followed silently. The professor said, as he lowered himself to the best chair, "The fact of which makes what *really* happens a crying shame, Ruben. Do you know that people in Guinea, in the nineteen seventies, have a life expectancy of only *twenty-six*? In Afghanistan, the Russians actually only need to wait; most Afghans die at *thirty-eight*! Why, in Turkey, a fairly civilized nation, it's only *fifty-four*!"

"And in the civilized countries," Ingrid remarked, "some experts think we're *losing* ground. Due to stress, smoking, the poisoned environment."

Ruben inhaled and let the smoke drift round his raised head. "Do we have any clear grasp on the causes of aging?"

Jacques leaned forward, hands clasped between his legs, to answer. "There are dozens of possible causes, Marteen," he said. "Immunological defenses collapse, cells die in massive numbers, the endocrine glands are 'told' to slow down by the brain—for reasons we don't understand. With the passing of years there are waxy deposits accumulated through the degeneration of tissue in the body, stacked between the cells until they, themselves, show signs of fat. Why, our muscle cells begin dying when we're *thirty*! And they don't renew themselves, my friend—not a jot! Half our tastebuds, at the age of seventy, have vanished along with one-quarter of the kidney urinary tubes—all these things showing us the *evidence* of an age process, without telling us quite why, or how to *reverse* it."

The most important thing of all occurred to Ruben. "What," he asked, "about the cells of our brains?" His mouth was dry when he asked it.

"They begin dying around thirty, also," Jacques said, his expression severe. "And we lose around one hundred thousand cells—everyday!"

Ruben blanched. "My God!"

Then Jacques chuckled. "It's not that terrible, *mon ami*. At that rate, unaltered by our experimentation, it would still take nearly three hundred years to use up the brain cells!"

"Cells double by division," Sinoway put in, ever serious, "some fifty times. Hm-m. But the only cell with the knack of doing it *indefinitely* is, I'm afraid, the cancer cell."

"It was cellular study that led me to my theory for living in accord with the planetary influences, Doctor," Ingrid explained, folding her arms across her breasts. "Many authorities believe that each normal cell of the body contains a sort of clock device which runs down at a predetermined rate. And this may well be one of *many* such 'clocks' in the body. True time is sidereal time, the time of the planets. Hence, if we are in *harmony* with them, we should theoretically be able to readjust—to *reset*—all those vital clock cells!"

"How will you know?" Ruben asked softly. "How will you be able to tell if your theory is working out?"

Jacques spread his hands in a happy gesture, showing how easy the answer was. "Our computers can detect whether any one individual present in our overall experiment is *remaining* more or less youthful than would normally be expected. Because of such modern technology as the computer, we don't have to *wait* forty years to see if the theory works!"

Sinoway reflected for a moment, then pounced energetically to his feet. His heavy brows curved, then lifted in decision. "Come, Ruben, come!" he urged. "Allow me to show you something!"

Ruben and the others followed the imperious Professor Sinoway down another corridor. He gestured ahead. "Down there," he said offhandedly. "Those are my, hm-m, private experimental labs. Off limits. But in here—" he opened a door to another hospital ward, with six old men in beds—"I'm trying to do something about senility."

They stopped beside a scarecrow of an aged man. "This pathetic fellow," Sinoway said with a careless gesture, "is Harry Pfeiff, eighty-some years old, with advanced brain disease—a senility so sweeping, hm-m, so *encompassing*, that Harry's had a good day if he remembers his name."

"Don't talk about him in *front* of him!" Ruben snapped, unable to stand it.

Morley Sinoway's hard brown eyes glistened briefly at Ruben. Then he lowered his head to look directly into Harry Pfeiff's placid, expressionless face. "Want a million dollars, Harry?" he shouted. "What about a woman, Harry—shall I bring you Charo, gift-wrapped with a glossy ribbon, hm-m? Could you use a nice porterhouse steak, Harry?" He paused. "Harry," Sinoway shouted, "you're a useless piece of excrement on life's shoals, a chunk of fleshy shit caught on the rocks—but I'm going to *save* you, Harry, I'm going to *save you from yourself*!"

"He simply didn't hear you," Ruben argued, furious. "It isn't just his poor mind, Sinoway—he couldn't *hear* you!"

"He heard every word I said but they meant nothing to him," the professor replied coolly. "He's a useless vegetable."

"*Why* did you bring me here?" asked Ruben, his fists doubled. "Just to watch you try to humiliate a sick, old man?"

Now Sinoway gave Ruben a smile that was almost sweet. He rested his balled hands on his hips. "To show you, *Doctor*, that compassion is meaningless, science is *all*. Very soon now—perhaps while you remain on Nommos Island—old Harry is going to be as good as new again!" He paused, reached down for a chart at the foot of the bed. He tossed it to Ruben, who barely caught it. "You can read, can't you, Ruben? *Memorize* some of that data. It indicates his skin elasticity, his heart and kidney function, the amount of cholesterol the old fool has managed to fill himself with, his maximum breathing capacity, the fluid pressure in his eyes, his grip strength—*all* that shit, Doctor!" He paused to glare at the other two people. "None of you care for my techniques, but I know what I'm doing and, when you see those statistics improve—very soon, *hm-m?*—you'll know I was right."

Ruben nodded, understanding. "You're treating this patient medically as well as astrologically," he observed.

"Precisely! Among other things," Sinoway continued, "I'm giving him exceptionally large doses of L-Dopa to make his glands secrete better. It's a building block of dopamine, which is *eminently* important—a transmitter of signals between brain cells. I'm giving him enormous injections of Vitamin E, in order to kill free-radical reactions, and mixing them—rather dangerously, I confess—with an inhibitor known at BHT— butylated hydroxytoluene. And today, finally, I've even used two-mercaptoethylamine."

Ruben's face clouded. "How can you *dare* try so many experimental methods on this patient?" he demanded. The professor's two burly attendants bunched their fists.

"He's *nothing* this way, hm-m?" Sinoway replied.

"But he's going to prove my scientific techniques are right!"

"You have no right—"

"Martin," Jacques said softly, touching his friend's arm, "Harry Pfieff is Morley's stepfather."

Morley Sinoway spoke again in his resonant baritone. "Creatures, large and small, have inhabited this planet for three billion years," he intoned. "During that period of time, *ninety-eight million* different species have been born and died. Man has no reason—no reason, at *all*, hm-m?—to think that *his* species will endlessly survive." He turned his bald head to look at Ruben. "What we are trying to do, at Solomon Studies, is *provide* man with that reason. After two hundred thousand generations, we're still a babe in arms. Compare it: bacteria has gone through ten *trillion* generations; the common horse has made it through twenty-seven million generations. We're a newcomer, Ruben, hm-m? And the jury is out on whether we will continue to inhabit the planet—or become the ninety-eight millionth-and-*one*!"

When they had completed the tour, Ruben continued to feel that this activity—at least, hidden by secrecy and the covering study of the paranormal—was somehow wrongheaded. But he could no longer be sure. The survival of his own species on the planet was as important to Ruben as it was to the next man. His own life, he had to admit, was precious to him; he would like to prolong it indefinitely. Perhaps it was only the fully experimental nature of what was happening here—or of the people who were in charge.

When they had returned to Ingrid Solomon's office, Ruben found himself quite naturally slipping his arm around the director's slim waist. "It was utterly engrossing," he said, "although I'd like to know what

Sinoway's up to in his private labs." He nibbled the back of her neck.

Jacques, in his mildest of tones, called to him. "Please do not do that to the lady, *mon ami*."

Ruben was surprised. "What did you say, Jacques?"

"The lady has been spoken for, Martin," Jacques replied. "Clearly you did not know that."

"By whom?" Ruben asked, stepping away from the woman who had twice come to his bedroom at night. "*Who* spoke for her, as you put it?"

Ingrid rubbed her hand over Jacques' chest, kissing the goateed chin. "Why, I thought you knew, Martin," she answered lightly. "I belong to your friend Jacques. We're married."

Nine

During the afternoon, Ruben visited the modish library in a corner of the first floor and richly approved. Although it appeared to have every new book or magazine or newsletter related to psychology, parapsychology and medicine, it also had a large "new books" section. He wished that he had more time to read for pleasure and was immediately scornful of himself, since he'd told nonreading friends that we *all* make time for what we really want to do. Toward the stacks, to Martin's surprise, he even found a small "rare books" section, protected by glass. There were a number of quite valuable old books, some limited editions; and he wasn't startled to find a first edition of a book by Sir Francis Galton.

He had to hand it to Ingrid, she believed in going first cabin!

Ruben looked up "eugenics" in several sources. The one he thought was the most accurate indicated that eugenics is a science of selective perfection. It was used either for breeding out and banishing the undesirables in society, or for striving by other means for the most desirable or "fit" members.

What a hero Ingrid had chosen, Martin thought with despair. Couldn't she remember what Hitler had done through experiments, or the series of twins put to death by people like Eichmann? He read, too, that Julius Caesar once tendered a thousand sesterces to each mother he chose as being most likely to produce "desirable" children. Augustus Caesar eventually made it two thousand but the powerful and rich, just as Plato once feared, either could not or would not "breed" the way "undesirables" did. To what extent, Ruben wondered, was Ingrid acting on the advice of her hero— or, like Adolf Hitler, did she merely *order* such experiments done?

The few volumes the library had on the topic of life extension revealed little that he hadn't heard already. Most people claimed that they wanted to live longer, he read, but only if they could retain their physical health, mental energy, and productivity, plus the financial resources to seek pleasure and hobbies. The authority Ruben was reading noted that a much longer life span would surely mean more marriages and other intimate relationships. That meant that a woman who lived, youthfully, to the age of one hundred and ten would— if her husband died when she was sixty-five—have forty-five years of life to go!

The expert also indicated that larger populations were likely through increased longevity, especially should the elderly woman retain her fertility into her sixties or seventies. War might become socially desirable, even acceptable, to hold the population down—or one might require permission to have children after a certain age. Since humankind stubbornly did what it pleased, a result of this might well be court-appointed abortions.

With great longevity, medical costs were bound to skyrocket, assuming that people went on getting ill. There was the question of the "human vegetable," who might now live to a hundred instead of fifty or sixty; did medicine then try to prolong life at such great economic cost? Retirement age would have to be postponed an additional quarter of a century, to eight-five or ninety, which in turn would cut down on the jobs that were available. A man could work seventy years on his job, neatly cutting out job opportunities for the young; which suggested that future crimes would involve young men killing old for a position!

Ruben frowned. The writer of the book seemed to be saying that he wasn't at all in favor of longer lives. Which was shocking to Martin since that meant the author *was* advocating death as a suitable alternative!

But he went on reading. Retirement would cost a fortune, with immense sums paid in for another twenty or thirty years—and if such a plan continued to pay for the balance of a life, from age sixty-five through one hundred and twenty, there would be more money paid *out* by far than customers currently pay in. What this might mean to an already embattled Social Security program, neither the writer nor Ruben could guess. But it was clear that aged people—after effective life extension—must become the supreme force on the planet. They would quickly become the majority and would remain consumers and parents.

If, that is, they were *allowed* to survive. Longer lives might lead to governmental euthanasia, with old men and old women obliged to *establish* to *prove*, that they led "meaningful, societally redeemable" existences. If they were just commonplace or ordinary people, a dreaded science fiction fantasy might come to life—or death. In short, mankind would have to adopt a synergistic scientific outlook: The whole would be considered always greater than the sum of its parts.

Weary of such extreme answers to problems that hadn't even developed yet, Ruben left both the library and central building to go in search of fresh air and exercise.

When he exited onto the front grounds Ruben was a trifle dazed by the July heat and sunshine. Everything shimmered; many yards at a distance he could make out the golden beach and Lake Triton beyond it, the ambience of the scenery rather disconcertingly unreal. How quickly, Martin thought, we get used to our routines, to artificial light and air conditioning. Certain forms of dedicated work that took place in a single structure developed a frame of mind much like that of a convict. In a sense, he thought with a grin, the con and the scientist, businessman or politician, couldn't be properly adjusted to society. All were eventually institutionalized.

"Have you been close to the mound yet?"

Ruben wasn't startled; after the past two or three days he wondered if anything could startle him.

He was looking down at Tina, the Eurasian girl whom Ingrid had said was a child-prostitute before coming to Nommos Island. Despite himself, he found he was staring deeply at her. While the green eyes were somewhat hard, or excessively self-assured, the tanned complexion, the rounded arms and calves, were youthful and oddly innocent. It occurred to him that if this gorgeous child had been corrupted, no one anywhere was safe from mankind.

"No, but I'd like that," he said after a moment, with a smile, "and your company."

She linked her arm in his and they strode unhurriedly past the funhouse and merry-go-round left behind by Boysangurls Amusements. She is barely too old, Martin thought, to sit on one of those funny animals and be captivated by tinny music.

Several people, children and adults alike, were already at the mound. The girls and boys looked to

Tina, most of them speaking, in the friendly but obsequious way of the very young addressing the nearly-grown. Ruben instinctively studied the faces of both adults and children, saw nothing unusual in their expressions, no indication that they were under any kind of spell.

"Do you know about *ley lines*?" asked Tina. She was wearing a bright-red halter and skintight shorts which did little to emphasize her girlhood.

"I think leys are mysterious lines of alignment between ancient landmarks," he said soberly, remembering how it offends the young to be taken lightly. "They're in England."

"A man named Alfred Watkins suggested them sixty years ago," Tina explained, "but they're principally connecting lines between things like churches, hilltops, King Arthur's Glastonbury, monuments such as Stonehenge, and Druidic sites. And they're not only in England," she added.

Ruben remembered and nodded. "That's right, the lines sometimes run for hundreds of miles and the combination of the leys and the precision of the sites on them totally rules out chance. Don't some people think they're prehistoric trade routes?"

Her lovely face was dark and serious now. "Yes. But today it's generally felt that they're *magical*, even *religiously mystical* lines, to keep the flow of natural earth sources going and to energize those who visit sites on the lines. One must be very, very cautious with them. People on leys have disappeared, right into the earth. Others have had strange births, or discovered exceptional talents—like the ability to fly, unaided." Her gaze sought Ruben's willingness to believe; it was grave, old beyond her years, and he thought that her I.Q. must be so high that for her to have had such a past was criminal. "Some call them . . . *dragon paths*, and say they've found traces or fossils of creatures that never, uhm, materialize any other place on earth."

Now the others who had stood with them had wended away except for a small, handsome black boy who Ruben knew was listening to their every word. He turned to stare at the mound. It was only an immense, brown swelling of earth, neatly roped off; but a word leaped to his conscious mind; pregnant, it looked *pregnant*. Or, at any rate, viable. The boy drew nearer to them, as if for comfort.

"Some say," continued Tina in hushed tones, "that . . . *things* which live forever dwell beneath the earth at connecting ley lines. UFOs in the Bermuda Triangle and elsewhere are sometimes said to rendezvous or even create landing sites on such ley lines." She shuddered. "And still others say that creatures exist in the earth, beneath leys, who are elementals, capable of bringing us a sort of *alternate reality*—a world like ours but hideously distorted."

"But, Tina," he probed gently, "what do *you* say?"

"I say that they don't exist only in Britain," she asserted boldly. "They have been traced to China for centuries, for example, and now they're here. And I know some *other* things you may find important, Dr. Ruben." When she glanced at him it was again with sensuality but also a distant, anxious glint in her eyes. "Things you don't know, but which I think you should know."

"And what are they, child?"

"This place—Nommos Island—is directly situated on leys. And that awful, ugly mound—" she pointed at it— "is directly at the *heart* of Nommos. That mound sits at the *precise center* of all the ley lines—the old dragon paths—in this continent. Except, in England, the sites are holy." Tina swallowed hard. "Here, th-they are *e-evil*."

For some time Ruben had been aware that he didn't actually find the mound ugly, as Tina described it. His feelings were new to him; he tried to analyze them but he was conscious of a confusing heat disturbing him. Really, there was something wondrously time-tested, *permanent*, about the curving, sloping mound. It had an almost feminine shape.

Suddenly he knelt and reached out, with his hand, to touch the rising foot of the mound.

"*No*, Martin!" cried Ingrid Solomon. "*Don't do that!*"

Instinctively he obeyed, yanking his arm back. He peered at the Director with irritation and perhaps a flash of guilt. "You have the most *disconcerting* damned way of appearing out of nowhere!"

She ignored his remarks. "Only crass Americans feel they must *touch* everything important before they can believe it's *real*," she exploded, her face near his. "Don't you understand this is a very ancient site, that it should be treated with respect, even *veneration*?"

"Oh, sweets, I simply *had* to get a handful to put in my pocket for luck," Ruben replied sarcastically. He was perspiring now.

"You *don't* come here at night," she said firmly, right index finger brushing tip of left for emphasis, "and you *don't touch* the mound. From ignorance, so many terrible things can happen around such an ancient shrine. Many years ago, the state of Indiana was populated by tribes of Amerindians. The state's name, and that of Indianapolis, of course, derived from the savages whom we rudely evicted. It was they who made the orders of the kind I've simply passed along, to you, and everyone. What the regulars do, Doctor, is come to the mound with their angers, their frustrations, their disappointments, and *project them* to the mound—theoretically allow *it* to absorb all their unhappiness. According to legend, when we leave, we have left our misery behind. And I intend that my people will *honor* the customs!"

Ruben had heard her but found his attention drawn to the small black boy who, possibly ten feet away now, continued to eavesdrop shamelessly on everything they said.

Ingrid sighed heavily, made ready to go. "Look, Martin, I came out here just to fetch Tina," she explained. "If I was rude, or overly direct, I'm sorry. You can't expect to know everything about the place after only a day or so. Come along, Tina, m'girl; I have some forms which need to be circulated to the others."

Martin watched as Ingrid led the Eurasian girl away—so he wouldn't hear more of her thoughts?—and was more annoyed than he'd care to admit. It wasn't the first time he'd met a woman who, having given him her body, felt that he was obligated to take any criticism she cared to level. But damn! they made an exotically beautiful pair!

"What's your name?"

He jumped, eyes leaping down to small-boy level. "Why, I'm Doctor Ruben, son. Martin Ruben, a guest."

"Some way to treat company! I, Dhombola." He had two immense black eyes with a thick foliage of beautiful lashes and an automatic, enormously winning smile. "This first time you come to mound?"

Ruben nodded soberly. "It is. Where are you from, Dhombola?"

"Country, new one. Called Oldannah, in Africa." A flicker of obvious homesickness glowed in his open eyes. He sighed and scratched his head. "Long way back home."

"Yes, it must be." He appraised the boy. He wore a short, lightweight dashiki of many hues and was barefoot, but his hair had been trimmed short and neat. "Did you hear the girl tell me about this mound? About ley lines?"

Dhombola nodded. "Dhombola have good ears. Know of leys 'cause we have legend about them, Oldannah, too."

Ruben nodded thoughtfully and reached out. "Let's have a little talk."

The boy paused, considering. Ruben wondered if he was using some telepathic talent to determine the adult's motives. But at last Dhombola put his little hand in Ruben's and permitted himself to be led to the nearby merry-go-round.

"You know what this used to be?" he inquired.

Dhombola nodded earnestly. "It went circles, lotsa times. Played music, almost like tin drum." He frowned. "I sense many, many children ride it. Some hurt. It not work anymore."

"I'll bet you'd like to ride it," Martin said, smiling.

The boy's grin was utterly scornful. "Ride toy animals? Not Dhombola! I saw all them animals, in life, way back home. Not need *toy* animals!"

Ruben saw the inanity of his remark and thoughtfully scratched his head. He took his seat on a plaster lion, almost as if showing the boy nobody would make fun of American toy animals, and looked up again. "You're terrified of that mound, aren't you, son?"

It seemed Dhombola would bluff, at first. Then he held his head high. "Not of mound—what's *inside*. Bad, there."

"Tell me. Are you precognitive or clairvoyant?"

Dhombola stared suspiciously at him. "I, Oldannah! *Africk!*"

Ruben smiled. "I mean, can you see the future? Is that the reason you're here, Dhombola, because you can see into the future?"

"No, not so." He shook his head, then peered down at his palms. "I here because I see into *past*. Know what happened. When Dhombola touch something, sometimes just be *near* things, I know what happened before. Long time back. Help find crook by having what he touched in my hand. I know 'bout him, then."

Now Ruben had what he wanted. He spoke carefully: "And what do you see has happened *here*, before, Dhombola? What's the past of this mound? What do you *see*?"

And Ruben trickled into the boy's palm a few grains of dirt he had picked up at the foot of the mound.

The child held it steadily, finally looked away, almost longingly. "I see woman, very, very beautiful. Small. She has—what you call it—sexy!"

"And what else?" Ruben pressed.

Because Dhombola had stopped speaking. Ruben could tell there was more, and waited as patiently as possible. Yet the boy did not go on.

"What's the matter, son?" Ruben asked gently, touching his forearm. "Is it that you do not know exactly *what* you're seeing in your mind?"

Another beat. Overhead, the sun bore down relentlessly and, beside this small ebon person, Ruben nearly expected to hear jungle drums. Then Dhombola looked up at him, excited. "Dhombola know *what* he see, not know how to *say* it." He paused, a part of his mind still turned inward. "Man and woman, sir—boom-*boom!*"

He stared at Ruben's puzzled face, then drove his small fist into a space left by his spread thumb and fingers, repeatedly. "Boom-*boom*, boom-*boom*! *You* know, bwana Doctor—man, woman, make sexy!"

Martin understood, and smiled. "All right. I understand you now. But there is more, isn't there? What do you see?"

Dhombola's eyebrows raised, first in surprise, then in fear. "The sexy first, sir—then . . . *the kill*! The awful way to die!" He blinked away the vision as well as he could, frightened of it; but he couldn't immediately make his mind let go. "Oh, bwana Doctor, many, many people have died *awful* from this mound! Many, many!" His dark gaze beseeched Ruben for an explanation. "*Terrible* deaths—from monster who lives in mound!"

He hurled the dirt in his palm to the ground.

It sizzled, and a little plume of smoke drifted upward, as Dhombola turned and ran.

Ten

He stayed awake as long as he could, but Ingrid didn't come to his room. He was left alone all night, and slept in snatches.

Ruben tried to tell himself that it didn't matter, that he wouldn't have touched Ingrid now, anyway. Now he knew that she was Jacques' wife, and best friends didn't go in for that sort of thing.

In point of fact, Martin was really angered with the beautiful director for keeping it from him. But the honesty of the better psychologists dwelled in Ruben and he wondered if he actually could have turned her away, before, even with the knowledge that she was Mme. Coquelion.

The blonde was utterly delectable. Even now, he could see her beneath him, twisting and thrusting; she really know how to "writhe" to the occasion, he told himself with a smile.

While he fought sleep, Ruben thought about the ancient mound at the center of the island. What Ingrid had described—the idea of permanent people on Nommos going to the mound to concentrate their fury, disappointment, or anger on the apparently innocuous hillock—was a strongly familiar element of psychology. Freud himself had enunciated it, in 1894, the concept of *projection* under which one attributes to others the drives, complexes or attitudes that belong to oneself. It was common enough in delusion of persecution, for example.

But it was quite new to him in the sense of *consciously, intentionally* projecting negative feelings. Theoretically, on the surface, it might be harmless enough, even therapeutic for those who could do it; but Ruben had never been a surface person. He wondered about such things as whether or not the people here were failing to cope, by getting rid of their pressures; and he wondered, despite himself, what effect the *bombardment* of adverse emotions on an ancient, presumably once-venerated mound might have.

He awakened halfway through the four hours of sleep he managed, to wonder as well if the whole approach to the mound wasn't a kind of sacrilegious prayer. It was bad enough to consider the tasteless impropriety of that; but the great megaliths and menhirs of Europe had apparently received prayer, and *they* continued to stand, to endure, for hundreds upon hundreds of years. What kind of longevity were the Solomon Studies people inadvertently granting a plot of ground?

He was just drifting back off to sleep when he realized he wasn't alone, after all.

For a moment Ruben thought he was experiencing another premonition; he had been trapped in that confusing twilight between sleep and consciousness, and blinked wildly as he tried to identify the noise. When he lurched sleepily into the front room of his quarters Ruben found Tina standing beside the door, her back to him. She was again tacking something to his corkboard.

Tina had not heard him and Ruben found himself in his shorts, staring at the Eurasian's well-rounded buttocks. It was a hot evening and she wore skintight shorts and a bra that looked like it belonged with a bikini. The long, black hair streaming down her back to her waist gave the girl an adult image of appealing sexuality, and Ruben had to make himself clear his throat and announce his presence.

She turned to him in a spinning motion, dropping the papers in her arms. Immediately she bent to retrieve them and Martin found himself looking down her bikini top at two small, round breasts between which he couldn't have inserted a pencil. Everything about her was deliciously bunched in curving, round strokes any artist would have admired.

Acting on instinct, Ruben had jumped to assist Tina. When her gaze lifted, he remembered that he wore only shorts and began backing away, partly aroused and partly flustered.

"I'm sorry I disturbed you," she said, her voice flat. She seemed unable to raise her stare from below Ruben's waist.

"That's all right," he said hurriedly, "I'm sorry I startled you. It's time I was up anyway."

"At five-thirty in the morning?" she demanded, giggling.

He glanced at his watch and smiled. "Well, you're up and around," he pointed out.

"It's my job, according to this month's schedule," she said. Again her emerald eyes trailed down his front before reluctantly returning to his face. She came forward, holding out a bare arm. "Here, now I don't need to tack it up."

Has the air conditioning broken? he wondered inanely, conscious of beginning to perspire heavily.

When her hand touched his, the impact was electric, shocking. And he could tell that the girl sensed it too. She blinked several times and momentarily lost the balance of those short, well-curved legs. Then before he could speak again or, as he feared he might do, reach out to pull her against him, Tina spun round and hurried to the door.

Ruben sank into a chair.

What's that?

He had leaped like he was wounded; his heartbeat, already hastened by the nearly naked girl, again accelerated. Before the door had closed behind Tina he had seen, from the corner of his eye, a large, black massing of *shadows*. Then it, too, was gone behind the girl and he was alone.

He tried to read the papers she'd given him but his hand was trembling. *Great heaven*, he thought to himself, *I almost made a* pass *at that child! Even now, I crave her body so much it's painful. What's the* matter *with me?*

And then it occurred to him that, while she had expressed her interest in him right from the start, it was *Tina* who had the courage—or wisdom—to flee! What's going *on* in this place?

He forced himself to read the papers in his hands. They were neatly typed and photocopied, and they bore his name and his personal schedule for the Leo period that began tomorrow.

And who, he wondered, has the *original* of this schedule? Ingrid? Jacques? That bully Sinoway? And why did they let a seventeen year old have the keys to every apartment?

Still feeling their behavior was highhanded, since he wasn't a member, yet, of the staff, Ruben saw that the schedule was in full keeping with his horoscope—two-hour period by two-hour period.

He studied it for logic. Leo itself rose at sunrise, around 6 A.M. That placed his Gemini planets four hours *before* dawn, beginning about 2:15 at night.

His Capricorn rising sign, fitted in appropriately at

3:50 in the afternoon, was used sensibly for a class he was meant to teach. Indeed, he was penciled in for classes from 3:50 through 9:50 P.M., utilizing in a practical way his public "face" or personality during its time of peak appeal. That meant he would be assigned a six-hour work day. Presumably, Ruben calculated, he would primarily teach students who *adapted* well to his teaching and who were in harmony with his Capricorn ascendant. Doubtlessly those students would *not* belong to Pisces, Gemini, or Virgo, but would have rising signs compatible with his own. That way, he wouldn't deal with them on the basis of squaring or mutually frustrating aspects.

He went on scanning the schedule. At 10 P.M., with his own squaring fourth House occupied by Aries rising, he was intended to return to his quarters for "rest or sleep," according to the printed instructions. Aha, he thought sarcastically, freedom! He could rest *or* sleep!

Then Ruben's gaze was drawn to a portion squared off in red—yes, the whole schedule was generally color-coordinated—and the schedule for 1 through 3 A.M. That was when late Taurus and early Gemini rose, and they called, incredibly, for something plainly indicated on his schedule: "sex activities." He was flabberghasted! Ruben slapped his forehead with the palm of his hand. My Lord, they even scheduled sex!

That was his Fifth House rising, at one during the night, the House that had intrigued little Tina when he first met her! At the recollection of the girl Ruben's mind's eye traced the rounded half circles of her hips, when her back was turned to him, hungrily; and almost simultaneously he remembered, too, his original premonitions—vivid snaps of danger and death involving the blonde who turned out to be Ingrid Solomon, clicking past his vision like slides on a pale white screen.

He made himself concentrate, wiped the back of his hand on his perspiring forehead. Round the bend we go, he thought wildly; going bonkers for fun and profit.

All right. Since Ingrid and Jacques had stated that everyone at Solomon Studies would abide by an astrological regulation, this schedule of Martin's implied that everyone old enough for sexual activity—*did* Ingrid even allow minimums?—would find it plainly scheduled—routinized; laid out by decree—on their personal wall charts. Right along with "rest or sleep" and "meal"! It meant that everyone he'd already met, at least those on staff, already *abided* by these regulations. And Ingrid, of course, clearly intended that he, too, would fully comply with this schedule!

Then Ruben lit the first Camel of the day, his fingers trembling as he continued to think it through. People who were astrologically compatible were undoubtedly paired off with others for the *same* scheduled period. Aquarians with Librans, Sagittarians, Geminians, and Arians during a two-hour segment; Scorpio natives with Pisceans, Cancerians, Virgoans, and Capricornians during another two-hour period.

That had to be what Jacques meant when he mentioned sending the chart through the computer for "matchups"! And it explained why Ingrid wasn't here again, tonight: Unquestionably she had failed to match up with Ruben, astrologically, and was elsewhere, driving some other man other than her husband to sexual extremes. Because, Ruben was sure of this, Ingrid Solomon would certainly practice what she preached!

Martin inhaled furiously, tried to be cool and rational. From a strictly logical viewpoint, it was—in theory—workable, even worthwhile. Set up in this fashion, there would never be any instant animosities nor lengthy courtships; just immediate shared magnetism and *plop*! right into bed. Because everyone would like those whom they were matched with right off, and most kinds of ongoing compatibility were guaranteed by the combination of ancient astrology and the modern computer. Unquestionably there would be people who fell into real love during these scheduled "sex activities."

But Lord, it was so damnably *cold*; and it was so damnably anti-freedom of choice! Here was no adventurous pursuit, no romantic first dating. And he knew enough psychology to know that with Solomon Studies taking the responsibility for it, an authority figure not only *endorsing* free sex but *insisting* upon it, many people would participate without another thought.

He stubbed out his Camel with an angry gesture. A man or woman had a *right* to make a mistake, even to make fools of themselves—a right to reach a stage when they might look back ruefully on the past and say, "How could I possibly have thought I loved that person?"

And while you were associated with Solomon Studies, these rights were suspended. Along with Ingrid herself, you simply sought perfection and got on with it.

This moment, he thought as he returned, dazedly, to the photocopy schedule, with the sign Leo presently rising, it was his own Eighth House and there on the schedule—as sure as death and democrats!—they'd indicated Eighth House matters: Church or synagogue attendance for the religiously inclined (Martin recalled having seen a tiny, drably nondenominational chapel here that reminded him of the chilly, unmarked rooms at the United Nations); study of life and death issues generally, from medical checkups to philosophical reflection, even meditation; and balancing one's personal books. All were typical Eighth House matters, in astrology. The entry on the schedule added, helpfully, "Et cetera."

So what, Martin old son, do *you* do with this two hours? It's still days until the plane comes to return people to the mainland; might as well try to get along. Irked, and vaguely worried, he stared out the window at the already steaming new day. No chance for more sleep, that's for sure.

In the distance he could make out the merry-go-round, the animals still frozen in docile waiting for riders who would never come, and a corner of the ancient mound. People, he saw, were already making their daily visits to it, already propitiating it with their projected problems.

He nodded slowly, his heartbeat quickening as he understood. Of course! *That's* an Eighth House invention, that bulging mound—doubtless, when there's nothing else to do at such times, one is *meant* to visit the mound!

He rested the schedule on the table beside his easychair with slightly trembling hands and looked glumly at the children already afoot, outwardly as normal as kids anywhere. *What happens if I* don't *visit the mound each day?* he wondered. *And what happens if I don't choose to obey* any *of their goddamned schedule?*

Almost as if he had been given an instant, grim answer—as if S.S. stood for something it used to, instead of Solomon Studies—there was a sharp, persistent knock at the door.

126

Eleven

Three men stood on the threshold, two in uniform. *Storm troopers*, Ruben thought fleetingly and with anguish, remembering the Holocaust.

But they were only Professor Morley Sinoway, resplendent in a three-piece suit that must have cost a fortune, and his two silent aides. Ruben moved away from the door, thinking about the paranoia of a man who went nowhere without two bodyguards. "Come in," he muttered.

"My, my, you've done nothing to fix your place up," the professor said in a chiding tone of voice. He went so far as to peer through Ruben's front-room window and move the coffee table two inches. He looked up at the parapsychologist with what might have been meant to be a charming smile. "These little places are adequate, as far as they go, hm-m? But one must ask a decorator to come over from South Bend to make them livable."

"I find it comfortable, Professor," Ruben murmured, indicating a chair. "You're an early visitor. Shall I ring downstairs for coffee?"

"No, no, I require no stimulants," Sinoway replied, arching his brows. "The dedication to one's work is quite the finest, hm-m, 'high' available to an intellectual mind." He settled into his chair.

Before Ruben could suggest the couch for the professor's attendants, they moved to the window and perched on the windowsill like the birds in Hitchcock's film: stoic, expressionless, watchful.

"This happens to be my study period," the professor began, carefully folding one tailored leg over the other and delicately leaning back, "and I decided—since it coincides harmoniously, by sextile, with your Eighth House schedule—to spend it with you."

"Your munifience is overwhelming, my dear Sinoway," Ruben said in his best Sherlockian manner, lowering his own lids warily to his guest.

The sarcasm was lost on the older man. "Not at all." He bowed his bald head. "I think that it may prove to our mutual advantage since we do share a common interest."

Ruben smiled sardonically. "Forgive me, old man, but I cannot for the life of me imagine what that might be."

"No? I'm surprised by your lack of imagination." The brown eyes beneath the bushy brows glittered. "I refer to the workings of the human mind."

"Ah. But I am inclined to appraise its involved operation from the *outside*, Professor, on a sheerly human level." He lit a new cigarette without offering the pack. "What I lack is the facility for seeing a man as a grab bag of assorted parts that happen to have been assembled in functioning condition."

Sinoway motioned with his hand, dismissing the objection. "Tell me, Doctor. Are you aware of the differences between the two hemispheres of the human brain?"

"Enough to be loosely conversant on the topic," Ruben admitted. "I know there has been considerable experimentation in the Sixties and so far in the Seventies that demonstrates that the *left* hemisphere of the brain is practical and fact-oriented, the *right* is more creative, illusory, and nonverbal."

"Excellent!" Sinoway cried, striking the chair arm with a large fist. "I've always admired the uncanny *resourcefulness* of the Hebrew brain! Its shrewdness, its manipulative character."

Ruben paused before answering. "Tell me, Professor," he said softly. "In your minute inspections of the brains, have you actually detected a *difference* between the Hebrew and the gentile?"

"Alas, hm-m, only between the male and female." Sinoway smiled with easy animosity. "You fellows are a little harder to get into."

Ruben blanched; he felt his scalp tightening under the sudden close scrutiny of Professor Morley Sinoway. It was as if the fellow would like nothing more than to produce a scalpel and dig directly into Ruben's brain.

"Permit me to be candid, sir," Ruben said coolly. "I'm aware that you do not like me, or perhaps my race. And despite your storm troopers there—" he flicked a thumb at the dispassionate duo by the window—"I'm obliged to tell you that the feeling is mutual. Almost any human brain, pickled in alcohol or brine, would have more warmth than you."

"We were speaking of the hemispheres," Sinoway said after glancing at his men. "I can use a good sounding board. Your definition of the two halves was adequate, as far as it went. In modern western society, the left brain has had little chance to develop verbal skills, so that when a creative man is asked how he does something, he generally replies: 'This way,' and *demonstrates* the talent. Moreover, the memories of the two brain sections aren't immediately accessible to one another—did you know that?"

Ruben met the gleaming eyes, alive with challenge,

with an expression of interest. "No, but I appreciate the data. And I can see its potential application in psychology."

"How so?"

"If your information is correct," Ruben replied, "a memory trace may exist that stimulates behavior, yet remains unknown to the portion of the brain capable of communicating it. If," he said lightly, "I've followed the track of thought."

"Admirable once more, Doctor." Sinoway scrubbed his bald head with a hand and sighed. "Clearly, I should think, a synthesis is required so that a man can fully know himself—and a synergy between him and his computer."

"Are there more examples of what you've learned which you'd recommend to me?" Ruben inquired, inhaling smoke and releasing it through his nostrils. "I've long believed it is possible to adduce valuable insight from a small child, even a vicious animal."

Sinoway laughed. "Ah, your Jewish sense of humor is delectable! Well, sir, you might find it interesting to know that brain left doesn't observe inflections or expressions in speech. The right does so, but the language expressed is less significant to it than the expression or pose of the body. Consider how these facts, Ruben, can influence a patient reclining on your couch—or a so-called 'sensitive' for that matter." He leaned forward as though confiding confidential information. "Your Mister Freud placed considerable emphasis on the dream state, I believe. Are you aware that dreams occurring in mind right, which are forgotten upon awakening, are not known to mind left—because mind right doesn't communicate the information!"

Ruben nodded thoughtfully. "I confess that I find

your work interesting. But I'm certain, though I know you only on short acquaintance, that this data has some direct bearing upon your *own* professional interests. Are you experimenting with psychochemicals to merge the two hemispheres, or what?"

The professor held his gaze. "I am not prepared to discuss any of my personal experiments in detail, Ruben, but I tell you this: I intend to determine whether a man lives longer who uses primarily the left hemisphere or the right, and whether he lives longer still if they enjoy a perfect union of the two minds."

"And do you *have* test subjects who predominantly use mind right?"

Sinoway sighed hugely. "Alas, hm-m, not nearly enough. With the exception of certain children from the wilder regions of this lunatic world, those who have not been indoctrinated by their pragmatic parents, my guinea pigs are largely left-dominated. Even the more genuinely versatile adults. That is why they have no respectable control of their gifts or powers: As a rule, what they can do surprises *them* as much as it surprises *us*."

"I believe, Professor," Ruben said tightly, his eyes shut as though in pain, "that if I hear you refer to human beings as 'guinea pigs' one more time, I shall have to determine whether I can get to your smug face before your uniformed goon squad reaches me. Please regard that as an admonition for tact."

"Do not trouble yourself with my choice of words, Doctor," Sinoway stood, seeming almost militarily erect despite his age. "My manners are terrible, and I'm aware of it. I also make no apology for my thought processes, since they are unfailingly accurate, if rude."

"Then I hope you will forgive me if I throw you—"

The two men were facing each other in growing anger

when someone rapped twice on the door, and then opened it. The men at the window turned alertly from Ruben to the new potential threat.

It was Ingrid Solomon, resplendent in a green pants suit with her light-blond hair shimmering in the light from the corridor. She was smiling more openly and happily than Martin could recall.

"I have outstanding news for you, Professor Sinoway, and you may as well hear it too, Doctor Ruben." She beamed on them, barely able to contain her secret a second longer. "We have back in our hands the results of Test Course BB-five-five-one."

The professor trembled at the news, his eyes staring at her.

"For the first time, we have absolute, *clinical proof*—proof that could be evidentially accepted anywhere in the world—that astrocosmological regimentation is working! The alcoholic test subjects? They've stopped drinking completely and have no interest in booze! The depressed patients under Doctor Coquelion's care show every indication of maintaining a constant level of poise and contentment! Our obese patients suddenly show significant weight loss and reduced interest in food!"

"Yes, yes, that's all very good," Sinoway snapped, excitedly and rudely. "But what of our overall Life Extension program itself? How do the results look?"

"How *dare* you challenge me in that manner, Sinoway!" Ingrid flared, nearly striking the old man. "How *dare* you forget that I am the Director of Solomon Studies! I will tell you what *I* wish you to know, when *I* am ready—and not a moment before!"

Suddenly Sinoway was ashen. To Ruben it was obvious that he would give anything in the world at that instant to know the results he sought. It was also clear to him that his aides were permitted with Ingrid's acquiescence, since they didn't flicker an eyelash at her attack.

"I'm s-sorry," the professor mumbled, turning away. "Sorry."

"Yes, progress is being made in that region too." Ingrid spoke to his back with no sense of compassion evident. Martin felt that she had planned to go this far and merely followed through. "Case study forty-eight-mmo-three survived another good night. Everyone in the crisis ward shows improvement."

Ruben saw Sinoway's expression lighten but couldn't resist it. "Ingrid," he began, "pardon me, but recovering from an illness is not quite the same thing as Life Extension—as living longer."

She gave him a frigid smile. "It's the same when you're speaking of terminal cancer, and heart transplant patients who've been given *days* or *hours* to live. And," she added emphatically, "when our *revised* prognosis indicates that they have months to live!" She took his hand briefly, squeezed it. "It's our breakthrough, Martin! It *is* working! *Will* you sign a contract with us today?"

He smiled. "Perhaps, but not just this moment. There is more that I need to know." He paused. "But I must admit I'm impressed. Results speak for themselves."

"Excellent," she murmured, patting his arm as she turned to the door. "You remain a logical man. Professor?" She called to Sinoway who, by now, was nearly apoplectic with the desire to know what she knew. "I suppose I may as well tell you now. Case study twelve-mmr-one indicates an especially marked improvement too. It's too soon for conclusive affirmatives, but I believe the patient is going to survive."

And the door closed behind her.

Ruben turned back to his guest and stared at Sinoway in astonishment. The rude martinet had buried his tearful face in his hands. As Ruben gaped at him, his shoulders shook in relief. "Thank God," he whispered. "Oh, thank God!"

Martin was touched. He leaned toward the older man. "I'm happy for you, Professor. Was it your stepfather to whom the Director referred?"

"No, you fool!" Sinoway exclaimed, looking up at Ruben with a tear-streaked, happy face. "It's *me*! It's me she's talking about! It seems that I may survive!"

And he resumed his joyful, tearful noisemaking, snorting and humming at the same time.

Even the two men at the window looked shaken by the old man's crying, glancing nervously at each other and then at Martin Ruben.

At last Sinoway pulled himself together and blew his nose honkingly into an immense, white handkerchief. "I suppose I owe you an explanation, Ruben," he said, trying to compose himself. "Yes, I'm dying. I'm really quite surprised you didn't know about us."

"About '*us*'?" Ruben repeated, puzzled. "Who's dying besides you?"

"Why, *everyone*, Doctor—everyone on *the entire staff*! Every medical doctor, surgeon, psychologist, psychiatrist, nurse, and technician—absolutely everybody." Sinoway paused as it dawned on him and his wrinkled brow showed his surprise. "Aren't you?"

Ruben sat on the edge of his chair, incredulous. "Not that I'm aware of," he replied wryly, shaking his head in wonderment.

"Well, well, the Director must really have fancied

you!"

"I was recommended by her husband, Dr. Coquelion," Ruben said stiffly. "He's an old friend of mine for many years. Tell me, please: *Why* has Ingrid hired only those personnel who are terminal?"

The professor sat back in his chair at last, still gripping the handkerchief in a hand between his knees. "It was the only way Ms. Solomon could get people of our exceptional stripe, our outstanding quality. Perhaps the *only* way, in some cases, since there are numerous people here who do not really accept the concept of the paranormal even to the degree *I* do." His smile was rare and Ruben saw why. His teeth were two uneven rows of corn-yellow. "Many of us had already ceased working, and were merely waiting to die. Others were discharged by hospitals or universities under one feeble pretext or another, but always, in truth, because they didn't want the embarrassment of a professional corpse cluttering up the place."

Ruben passed a wondering hand over his eyes. "I still don't—"

"It should be obvious, man!" Sinoway snapped. "Ms. Solomon's conviction was that people under a death sentence will work vastly harder and with greater dedication and industry to *find* a way to prolong life when they themselves are *dying*!"

It occurred suddenly to Ruben that he was appalled he'd even slept with the woman while he simultaneously saw that he had, while respecting her, underestimated her genius. Then another thought occurred to him. "And Ingrid herself," he asked; "is *she*—?"

"The *Director*?" Sinoway demanded, incredulous. "*Dying*?" Abruptly he howled hilariously with laughter that included a sucking noise in the nostrils and showed his pink gums in a terrible grimace. "My God almighty, man! what an absurd question!"

Ruben stared at him, uncomprehending.

Sinoway calmed down to a grin. "I should think it's perfectly clear that Ingrid Solomon is in sparkling good health. Especially," he added after a cunning pause, "*for a woman who is sixty years old*!"

Now Ruben was reeling. "*That* beautiful woman?" he demanded, confounded and stunned. "*Sixty*?" Fantastic!" He blinked and sought to follow the logic of what he was hearing. "Then, her concept of astrocosmology, as she calls it, was *hers* from the start—and I suppose she'd practiced it for years?"

The professor nodded. "Certainly. She'd lived under its tight regimen for over forty years, I understand. I'd have to say, hm-m, she's her own best advertisement for the peculiar practice. In turn, you see, she gave the concept to her organization. To Solomon Studies, knowing it would be effective."

Now Ruben's mind was working swiftly again. "Yes, she's intelligent enough to know that, though she remains vastly younger in appearance, her life span at sixty must remain relatively short."

"Ah-a, you're coming about, you're coming about!" Sinoway chortled. He was still, understandably, ecstatic over Ingrid's news of the morning. "The Director saw her life span was running a trifle low and wanted *us* to find ways for *her* to live forever. Or at least, for many more years than she anticipates. But no one enlists the full-fledged support of three dozen top experts under ordinary circumstances; hence S.S. And in return, why, we receive excellent jobs at a fine facility, reasonable pay, all the fringe benefits you've obviously enjoyed—and the prospect not only of saving our own lives but of

Ingrid Solomon herself, living . . . eternally!"

Martin shook his head in genuine awe. "Great heavens, Sinoway, she's utterly brilliant. I suppose she must be the most brilliant human being I've ever known."

"Quite possibly," the professor agreed, bobbing his head. His eyes shone with unnatural brightness. "Which is what one would, hm-m, expect, after all."

Ruben frowned curiously. "Why? *Why* is that 'what one would expect'?"

Now the professor saw that he might have gone too far, but decided to finish. He tapped his manicured fingers on the chair arm. "Well, Doctor, Ingrid Solomon does not speak readily of this. She knows her views might sound preposterous to the man on the street. But she, hm-m, totally accepts the concept of reincarnation."

"Yes," Ruben prompted. "So do I. What does that have to do with anything?"

"The Director has ordered certain elaborate, quasi-scientific tests in the past—I participated reluctantly in a few of them myself, I confess—which convinced her that she was correct. That she is, hm-m, the reincarnation of a brilliant king of antiquity. A man whom numerous occultists claim was, quite possibly, history's first magus or sorcerer."

Ruben stared at him as he understood, unable to speak.

Sinoway smiled at his dazed condition. "Yes, you're right in the conclusion you're beginning to draw just now. Absolutely right, Ruben. Our Director is quite *convinced* that she was once the wisest man who ever lived, reincarnated in the wholly exotic female flesh you, hm-m, know so well. That legendary man who once almost cut a baby in half to determine its true mother." The professor's horrible smile glowed yellowly. "I refer, of course, to King Solomon of Israel."

Twelve

Things were beginning to happen at a dizzying pace, Ruben felt, so quickly it was hard to sort things out. With a shrieking headache plaguing him, he succeeded in urging Sinoway out of his quarters and, trying to relax and think, took a quick shower.

He realized that when he'd last heard Ingrid utter Biblical lines, he'd been correct. They weren't from the *Song of Solomon*, that beautiful and rare old tribute to love and passion. They were, instead, the words of Solomon himself, from *Ecclesiastes*.

Drying himself, half-wondering whom he might find waiting for him when he again returned to the front room, Ruben had a mental image of the brilliant blonde poring through the Holy Bible, memorizing words that she believed she had once spoken herself. Thousands of years ago.

Don't judge her, he thought warningly, not yet.

He located a Bible in the study alcove of his apartment, thinking wryly that he was literally doing what Ingrid wanted him to do, during this two-hour segment of the morning. His Eighth House was still rising; it allowed religious study. Did this suggest, he wondered, that he was beginning unconsciously to obey the doctrine of astrocosmology?

By assiduously using his own small knowledge of the

Bible and scanning it with a college professor's keen eye, Martin felt that he was learning more about the private motivations of fantastic Ingrid Solomon.

Her urge to create the organization she'd called Solomon Studies could be intuited in I Kings: "Moreover, the king made a great throne of ivory, and overlaid it with the best gold . . . and two lions stood beside the stays." Jacques and Sinoway, Ruben thought, and remembered too that Solomon built the first great Temple in Israel. "And all the earth sought to Solomon, to hear his wisdom, which God had put in his heart." It didn't surprise him to read that and realize that part of Ingrid's ambition included power and fame, "the earth" seeking her for the wisdom of longevity. In the words, "But King Solomon loved many strange women," he thought there was an endorsement of Ingrid's attitude toward sex.

The original Solomon had belived in routine, in order. ". . . Daily shall he be praised," reads the 72nd Psalm, attributed to the ancient king. Her fascination with the world of ideas—especially "forbidden" knowledge—was recalled as well: "And I gave my heart to seek and search out by wisdom concerning all things that are done under heaven . . . I made me great works: I builded me houses . . . I got me servants and maidens, and had servants born in my house."

Even Solomon's abhorrence of dying seemed to prefigure in Ingrid's own fear: "There is no remembrance of the wise more than of the fool for ever; seeing that which now is in the days to come shall all be forgotten. And how dieth the wise man? as the fool." Ruben paused at the following thought: "Therefore I hated life." If she closed her eyes to questionable practices on Nommos, it would be entirely in keeping with her earlier life.

Ingrid's absolute devotion to her tasks? Again, Solomon: "I perceive that there is nothing better, than that a man should rejoice in his own works; for that is his portion . . ." Ruben read the next words five times: ". . . *A living dog is better than a dead lion.*"

That, he thought, said it all.

Now, Ruben asked himself, closing the Holy Book, what did all that *mean*? Did it make Ingrid Solomon mad? Did it make her evil? Did it make her work wrong-minded or worse?

He dressed slowly, considering. There were a number of professional assumptions he could draw. Nice, pat arguments indicating Ingrid's aberrative condition—concluding that she was ill. No doubt of that. He peered at his face in the mirror and decided, on the spot, to grow a beard. It might cut down on the number of people who took him for Sherlock Holmes. He put his electric razor back in its case and sat down on the edge of the bed to put on his shoes.

What, in the last analysis, was Ingrid doing that was *wrong*? So far as he knew, the Director had no intention of hoarding her discoveries. She could not become famous and draw the world to her by living in silence. And if the discoveries benefited mankind—if they meant, to the average man or woman in Milwaukee or Syracuse, Jacksonville or Pittsburgh or Carmel, that they wouldn't need to concern themselves with death for upwards of fifty or sixty years—that man or woman couldn't care *less* if Ingrid Solomon were mad as a hatter!

And what kind of hypocrite would he be, since he accepted the concepts of reincarnation himself, to conclude, automatically, that her claim was invalid? *Why* did it have to be nonsense?

It was true enough that the institutions were full of

madmen who believed they once were Napoleon, Moses, St. Peter, or Adolph Hitler—but if every human being *was* reincarnated, didn't that mean that Napoleon and the rest *had*, in point of pure logic, returned to earth?

He had become weary over the years of investigating reincarnational claims to his patients being ex-generals, ex-queens, ex-apostles, ex-inventors and ex-authors. Logic suggested that *some* of the people walking around today had never been famous in a previous existence, since ninety-nine percent of the population over the decades never approached an iota of fame. But logic also insisted that Benjamin Franklin, Shakespeare, Martin Luther, and Thomas Alva Edison *had* been born again, if there was anything to reincarnation!

It was a neat problem, what Holmes would have called a "three-pipe problem." But in Ingrid's case it boiled down to which came *first*: Her appraisal of the Bible and subsequent emulation of Solomon, which indicated schizophrenia; or a lifelong, inner *psychic knowing* of her former existence which only seemed corroborated by a reading of the Bible. In short, it plainly wasn't possible that she once had been, quite literally, the King of Israel.

Regeneration came in various ways, Ruben thought, and chose a tall glass of iced tea. He located Jacques Coquelion at a table in the cafeteria and took a chair beside him. The Belgian's greeting was warm and hearty. Not only that, Martin thought, but he looked much better.

"Your wife told me that the progress lately is substantial," he remarked, studying his friend's good color. "She said that addicts are losing their addiction, drunks have dried out, the terminal are receiving promising new prognoses. That *does* include you, I think, if I judge correctly."

Jacques laughed lightly and flushed. "Yes, *mon ami*, I believe it does. The tests Ingrid spoke of?" He paused, beaming happily. "They included mine."

"I'm very, *very* glad, Jacques!" Ruben shook his hand. "Is it simply the astrology or is there more to your recovery?"

"There's more. Sinoway developed a program for me that included lowering my body temperature as well as lowering my food intake."

"How does that work?" Ruben inquired, curious.

"Well, there is considerable evidence that the so-called 'normal' body temperature of ninety-eight point six degress isn't the end all and be all, that it's not immutable. Sinoway proved that, knowing that life is automatically lengthened with a lower temperature." He shrugged. "Some connections of his at Michigan State helped out. I've been on an experimental drug that causes my temperature to drop to that of the surrounding air." Jacques smiled. "Ingrid keeps this place a trifle warm, as you know, and that's for my benefit. It's always eighty-two degrees here, and that matches my *own* temperature. The results, you already know."

"Fascinating," Martin murmured. "Tell me, why didn't you inform me that everyone on the staff except your wife was operating on a death sentence?"

"I simply didn't think you would want to come here if you knew that. I'm enough of a psychiatrist to know that dying people don't exactly cheer one up."

Ruben looked sharply at the Belgian. "And besides that, Ingrid told you not to. Correct?"

Jacques smiled shyly. "Observant as ever, Doctor." He rubbed his goatee thoughtfully. "I've always had a sort of boyish admiration for genuine brilliance. I—I never met anyone as intelligent as Ingrid."

Ruben hesitated, sipping his iced tea. "But was that enough for matrimony? I suppose what I'm asking you, Jacques, is—how do you really feel about our brilliant Director?"

The other man was troubled; he sighed and averted his face. "I'm not certain it is easy to feel anything at all for my little woman except admiration and lust. She—isn't a simple person to know well."

"Because she believes she was once Solomon?"

Jacques' head spun in surprise. "How did you know about that?" he demanded.

"Dear old Professor Sinoway."

Jacques frowned. "I should have known. Well, Ingrid *believing* that doesn't disturb me. What bothers me is that she *was* Solomon. I've come to accept that."

Ruben pursed his lips. "My respect for her intelligence continues to grow," he said. "You're afraid of her, aren't you, Jacques?"

For a moment it seemed the psychiatrist would explode in anger. Then he shrugged his shoulders lightly. "Some, perhaps. A *soupçon.*" The lines on his forehead deepened. "It isn't hard to be afraid of someone who has the power of life and death over you."

"What does *that* mean?" Ruben asked surprised.

Jacques gestured with his hand. "Only that, if she willed it, Sinoway would refuse to treat me any longer. He never wanted to do it, anyway. He regards me as an interloper, since I'm quite certain he once planned to marry her himself." Jacques cleared his throat. "I know, by the way, that she went voluntarily to your room, that it wasn't your idea. I know that you made love."

Ruben was embarrassed. "Made *sex*, perhaps. My dear friend, I'm so terribly sorry. I had no idea that you were married to her."

"Ah, well, you weren't the first who helped her cuckhold me, old son. Nor will you be the last. Tonight I'm sure, during the proper two hours . . ."

"But how do you *stand* it?" Ruben demanded. "*You*, Jacques, with your history of commanding every relationship in which you were engaged! The finest Casanova since the original!"

His brows lifted. "She was fair about it, *mon ami*. Before we wed, she informed me that it would be this way. If the truth be known, Marteen, I—I am grateful that she consented to marry a dying wreck of a man."

"But *why*? Why would you ask her? You've never had any problems getting women before."

Again Jacques shrugged. "Part of it is that I needed her money for my debts, including soaring medical bills. And money for a teen-aged son who does not know I exist." Now Jacques' eyes filled with tears. "But the major part, my dear Marteen, is much simpler than that. You see, I *love* Ingrid. I love her with all my heart. It is the fondest dream of my heart that, one day, she will be able to feel more than sex for me—that at last, some magical night, she will love me, too."

Martin was more touched than he could say by his old friend's admission and his terrible plight. But this, after all, was none of his business. When he could, decently, Ruben excused himself.

Shortly before noon, when he was taking a scheduled exercise break—not because he'd decided to be obedient but because working out suddenly, strangely sounded enjoyable—Tina the messenger-girl came to fetch him.

She discovered Ruben flat on his back beneath barbells and stared in open surprise at the rather aesthetic parapsychologist as she told him that the Director and Professor Sinoway desired his company.

"Where are they?" Ruben asked, remaining where he was. The barbells appeared to be plowing a furrow in his narrow chest but he made no effort to remove it. He seemed content for it to become imbedded there.

"In Section Three C," the Eurasian girl replied, watching the way Ruben's face continued to redden. She shifted her weight, one hand on a round hip. "You want me to show you the way?"

"Ah." He paused. When he spoke it was with greater difficulty. "Ah, no. But thank you."

She shrugged, a trifle taken aback, and turned away.

Behind her there were a variety of strange snortling noises and she had the impression of great effort being exerted.

Tina looked back and the sounds instantly stopped. Ruben smiled pleasantly at her, perspiring freely. She pointed. "You can't get out from under that thing, can you, Doctor?"

He glanced deliberately right then left. There were no other men near him in the gym.

He cleared his throat. "As a matter of pure fact, my dear, I cannot."

"Oh." She said it lightly.

Then she approached the bench and lifted the barbell, with one careless hand, from the prone parapsychologist's chest.

He struggled shakily to his feet as Tina, grinning from ear to ear, replaced the exercise tool in its rack.

"Physical conditioning," Ruben muttered hoarsely, passing her in quest of a towel, "has to be the *worst* pastime for man on this globe!"

She resisted a tendency toward giggling.

Martin didn't want to waste time changing clothes, and besides, he felt suddenly quite athletic and light. He followed Tina through winding corridors to an elevator, wearing his sweatclothes and a towel. En route, he recalled that Section III-C housed a large sampling of Sinoway's critically ill patients.

The professor and his entourage met him at the nurses' station, his brown eyes sweeping the sweat-stained body from head to toe in obvious scorn. "This way," he grunted in the tone of a man reluctantly obliged to guide a sewer cleaner.

Is it my imagination, Ruben thought, moving on airy feet, *or do I already feel better on this regimen? I'm ready to take on Sinoway's bodyguard!*

Ingrid was sitting beside a bed and looked up to greet him with a luminous smile. It was palpably impossible to consider her sixty years of age. Thirty-six or -seven, perhaps; no more.

The room was familiar, he realized, as he moved toward the foot of the bed.

"I thought you might like to be part of this, Doctor," she said to him.

It was senile Harry Pfeiff, at whom Morley Sinoway had shouted insults.

But *this* Harry, Martin thought, wouldn't put up with it. He was sitting up in bed, grinning a bit foolishly with a light of obvious intelligence in his gray eyes. "You're Doctor Ruben," he said brightly. "How do!"

The full impact didn't strike Ruben at once. He took the arthritic hand extended to him and shook it, smiling, before he understood.

This old man, just the day before, had been nearly comatose with advanced senility, incapable of speaking a word relevant to the 1970s! He didn't know his own name, let alone Ruben's! This much improvement so swiftly was nothing short of incredible!

"How are you feeling today, Mister Pfeiff?" he asked, testing.

"I haven't felt this good since old Harry S showed Tom Dewey a thing or two about politics!" Harry beamed at him toothlessly.

Sinoway allowed himself a smile. "Part of it is the L-Dopa, as I discussed with you. The glands are secreting vastly better today."

"But primarily it's our special regimen," Ingrid declared, flushed with delight. She didn't see Sinoway's disapproving frown. "It is adhered to faithfully even in the hospital wards. And I allowed the Professor an extra injection last night. You see the results."

The bald professor lifted a bushy eyebrow. "We must be cautious, of course. In many elderly patients, L-Dopa has an almost aphrodisiac effect."

Old Harry grinned at Sinoway and then directly at Ingrid. He threw back his sheets. "You mean," he demanded, "like *this*?"

Ruben registered astonishment. The old man's gown was pulled above his waist and his aged member was erect, mammoth and ready.

Ingrid disappointed Harry by refusing to blush. She replaced the sheet and scolded him. "You have to make up to me for that, you old bastard," she snapped, hands on hips. "You'll just have to answer some questions."

Suspicion cooled Harry's gaze. "Like what?" he asked.

And Ingrid fired a battery of questions at him, barely waiting until he had answered. "Who is the President of the United States? Who is the Vice President? Who won the National League baseball championship last year? Who won the World Series in 1955? Who was Earl Warren?" She continued to ask him queries: "Who played in the Super Bowl last January? How many grandchildren do you have? What are their names? Who was President in 1968?"

Martin Ruben watched in astonishment. As fast as Ingrid could frame a question, old Harry Pfeiff fired the answer back at her. It was with difficulty that he remembered the old boy could not, just yesterday, have known the day of the week. And for the first time, Ruben felt affection for the beautiful Director. Her interest in Harry was obviously sincere. Perhaps he was only one of many statistics to Ingrid Solomon but, just now, in old Harry's presence, he really felt that she cared about him.

When she was convinced that the treatment had worked, she led Ruben aside. Her cheeks remained flushed and her generally perfect hairdo revealed a rebellious curl or two. "Harry here is one of nine senile men who've come around today," she declared, almost breathlessly. She paused as if ashamed to admit what she was about to say. "He reminds me so of my own father, Doctor. The poor man died the way Harry was—yesterday."

When the three of them were moving outside, Harry's voice trailed after them: "Morley, you never were worth a good goddamn before!" he cried, the jubilation at his own restored health evident in his tone. "But now I got hope for ya, son!"

Sinoway looked at Ruben, coldly. "Of all the people to cure," he said, "we had to cure *him*!"

Ruben laughed. They were drifting nearer the nurses' station, as he caught Ingrid Solomon's arm. "Madame Director, do you have it on your person?"

She looked blankly at him. "What?"

Ruben smiled. "My contract." He took a deep breath. "Your father wasn't the only one whom Harry reminded me of, Ingrid. I take it you'd still like me to head the parapsychological teaching department?"

Her violet eyes had tears in them. "Very, very much,

Martin Ruben."

He sighed. "Well, your methods are more than a trifle unorthodox. Some of your views seem virtually Druidic, shades of Wicca!" He kissed her forehead. "But I'd consider it an honor to work where people are not only making progress for other people in the future but actually doing wonders for them today. I'll try to live by your rules."

As Martin rested the contract against the wall and was affixing his signature, he caught a glimpse from the corner of his eye of Professor Morley Sinoway.

It was the most inexplicable, truly complex expression on the other man's face. It was—unreadable. And when he peered again at Ingrid Solomon, he saw that her expression was the same.

Maybe she *is* King Solomon, Ruben thought with a last-minute pang of doubt. She's at least as enigmatic.

Thirteen

Shortly after 3:30 P.M., Ruben was in his appointed classroom on the first level, prepared for his initial class to begin at 3:50. Instead of the arenalike hall at Badler University, he found himself in a large, airy room with plenty of natural light and seating for no more than eighteen pupils. He liked his surroundings immediately; a teacher could *reach out* and *teach* such a group. He felt some of the excitement he'd experienced, years ago, when he'd readied himself for the first class at Badler. At his desk he shuffled and reshuffled notes he'd hastily assembled, then glanced through the large textbook from which he was meant to teach.

The book was an anthology of some of the best writing on the paranormal by people such as J. B. Rhine, Colin Wilson, Hereward Carrington, Karlis Osis, John Taylor, Lewis Spence, Francis Hitching, C. G. Jung, William James, Charles Berlitz, Harold T. Wilkins, Stuart Holroyd, and Georgei Gurdjieff. A special astrology section—the implication of that didn't escape Ruben—pleased him by containing contributions from Charles E. O. Carter, Mary Neal, William T. Tucker, Sybil Leek, Nicholas DeVore, and Dane Rudhyar. This was not dreamworld, ephemeral astrology, it was a compendium of what *worked*.

Best of all, he had learned from both a syllabus and

hurried conversation with Jacques Coquelion that there was nothing hidebound about either what he taught or the nature of his classes. Students were to be instructed, not graded. Instead of being assembled by age or grade level, the classes were (as he had expected) composed according to astrological harmony. The intent was both to enhance his own communication to them and to stimulate the kind of camaraderie that resulted in good give-and-take.

Ruben soon found that the system worked. If the younger children, such as Dhombola, didn't understand a point they simply *said* so, and Ruben or another pupil examined it. Not that Dhombola required much assistance; like the others, he was exceptionally eager and intelligent. Wiping his forehead with a handkerchief after the first class, Ruben couldn't remember a brighter bunch. They were the kind who pushed a professor to be at his best, to *think* along with them rather than merely restating drab facts. They were, he grinned, students in the truest sense.

He found it was impossible to gauge how much the success of these classes arose from the quick bonds that were established, not only between him and the pupils, but among themselves. Really, he thought, flushed with pleasure, it didn't matter. He was finally seeing astrology put to its penultimate productive use, not merely to handle such questions as "Joe's a Leo and I'm Taurus, so are we a good match?"

Ruben ranged over a wide field of knowledge, partly to convince these bright people that he knew his business. He told them how, during the reign of Clovis I in the fifth century, the Salic Franks had a law called the Lex Salica that stated that "a witch, having eaten human flesh, and being convicted of this crime, shall pay eight thousand dinerii, i.e., two hundred gold pennies."

Then he asked his class to comment on what was unusual about that.

A moon-faced little girl of thirteen or so grinned. "Even without inflation, that isn't much of a fine for such a terrible crime!"

"Exactly," Ruben nodded. "Strangely enough, in those days the fines for evil magic were usually lower than those for unproved accusations that a person *was* a witch. Our use of the word 'defamation' derives from that period," he continued. "Two hundred years later, this kind of thinking still obtained. The *Liber Poenitentialis*—a church law of Saint Leonard—recommended this penance for a sacrifice to devils: "'One year of penance, if he is a clown of low estate; if he be of a higher degree, ten years.' Who can comment on that?"

Dhombola's brown arm shot up. His teeth flashed in a smile. "Chief's harder on bigshots than regular people. Musta thought bigshots should know better!"

Ruben had nodded, pleased. "Until the past century or so, little distinction was drawn, if any, between psychics or sensitives and so-called witches. What you've heard also suggests that civilization did not improve in its treatment of witches with the years, considering the Inquisition and Salem. Learn from this, please. The views which are new are not necessarily better than the ones of a hundred or two hundred years before simply because they are 'modern.' And bear in mind, too, that the public attitude toward topics of the paranormal—well-intentioned, or evil—fluctuate even more than political views do. Today, as we embark into the transition to the new Aquarian Age, your exceptional talents tend to be acceptable. But that can change almost overnight if those in control become more repressive."

At ten, wrung-out from his teaching efforts, Ruben saw the last student file out of the classroom and pulled his schedule out of his desk drawer, glancing at it.

He was supposed to "rest or sleep" until 1 A.M. when "sex activities" were scheduled. He grimaced and tried not to think of that, since he'd made no plans for it and imagined that he would simply sleep through the two-hour segment.

As for resting, just now, Ruben was far too exhilarated to lie down. He had never been a man who could cease work and instantly fall asleep. It was a personal maxim of Martin's that, if the work was worth doing to begin with, a man would be too stimulated when he stopped to collapse into bed. He required time to unwind.

He sighed. Soon, he thought, it would be necessary to phone Badler and make arrangements for his final break. That would not be easy. He had many associations he'd richly enjoyed, and he knew that he would miss them. Although the day's work, following his witness of an incredible improvement in old Harry Pfeiff, had been a delight, it occurred to Ruben that he was rather relieved about a clause in his Badler's contract. It gave the Board the option of making a counter offer before giving him a formal release. If they decided to fight for his services, they could tie up everything for weeks, even months.

Which meant, he saw, that his impulsive signing of the Solomon Studies contract could place him in one hell of a legal jam.

He stood, stretching and inhaling. Probably he was simply anxious about 1 A.M. What was he supposed to *do*—walk around the corridors or the grounds until he saw a woman who appealed to him, and pounce upon her? He doubted that Ingrid's endorsement of sexual freedom extended to rape! And the very idea of his personal affairs being that routinized continued to be positively abhorrent to him. The best in human relationships, he thought, happened spontaneously, often as a full surprise to both parties.

Instead of returning to his quarters the way the schedule called for, Ruben found himself wandering outside, into the island night. He also found himself irritatingly *silent*. He was almost sneaking from place to place, like a naughty teenager after curfew. It was still on the grounds around the central building except, at a distance, Martin could hear voices of others who were, presumably, scheduled to be up and around.

Moonlight flooded the more open areas of the island like opaque water. The grass appeared almost beige, unreal. It was hot and humid tonight, and perspiration began to trickle down his neck from behind his ear. When he turned in the direction of the mound Ruben saw, with some surprise, a figure just beyond its roped area. By now he knew it was strictly tabu to be approaching the ancient landmark at night and wondered who the daring interloper might be.

When he had padded nearer, he stared in further surprise: The figure seemed to be that of a pygmy, at least a midget or dwarf. It was scarcely taller than the rope that hit Ruben slightly below the waist.

At the instant that he stepped on a fallen tree branch, the *crack*! a reverberating thunderclap that seemed deafening, the little man whirled to face him. Ruben had time to see that the thin, little fellow was absolutely naked and had the most ugly face Ruben had seen in ages.

Then the unknown creature had bolted, running agilely on tiptoe, circling toward the distant part of the island where the farm operation and generators were situated.

Now, what was *that* all about, Martin wondered?

He wasn't sure, but he thought the tiny man had been down on his knees before the mound. He had buried something there, perhaps? Or was he trying to learn what *was* buried in the mound? Ruben thought of the way nudity indicated savagery and mused briefly on the possibility that the mound was, indeed, Indian and so was the small interloper. Could there be a crazed witch doctor or medicine man's bones lying there for centuries?

As he thought, Ruben's feet quite naturally drew him nearer the swelling mound. He became conscious of warmth, as though the temperature had suddenly shot up nine or ten degrees.

More than that, Ruben was aware of other sensations. He *needed* something, he realized; there was something he *wanted*—but he could not imagine what.

Since he was at the mound he tried to do what was recommended and to project his frustrations and overall sense of confusion to the hillock: Confusion, in part, over whether he'd done the right thing in signing Ingrid's contract. Strangely, the mound seemed to give him back a certain feeling of peacefulness. It seemed almost to—*understand*. Yet the need, the unformed desire, remained with the heat in the parapsychologist's veins.

He went on trying to project, to *aim* his feelings at the mound, to let them go there until they were left for good with this ancient plot of ground. Sweat broke out anew on his forehead as he made the earnest effort, without knowing quite why he bothered.

And he didn't stop projecting and became filled with a thrill of supernatural fear until as he stared at it . . .

the mound finally *stopped* breathing.

Impossible, he thought, gaping wide-mouthed; he must have been wrong....

"I thought I'd find you here."

Ruben whirled in terror. But it was only the Director of Solomon Studies, no longer an eager and willing bedmate who was cheating on her husband through her husband's best friend, but Martin Ruben's employer. A person who owned every building, mound, tree and twig on Nommos Island.

"You signed a contract with us, Doctor Ruben," she began coldly. "We were both pleased, very pleased, I think. But I fully expect the terms of that contract to be honored—not just by others, but by *you* as well."

"I taught my classes when I was meant to," he replied mildly. "They went very well."

"If that means that you think all you need to do to comply is *teach*," Ingrid snapped, moonlight behind her haloing her lovely face now and turning her anger to freezing fire, "then read the small print in your copy of the document. I have no doubt about your teaching, which is exemplary. But you also agreed to abide totally by the schedule posted at the beginning of each zodiacal period. *All* of the schedule."

He was on the verge of mentioning that he had only trailed after an earlier, preceding visitor to the mound and ask who the tiny fellow had been when he realized that she was genuinely angry. "I had hoped we could be civilized about this," he said slowly. "Anyone who used to live as Solomon, antiquity's most wise and brilliant man, should have a knack for reasonableness."

Her lips opened in astonishment. "H-How did you know about that?"

He never understood why he protected Sinoway. "It just—gets around. But, Ingrid, you needn't be ashamed of it. There have been many times when I was fairly convinced I'm Sir Arthur Conan Doyle. I imagine most people who believe in reincarnation have times when they're just *sure* they were Alexander the Great or—"

"There is nothing King Solomon could do that I can't do!" she exclaimed. "I've tried the magic attributed to him and it's entirely *natural* to me." She hesitated, her bosom rising and falling and her violet eyes confused for the first time. She looked—magnetic. "I don't know why I'm defending myself to you. I *know* who I was in a former life. What you believe is entirely your own affair."

Impulsively, Ruben reached out for her, pulled her tall body against his own. He was hot now, confused about his motivations, as he kissed her full on the lips.

Ingrid struggled away, astonishingly. She pushed hard at his chest and staggered back like a virginal ninth grader. "We could have sex before only because I didn't know your horoscope," she hissed, her eyes blazing at him. "Not anymore! We're not compatible sexually and what we did will never happen again, Doctor—never!"

He didn't argue, just looked baffled as Ingrid headed toward the buildings.

Then she paused and, without turning back to him, said coolly over her shoulder: "Neither of us should be here, Doctor. Get back into the central building, *at once*! Don't let me ever catch you out here again at night! Those who disobey me unfailingly regret it!"

She was gone.

Ruben groaned. With a dull, aching anger dawning inside, he began to walk slowly toward the main structure. You're the head of a major department, full of eager, bright students, he told himself firmly. You're going to make more money than you ever *knew* existed in the world! Why, Ruben could become wealthy, finally live up to the haunting expectations of red-cheeked old Max Ruben, who'd wanted an eminently successful doctor. And all that he had to do was follow a schedule that, according to his personal observations and experience, probably would serve him handsomely in the future—and might even mean an extended life span.

But, oh damn! He stepped into the elevator and, in privacy as the doors shut, slammed his fist against the moving wall. It was so *hard* to work for a woman who behaved as a domineering mother to a not-very-bright child!

He stretched out on his bed and tried to sleep. Oblivion for awhile would be nice, he said sardonically to himself. He could think about it all tomorrow when he arose.

For quite a while sleep would not come but relaxation slowly crept agreeably along and he was drifting off soon after midnight.

. . . Jacques' eyes stared at him, pleading for help. The Belgian could not speak, just as the others were obliged to remain silent. He made out more faces beside Jacques'—Sinoway, his student friend Barry Caldwell from Badler, little Dhombola from Africa, the neonatologist Julie, a little white boy he didn't recognize but whom he knew was named Robert, even Ingrid—*all* buried to their necks in dirt, their mouths and nostrils gradually filling with dirt. Poor Jacques seemed *bloated* with the stuff, mumpish, his eyes forced out by the pressure until Ruben thought they must pop away from their sockets. Above them, on top of the mound in which, like quicksand, they seemed to be drowning, a shadowy, naked little man danced insanely and called—or chanted—a mysterious name: *Aloha*, it might have been, or not, not that; *Al Lock,* something of that kind.

And as Ruben stared in horror, each of the people buried in the dirt pit began to turn red in the face, coughing themselves to death in a silence that was worse than a scream. . . .

Noise; some *noise* awakened him.

Ruben sat bolt upright in the dark bedroom, momentarily thinking he was back in his Indianapolis apartment. But the shadows were all wrong; his dresser was not where it should be, and *these* quarters were comfortable, tidy. . . .

Knowledge came. He smiled to himself but, when he reached out to turn on a lamp, his hand trembled. *One-oh-three*, the clock said.

Nighttime, he muttered; it's deep nighttime.

Ruben turned over on his stomach with weariness, sighing.

A *giggle*. Ruben's eyes shot open, staring at his pillow. *A female giggle*.

That was when he felt the hand on his right buttock.

Then it was stretching, higher, fingers locking beneath the right leg of his shorts—gentle, womanly fingers.

Martin turned quickly onto his back and looked down in panic.

A bare brunette of perhaps twenty-two or twenty-three, with the largest breasts he'd ever seen in his life—he thought of collegiate globes of the world—had clambered over the foot of the bed and inched her way up to him, the manner almost that of a predator. Her expression was sincere; it meant business as her deep-brown eyes swept his body hungrily; it hadn't been her that giggled.

He sat up, unable to speak. From one side of the bed a charming female head had appeared, fringed in reddish curls, short-trimmed and adorable.

She was perhaps a year or two older than the brunette; her breasts weren't nearly as large. The nipples were tiny, no larger than a dime, but the centers protruded a good quarter inch in their owner's eagerness. When she saw that she had his full attention, the redhead stood beside his bed, slipping one rounded knee over the edge. The center of her femaleness peeked through a mass of bright auburn curls. "I'm Debbie," she said in a high, amused voice that was certainly capable of giggles. "Hi, Martin!"

That was when the arms came around the bare chest, *other* arms; he was squeezed in a tender trap. Two sweet female breasts were pressed close to him. Martin turned enough to look back over his shoulder incredulously.

It was Tina, the Eurasian. She was quite gloriously naked, squinched between him and the headboard with the faces of her grouped breasts uptilted to his face. Her hands slid then in unison down his chest and stomach, reaching, ducking beneath the waistband of his shorts.

There they met another hand also arriving, each cupping.

And Ruben remembered. That preference test he'd completed. He had told them that he "couldn't get off" without at least three beautiful women! Great heaven, they gave you *exactly* what you asked for on Nommos Island!

But what could he possibly do with three gorgeous nude females?

There was pressure against his foot. Wildly, he peered down again, past the brunette and redhead.

A fourth girl, possibly nineteen, had stepped from his closet to kneel gracefully beside the brunette. She was another natural blonde, not pale like Ingrid but magnificently tanned. Where Ingrid had almost no pubic hair, this lass sported a veritable forest of tangled gold. She was indescribably lovely. Her eyes were sky blue—he'd said his favorite color was blue!—and as mocking as the brunette's were serious. She leaned forward, parting her rather long and pendulous breasts with his thin ankle to gently kiss his calf. "I'm Rhonda," she said and laughed lightly. "We're *all* compatible with you, Martin."

He didn't doubt it for a moment. Her action triggered some resentment in the brunette with the enormous bosom and she kissed higher. Martin's knee bent spasmodically. The blonde, whom he saw had the lightest-pink nipples in memory, responded by kissing him on the inside of his left thigh.

Finally they found a common ground, the location left when Tina stripped his shorts away. The redhead briefly joined them and Ruben felt three soft female tongues moving along his tremulous and rockhard penis.

"Girls," he gasped, unsure what he was trying to say. "*Ladies*! Th-there are *four* of you!"

The brunette's tongue curled around the tip of his shaft. "We can get a few more, if it's not enough," she said when she paused.

He was speechless. The old line about, "When rape is inevitable," occurred to him. Tina swung her short, plump leg across the bed to straddle his upper chest until she had—with an attitude that appeared proprietary—lowered one of her utterly round high breasts against his lips. A small girl, her bare lower body was furry-warm, light on his panting chest.

Then the redhead perched lightly beside him at the top of the bed and trailed her tongue along his jawline. She took his face between her hands and coaxed his lips away from Tina to her own elongated nipples. They weren't rubbery; instead, she tasted like some exotic food. She and Tina each took a hand of his and placed it between their thighs, high and, as his fingers stretched, quite deep.

The tiny Eruasian girl began to move at once on his chest. It pained his wrist but Ruben didn't mind. His mouth locked on the redhead's thrusting nipple as Tina began to throw her head back in delight, her hips slapping against his raised fingers.

"There's just one thing, Doctor." It was an unwelcome voice from nowhere or, more precisely, from an area Martin couldn't see with Tina and the redhead in the way. "We have a message for you from the Director."

He recognized the voice of the blonde. When she paused to think, she dropped her head against him and her long hair cascaded across his lower body so that the brunette also stopped. "She said, '*This* is what you will get so long as you live up to the letter of our contract.'"

The brunette held him in one hand and finished the message. "And she added, 'I advise you, sir, never find out what happens if you seriously violate it.' I think that's all there was, Martin."

"Thank y-you," Ruben managed, always polite.

He was incapable of hearing her reply. She had resumed the use of her incredible tongue, dipping at the tip of his penis as the blonde, on the other side, just as artful and dedicated, swept her tongue and hair over his taut testicles. When they each began to nibble ever-so-gently on either side of his penis Ruben knew that he must soon explode. It would, he felt, leave nothing of him but steaming-hot little pieces of flesh that bounced like rubber balls. That was when they stopped, almost as if on signal, although he suspected vaguely that Tina was in charge.

As he watched in a crimson haze, unable to say a sensible word, they began to alternate positions, a quartet of beautiful, bare women working as a team to please one man.

When they had settled in, the effect was almost of *another* four, new nude women cavorting on his bed. Now the giant breasts of the brunette were squashed against his face as she urged him to kiss them all over. The blonde was impatiently seated beside her, the forest of her pubis awaiting his attention. Beneath him, the redhead's tongue swept over his testicles and the Eurasian's moist lips closed around his penis like a velvet vice, darting up and down it with only the slightest sweet pressure.

The chill Ruben had experienced along his spine when he heard Ingrid's frosty message had lasted only a moment. He was human. What was happening to him, he knew, happened rarely to any mortal man. It was the experience of someone of incomparable fame or wealth, of a god in man's form. And later, when he had miraculously found the resilience and restructured rigidity to sample the orifices of all four young women, lost in a gorgeous tangle of eager arms and curvacious legs, he nearly forgot Ingrid's message entirely.

But the thing about sex is that, regardless of numbers or intensity, one can never lose himself in it forever. There came a time when he was left in his bed alone, feeling not only deliciously spent but also *used*—used, machinelike, turned into a plunging automaton, a human piston, of no further use when the engine would turn over no longer.

The aftertaste of this orgiastic menu was more bitter than he cared, just then, to confess to himself. Their femaleness scented every inch of his body, his sheets. He knew he would never forget it, would even reach a point when he treasured the memory, and might find it impossible not to tell of it to a male friend.

But in the blank recesses of early morning Martin Ruben also knew, deep inside, that some force of nature does not allow such a calory-heavy feast without eventually leaving the man with a hangover and terrible indigestion. Sooner or later, a Cosmic Waiter would hand him the bill. . . .

PART TWO

_____Fourteen

Weeks of pleasant work by day and dazzling sexual experience by night passed for Martin Ruben as if a new kind of calendar had been invented. In a way, he supposed, the world had become the fulfillment of lifetime dreams: The admitted, conscious dream of heading a parapsychology department and being permitted to teach the way he wished to intensely interested, highly gifted students. And a never-voiced, very private dream of unrestricted sensuality mingled with the richly stimulating quality of *every* man's nocturnal dream.

It was a world in a way too ideal for any man to survive endlessly. There was the intellectual flavor, his mind daily stimulated to new levels of inquiry and frequently subjected to remarkable insights from the experimental parapsychologists, who were quick to share their discoveries with him. There was the texture of improved physical health, since, under the routine of astrocosmology and his daily workouts in the gym, Ruben soon found himself in better shape than he'd ever been. Every few days he played two hard sets of tennis with Jacques Coquelion, and it was a marvelous moment when he finally defeated his Belgian companion. As well, the sensuality was of many parts, soothing the spirit and making it believe it was eternal. Undoubtedly, he thought, Ingrid meant her people to feel that way.

Ruben found that he could eat whatever rich foods he wanted in a cafeteria any film star would have reveled in, since he quickly worked out to rid himself of unwelcome calories. When his first paycheck came—the largest of his life—he took the returning plane in to South Bend, with several others. There, he bought the finest wardrobe of his life and for the first time didn't have to worry about the bottomline. His beard grew rapidly, luxuriantly; dressed in his splendid, new sportswear and swinging a gold-tipped stick he'd decided to affect, Martin Ruben became a familiar, well-liked figure on Nommos Island.

Even the daily visits to the mound fitted into his routine painlessly. For him, they became Solomon Studies' version of the daily business conference, no better and no worse. Since he stopped disobeying orders and was away from the strange hillock at night, he saw no more mysterious little men and no longer imagined that the mound was breathing.

By night, though he didn't get three women every time "sex activities" came up, he used the same questing, exploring mind he utilized in the classroom in ways that his father, old Max Ruben, never conceived. Twice he asked Jacques in, not for homosexual encounters but to relieve him with the incredibly nimble and dexterous pair of women who had showed up that night. There were a few curiosity-provoked flings with bisexual women, who brought along their companions and virtually flabbergasted Martin into shock. Once he tried taking pictures, but his old moralistic upbringing let him down; he lost interest at once in amateur pornography. The "sex activities" segment when he and a six-foot brunette dressed in costumes and pretended to be Caesar and Cleopatra ended with Ruben in tears of helpless laughter and the amazon angrily tromping off.

In short, all was not only well but fantastically well for him until the late-August luncheon when he realized how much he liked Julie Lyle, the neonatologist. He'd had so many women who were virtually strangers that he was relieved and rather pleased to learn that he still could see a female as a real person. But when he tried to persuade her to go with him to a first-run film in the theater-and-sports center, she shook her head reluctantly.

"I might have been around already," she told him shyly, her lids lowered, "except that we aren't compatible."

"*Who says?*" roared the newly self-assured and fastidious Ruben, so irritated he dragged an ornate cuff-link in the roquefort.

But he knew her answer: the computer said so. And nothing *he* could say would change Julie's mind or, worse, the computer's.

"Well, I didn't ask you to *sleep* with me," he protested, "only to go to a movie."

"Solomon Studies rules stipulate that those who are not compatible may socialize only in public conditions such as a luncheon," Julie pointed out.

"I don't give a damn what the regulations say!" he told her fiercely, reaching for her hand.

She pulled it away, stared silently at him. "Possibly *you* have the influence around here to bend the rules. I don't think I do." She touched the top of his hand. "I've learned that my tests show I've finally recovered from leukemia. There are—other problems, but I'm going to live. I'm going to stay alive. Martin, I have a duty and responsibility to people who saved my life."

She leaned forward to kiss him quickly above the brow and then, quite quietly, departed.

What "other problems"? he wondered. Ruben sat there a long while, poking at his strawbery shortcake and sipping his customary iced tea, trying to sort it out. Any job had its drawbacks, he reminded himself. Julie was right; it *would* be ungrateful to dispute an organization that gave one so much. Why did he continually feel that he was giving *up* personal freedom when the S.S. organization was providing him so much? Why, his classes *alone* should make it all worthwhile—if he'd had to grade these kids, Ruben would have had to figure out who did the *poorest* A work!

He wished he could relax and enjoy it, stop fighting the system. But he no longer doubted that strange things were happening, behind the scenes. He still wanted badly to learn what Morley Sinoway was doing in the privacy of his laboratory area. But taking direct action simply made no practical sense. His old employer, Badler University, had urged him to stay with S.S. through the summer until just before the beginning of the fall semester. That way, if Ruben changed his mind, he'd still have a place to go. In the meanwhile, his weekly paycheck was a fifty-secondth of more than one hundred thousand dollars; commonsense continually urged him to obey the rules and mind his own business.

In late August the Virgo period began and his schedule went *back* two hours. Now Martin was teaching from 1:30 to 7:30 P.M. daily, his rest period set for 8:00, and the segment for sex was scheduled to begin at 11 P.M. This allowed him a more normal sleeping time, and the mere change of hours kept life from having any inclination toward dullness.

And after September 1st, when they found the first body, it wasn't at all dull. Not ever again, on Nommos Island. The body belonged to Juan Emmanuel, a Mexican farmer of Mayan descent who toiled in the agricultural section. No one knew why he took his life; the circumstances of his death were unrevealed. But there wasn't much attention paid the tragedy in the central building, anyway; few members of the psychiatric or medical staffs even knew his name.

Three days later, however, Nellie Hermann, a nurse on the late-afternoon shift who worked in the Crisis Prevention Center, methodically swallowed every pill in a bottle she took from a locked cabinet to which she had the key. Like Juan, Nellie left no note. And like Juan, too, Nellie's body was removed instantly at the direction of Ingrid Solomon and the autopsy report, if any, was not made public.

Immediately rumors began, as they will in any tightly run operation. It was whispered that a murderer had emerged on Nommos; that Nellie and Juan were having an affair made impossible by incompatibility; that some secret virus causing intolerable depression had somehow been spread. Only Ruben, who didn't believe the rumors in any case, bothered to wonder if Sinoway might have let an experiment get out of hand.

The day after Nellie's body was found Ruben was sitting alone at his desk, smoking quietly, wondering. He'd completed his last class of the day and was troubled by the fact of two suicides in such a short period. He wondered, too, why he never could locate the little, naked man who preceded him to the mound a few weeks ago. Could there be a connection, he mused, between that odd fellow and the surge of self-destruction? The only places he hadn't gone to look for the tiny man were the hospital area—he had no desire to see Julie Lyle now and even less to encounter Sinoway— and the prayer room. He rather doubted that he'd find the fellow in civilized prayer; his demeanor had suggested something wild and free.

He rather wished Ingrid would approach him for a psychological opinion of the two suicides, but she hadn't. He sighed, decided to go back to his room. Rest was scheduled now anyway. He'd taken a few good novels by Craig Jones, Bernard Taylor, and Robert McCammon from the library and thought he'd spend his time until sex break reading.

But as he rose and moved toward the classroom door, he was surprised to see Dhombola, the African boy, dashing in. He looked like a child who was about to cry.

"What can possibly have gone wrong since the first class?" he asked the lad, rumpling his hair affectionately. "You look worried, son."

"My friend, *Docruben*," he answered quickly and a bit breathlessly. "He very, very sick! In hospital now."

"Well, I'm sure they're doing what they can for him," Ruben said kindly. "Who is he?"

The boy shook his head. "Not know the right magic to heal him, *Docruben*. But *you* can help him mebbe." Then he realized he hadn't fully answered the question. "Pigo, his name—Pigo, that all. Sir, you come—help my friend?"

Ruben paused. Physicians rarely like it when psychologists butted in. But he had been ignored in the suicides when he could have assisted. Besides, a visit would make the tiny African feel better. "Sure, son; I'll go. Show me where he is."

Dhombola tugging Martin's hand, they hurried down the corridor to the elevator and rode up to three.

Before emerging, the boy looked up at his tall friend and mentor. His expression was newly anxious. "Not let docs get mad at Dhombola, h'okay? Things—good, here, 'cept for mound thing. Not want to spoil everything, Docruben."

Martin peered down and wondered again how old the

child was, and how anyone could conceivably become angry with him. "I'll take the responsibility, son," he said. "Your friend, Pigo: Where's he from here? Do I know him at all?"

Dhombola shook his head. "Not here long. From far, far land, called—" he paused to form the word correctly—"called Au-stra-lia. He part of a tribe, like Dhombola. Not black really but still, some like me." He swallowed hard. "I not see him since he get sick but he *call* me, *Docruben*—in mind. Tell me he's *dying;* ask Dhombola to help."

"I'll do my best," Ruben promised, thinking. This lad's psychic gift involved interpretation from his *touch* of articles or, as Dhombola had put it, looking into the past. Now he was telling Ruben that he'd had a telepathic message. Curious.

They found Julie Lyle on duty outside the three-bed room. "I thought you handled only infants," he said lightly to her. It was the first time they'd spoken since she refused to see him. "What're you doing here?"

"Nellie's death left them shorthanded," Julie said, studying her chart. "I volunteered to help out." Finally she did look at him, curiously. "How do you happen to know Pigo?"

Ruben indicated the boy at his waist. "I'm consulting as a favor to this one. They're friends." He followed her as she led them into the room, curtains drawn on the late afternoon sunshine. "What's the matter with Mr. Pigo?"

Julie's glance was one of helplessness. "No one has any idea. Medically, he gets a clean bill of health. But he's *convinced* he's dying. And Martin, I think he is."

Sounds like voodoo, Ruben thought to himself, stepping to the bedside.

Dark against the snowy sheets, it was the little man

whom he had seen at the mound. He was not a child like Dhombola nor was he a pygmy, Martin realized with interest, but a full-grown, native Australoid. His aborigine mates had lived for hundreds of years without a shred of civilization altering their truly stone-age existence. Once numbering in the millions, Australoids now numbered no more than fifty or sixty thousand in the whole world—a phenomenon, indeed, considering that they represented the fourth major division of mankind and were not Caucasian, Negroid, or Oriental.

Ruben studied the tiny man carefully. Pigo's age was impossible to estimate; it might have been anything from twenty-five to fifty. Bodily, the poor creature was emaciated, his arms and legs positively spindly. Facially, by Caucasian standards, Pigo's outthrust, sloping brow and flat nose made him downright ugly.

The next half hour was one of the stranger periods in Ruben's life. He hung on every word, fascinated.

Pigo, it developed, was conscious but too sick to open his eyes or to speak. Besides, among Australoids most conversation was carried on by "finger talk," a marvelously intricate and expressive series of gestures with fingers and the muscles of the face. And so, he would tell his story telepathically and with accompanying digit-gestures through his friend Dhombola, who was neither telepathic nor able to understand the dialect or motions under normal circumstances.

To make matters even more incredible, the psychic bonds between the three males—tiny Pigo and Dhombola and the attentive Martin Ruben—were forged so strongly that little Dhombola told the unusual story in acceptable English.

"In his Australian jungle," the boy began, barely above a whisper with his nearly mesmerized eyes moving only from Pigo's hands to his face and back again,

"Pigo broke a tribal rule. To us, it would seem unimportant; to them, it was a capital offense. Since they do not like violence, they execute criminals by means of *bone pointing*—aiming something he calls a *kundela* at the convicted man, who knows—*accepts*—that he now must die."

Ruben felt Julie's hand slip into his, not in intimacy but a sort of fear of the unknown. Beyond the windows with the drawn curtains it was growing dark with gathering clouds and the distant, ominous rumble of thunder seeped into the room.

"A *kundela* is made from a human bone, cut to eight inches long with a hole in the end and through which is threaded a length of hair from a virginal woman." Dhombola nodded occasionally at Pigo, to show he understood, even though the little man's eyes remained shut. "The hair is intricately braided in preparation and the tribal doctor fills it with a spirit missile.

"According to custom, the convicted man flees, tries to stay free, and that is how Pigo was met by Director Solomon's people and brought here—partly to help him escape his fate.

"But while he was fleeing his village," Dhombola continued, "he was pursued by three executioners called *Kurdaitcha,* fierce and naked warriors with kangaroo hair adhering to their skins by dried human blood." The boy gulped, despite himself. "Emu feathers cloak their faces and they move like shadows through the jungle. Only one *Kurdaitcha* is the true executioner, the others acting as trackers or beaters; and when the escaped culprit is located, the executioner *freezes* him to the spot and, as he points the *kundela,* repeatedly chants: 'You die! You die!!' " At that moment little Dhombola's earnest face swiveled to face Ruben. "And . . . he *does*," he told Ruben. "He dies horribly, exhausted of all energy, nauseated by food, eventually running a fever and unable to control his bowels and bladder. He vomits incessantly. And he dies, lying in his own terrible mess."

Ruben thought that was all and again searched the Australoid's ugly face for a clue as to how he might be helped.

But Dhombola and Pigo weren't through. "Pigo says that he *was* pointed, and even though the Americans brought him here, to safety, he still must die. That, he says bravely, is all right. Dying is acceptable. But he is afraid for his soul, because, without knowing where he was going he visited the mound on his first night here. He approached it, and is fearful that the monster dwelling there may swallow his soul. That is why he contacted me."

"How did he d-do that?" Julie Lyle asked, the little redhead utterly absorbed by the bizarre tale. "He hasn't left the hospital in weeks."

The boy again watched Pigo's incredible hands gesture swiftly, saw the way Pigo's cheeks moved in and out, lips pursing, forehead crinkling. Dhombola's own eyes remained half-shut, half-possessed. And then he spoke again: "In Australia, *all* his people have the gift of ESP. Each member of the tribe has a totemic animal he calls a *djurabeels,* which may be any animal and which the tribal person never hunts or eats once it is chosen. Indeed, he must *protect* the *djurabeels* always, since it may one day save him."

"What does the *djurabeels* do for someone like Pigo?" Ruben inquired softly.

"At a time of danger," Dhombola replied, eyes not leaving Pigo's gesturing hands, "he can telepathically tell the animal—the *djurabeels*—of the crisis and it is passed along, through its fellows, until word has been reached by a man who can help. He then comes and saves the tribal member." The boy paused, partly smiled. "*I* was chosen by Pigo as his *djurabeels* because he did not know the animals here, and knew only me. That's how I received the request to bring you here."

Remarkable story, Ruben thought, closing his eyes almost prayerfully. It might sound impossible, but the fact remained that he was here.

He touched the lad's hand. "Can *you* communicate with Pigo, talk to him?" Dhombola nodded. "Then I shall do all I can."

Ruben began to "speak" with plain little Pigo, asking questions and listening attentively to the answers. He knew it was useless to question *pointing*; from his study of voodoo, Martin knew that the belief of a tribal member could be so strong that "white man medicine" wouldn't reach the illness.

But what Ruben thought he *could* do, through hypnosis, was convince Pigo that the guilty verdict or curse had been *removed* from him; that the witch doctor had declared him innocent at the last moment.

With the aid of Dhombola's telepathic translation, Ruben began his most difficult hypnotic session ever, thinking how appropriate it was in such circumstances, on such an island. Egyptians used hypnosis as anesthetic in surgical operations four thousand years ago, he knew. Ancient Greeks even had hypnotic clinics called *therapeutae,* or "sleep temples," to treat patients who had nervous disorders. Long before the birth of Franz Mesmer, Indian yogas and Chinese doctors used hypnosis. And what he was combating, here—was it not a form of *counter*-hypnosis?

It was also oddly like an exorcism, Ruben felt, midway through. The evil beliefs that possessed poor Pigo were, in their fashion, just as pervasive and certainly just as destructive as demonic possession.

After more than two hours, when it was nearing 3 A.M., Ruben brought Pigo out of his trance. The little Australoid instantly gave him a feeble but happy smile as he opened his eyes. And he acknowledged, promptly, that he realized the witch doctor had, indeed, released him from the pointing execution. Exhausted but glad, Ruben rumpled Dhombola's hair and rose to go.

But Pigo was tapping the boy's arm and Dhombola was tugging suddenly on Martin's sleeve.

"The mound, doctor—it *kills.*"

The words came from Dhombola's lips, but it was clear that Pigo was now able to speak for himself. The little African watched his hands, face, and eyes intently.

"Among my people in Australia, we often commune with the spirit world. It is called 'the Dreaming.' At such times we do not see the future or the past, but *all time,* spread before us like the white sheets of this bed. During Dream Time, however, we must ever guard against the evil ones—and I, Pigo, have met the demon of your mound." A sigh racked both the boy and the Australian. "It is very ancient, Doctor, and very bad. During the Dreaming, too, we sometimes see that which is called a 'Dreaming Place.' It is unfailingly a site of absolute terror, Doctor, of hideous death and most impure evil."

Now Ruben saw the frail Australoid lift his hand, pointing this time in the direction of the mound as Dhombola's lips moved in translation. "It has murdered here, already—and it shall kill again. *Soon!* Belch-doctor is first; then more—many more. Students . . . staff . . . *everyone.*" Ruben felt their four eyes on him now, intensely. "*You*, Doctor, will also be chosen. For awful death."

Ruben frowned. "What can I *do?*" he asked.

"Leave, sir! You must leave Nommos *forever!*" Pigo and the boy again paused. "The evil Dreaming Place, Doctor, which I mentioned; I did not mean the mound *alone,* sir. I meant—*the entire island of Nommos!* For the evil has *already spread!*"

It wasn't until the weary Ruben staggered into the elevator to head for his rooms that he realized whom Pigo had described by the quaint term, "belch-doctor."

He meant, "Belgian doctor."

Ruben's friend, Dr. Jacques Coquelion.

Fifteen

After four more days passed, Ruben and everyone at Solomon Studies became shocked and concerned by the discovery of three additional suicides.

And again, as in the preceding instances, the unhappy threesome was collected quickly at the Director's orders and taken to some unspecified place for an autopsy. This time, however, it was whispered that the trio had been found, covered with some kind of mold.

Ruben hadn't really thought of Ingrid Solomon as an evil individual capable of countenancing murder. Now, though, he wondered. Was it even remotely possible that she'd allowed one of the antisocial Sinoway's experiments to get out of control!

Since Ingrid considered herself the living incarnation of Solomon, he began digging into that Biblical period. His own occult literature had been flown in by the most recent plane, and the books were like seeing old friends after years of separation. He immediately learned that history may have recorded *two* important figures named Solomon. At this late date, experts said, it was impossible to know if Israel's wise king was the same man as a brilliant magus of antiquity with the same name.

Despite this confusion, history recorded that a monarch named Solomon did possess a magical root—perhaps mandrake—with which he banished devils.

Martin smiled, wishing Ingrid had one. Solomon, he found, had written several documents that still existed: *Testament of Solomon, Key of Solomon,* and *Lemegeton*. In these ancient writings the man had offered weird *grimoires,* collections of bizarre incantations and spells.

Ruben learned that the original Solomon wore a ring bearing a pentacle, the five-sided occult ring of power known by sorcerers for centuries. He thought, couldn't remember ever seeing a ring in Ingrid's possession. It also was said that Solomon urged all those who wished to invoke angel or demon to be humble, solemn, even chaste—things he'd certainly never associated with beautiful and passionate Ingrid!

But Martin's interest picked up when he found that Solomon was said to have control of *elemental spirits,* creatures of insubstantial nature capable of unbelievable mischief. If Ingrid believed she was the Israelite king, did she *also* strive to summon spirits? If so, might she have succeeded and could it now be behind this rash of suicides?

Martin didn't really think so, primarily since he couldn't believe in elementals. But he went on studying, reading of Solomon's fondness for winds (which he could command), and birds. Unfailingly, Ingrid has her office windows wide open. And she kept two colorful, little birds in a cage. What minimal affection she had in her, she lavished on her feathered pets.

Then Ruben read that demons were said to have conspired to ruin King Solomon's once-spotless character; again he paused to think. It was true that the wise King's career ended in ruins. If Ingrid were guilty of no more than what he had learned, she was probably, fundamentally, a power for good. But *if* some evil creatures actually *did* lurk in the mound—*if* some force was starting to drive Nammos' personnel to suicide—wasn't it possible that these forces were somehow *attracted* by the lovely Director—even unintentionally—to enact and complete a terrible confrontation tracing back three thousand years?

He closed his final book, sighing heavily. There were far more questions here than answers. How could he possibly conclude that astrocosmology was wrong, when only a single woman on a death sentence had actually died? Aside from the suicides, everyone else appeared to have improved his or her health—including Ruben himself!

For about a week Jacques Coquelion appeared to have been avoiding Ruben. He had broken both luncheon and tennis dates. Hence, it was startling, when Martin returned the books to the library and, coming back to his quarters, found Jacques waiting for him with an apologetic smile.

"What a pleasant surprise!" Ruben exclaimed, shaking hands.

Jacques' palm was clammy, his handshake light, somehow frail. "I cannot stay, Martin," the Belgian began, simply standing beside the door after Ruben had unlocked it. "But the truth is, *mon dieu,* I need an ally badly just now. You're—the only man on the island whom I can rely upon."

Martin was shocked by his friend's appearance. The words of the tiny Australoid filtered through his mind. Jacques was nearly trembling where he stood; he appeared cold as well as ill, and Ruben wondered if he'd had a relapse. "I'll do whatever I can to help, Jacques," he pledged honestly.

"I have not been completely guiltless about certain things which occur on Nommos," the Belgian said just as honestly, tugging nervously on his gray goatee. "But

I've always had my limits. Now, Martin, I have learned certain things that are . . . frightening. Frightening and, I feel, almost diabolically wrong."

"Can you give me an example?"

"Murder, I think, among other things." Jacques lowered his gaze to his folded hands. "No—I *know* that there has been murder. Murder which has already happened while more is being planned." He shuddered. "Of a particularly, ah, loathsome kind."

Ruben spoke in lower tones as he clasped his friend's shoulder. "Why don't you come inside and talk? Like the old days."

"I can't. Ingrid expects me for a meeting." Jacques finally met his companion's anxious gaze. "Sinoway, and his—people . . . They're doing things with my wife's tacit approval. Things I could never condone." Suddenly Jacques shook his handsome head furiously. "Despite all I can lose, Marteen, I *must* oppose this—*stop* it!"

"We will, we will," Ruben comforted him. "But I must know more details in order to help." Ruben tried to adjudge how much of Coquelion's attitude might be based on simple hysteria. "Can we meet later?"

Jacques glanced at his wristwatch. "Yes, of course, we must. Perhaps the two of us can prevail on Ingrid and thus avoid shutting this place down. There may still be time, and I still feel much good can come from Nommos. Look, when your classes are over, may we meet outside the central building? By the east entrance?"

There was barely time for Ruben to murmur his assent before Jacques was half-jogging down the carpeted corridor. Clearly, he continued to fear his wife and could not confront her without an ally.

Ruben worried about his old friend the rest of the

day. For the first time, none of his classes went smoothly. He didn't doubt for a minute that his own worried, curious disposition adversely affected these sensitive young people, and regretted it.

At 7:35 that evening, Martin slipped out of his classroom. The last student had exited minutes before, and the corridors were clear all the way to the front grounds. There, looking both ways to see if he were observed, he headed east, heart thumping in his chest. What in the world could Jacques have to tell him? What dreadful things had occurred to make Jacques turn against his beloved and faithless Ingrid, even for an instant? Whatever it might be, Morley Sinoway was now verbally indicted by at least one person Ruben trusted. His instincts had been right in adducing that the professor was far more than merely rude or bigoted. It wouldn't have surprised Martin if Sinoway turned out to be a literal megalomaniac, capable of anything. Anything at all.

With the early days of Autumn, the temperature had remained in the seventies but rain was starting now to drizzle on the island as Ruben began half-trotting toward his rendezvous point, his gold-tipped stick in his hand. Off to the left, scarcely visible in the drifting sheet of water, he could make out the omnipresent mound. It seemed almost to sizzle as increasingly huge drops beat upon its breast. Even at this range Ruben felt that it was hypnotic, beckoning—for whatever mysterious reasons might lie buried there.

Then he had stopped trotting and was staring up the east entranceway, frozen in concern.

Jacques Coquelion was there, staggering. He had taken three or four normal steps out the door and then began to totter, one hand shooting to his chest. Something in the other hand slipped to the ground as it reached agonizingly for his face. Paralyzed, Ruben stared and saw in the scant light a streaking, crimson gush of blood spurting jaggedly from his friend's nostrils. A moan reached his ears.

"Jacques!" he cried, running. "Don't try to move!"

He reached the affable Belgian only in time to help break his tumbling fall to the cement walk.

Ruben didn't know a lot of medicine but he could tell, at a shocked glance, that Jacques was suffering some kind of heart attack. He looked up and around, seeking help; saw no one. Coquelion's fingers were clutched at his heart as if striving mightily to hold it in place, and as if the heart was determined to burst free. The eyes he turned to Martin were agonized. "Fibrillating," he choked the words out, "my heart is fibrillating!"

Again Ruben searched wildly for aid. Instead, he found only the yellow folder his friend had brought. Ruben instinctively retrieved it, his gaze turned in pain to his poor friend.

"Les enfants, Marteen," gasped Jacques, eyes shooting toward the folder in desperation. "Save—save the new ones, at least." His hand went from his chest to Ruben's arm, the clutch like steel. "You'll *do* it, *n'est-ce pas?* Please—*save the new ones!"*

There was a final, choking spasm, a spurt of blood from nose and mouth, and Jacques was gone.

For a long time Martin Ruben simply held his dead friend's head and shoulders above the soiling walkway, his own head bowed in a simple prayer. At last he looked down at Jacques, cursing. That damned medicine Morley Sinoway had been giving him—by injection or pill—to lower Jacques' body temperature. The Belgian had told him Ingrid always kept the interior temperature at a steady 82 degrees when he was being medicated, to match his body temperature.

And out here on Solomon Studies ground, in this young September night, the temperature was only in the seventies . . . .

There'd be no way to prove Sinoway had intentionally killed Jacques, Ruben knew that. The professor could even *admit* he'd treated Jacques an hour ago, simply by shrugging and claiming that he had no way of knowing Jacques would venture into the night. Knowing something of the way Sinoway's mind worked, he might even say that Jacques had committed suicide!

If he had, it was because the information he had to give Ruben was so urgent, so tragically important, it was worth it to Jacques.

Ruben stared dully at the folder in his hand, then opened it and looked inside. From it he produced an eight-by-ten, glossy photograph. It had the most stomach-churning subject Martin had ever seen.

Pictured was an infant perhaps eight or nine months old. The child's head was ridiculously, sickeningly huge —the largest Ruben had seen, even on an adult body— fully as big as the entire remainder of its little body.

That would have been bad enough; but it wasn't all. The baby's brown eyes, staring up at Martin from the shiny photograph, were serious and dark, glinting with a faint, strange glow, and filled with abject terror. The child's eyes were *also*—Martin could swear to it—*the eyes of a particularly intelligent, maturely aware, competent, fully grown man.*

The woman's screams in the night. For the first time Ruben thought he knew *why* she shrieked her misery.

Stumblingly, he hurried off in search of the Director without noticing, in his fury and disgust, a rustling and shadowed form. It detached itself leisurely, almost ruminatively, from the corner of the main building and moved with graceful but deadly intent across the deserted grounds.

Sixteen

The meeting with Ingrid Solomon was brief and, for Ruben, infuriatingly upsetting.

When he had gently broken the news, the Director's first reaction was to lift the phone on her desk. "He's on the steps by the east exit?" she inquired. Speechless, he could only nod. She gave cool instructions into the mouthpiece for her husband's body to be removed. For Martin, it was like listening to a sanitation supervisor order a truck out to pick up uncollected garbage.

"I know, Doctor," she said calmly, intertwining her fingers and looking quietly at him across her desk. Behind the Director, wind and rain gusted noisily and a trace of water shone on the floor. "You want me to collapse into tears like any weak-minded woman would do. Recall all our wonderful good times together. Rush to view his poor remains."

"I hope I'd never want a woman to be in that state," Ruben replied tersely.

"But you would find it natural, and you find my reaction *un*natural." Her smile was maddeningly forgiving. "I can understand that. But you see, Jacques was far too emotional, too high-strung, and too easily *involved* for his own good. Or mine. I may as well confess that, despite his genius both in psychiatry and medicine, he was sometimes an embarrassment."

Ruben couldn't control himself. "You heartless

bitch," he said softly.

"Perhaps. But not mindless." Ingrid turned slightly in her chair to make chirping sounds to the birds caged within feet of her. She spoke as she extended a friendly finger to them. "A rational person would expect a man like Jacques to die so stupidly, given his ill health. And I *am*, you recall, blessed with a reputation for wisdom. Surely you still believe in reincarnation, Doctor?"

"I tend to," he said tightly, his calves suddenly springy with the nervous urge to get out of her presence. "But I have no idea whom I may have been in the past. I'm not certain anyone has a right to know that."

"That is *your* loss, *your* hangup, Martin. I *know* whom I've been—*all* my previous incarnations!"

"God help you in your *future* ones," he observed, smiling for the first time. "If there *is* such a thing as karmic debt, you're going to tote quite a load in your next existence."

She stopped playing with the birds and faced him, her face a glacial mask. "That is precisely the point, my dear Ruben. In my earlier role as Solomon, I made the mistake of losing my God's endorsement—His gifts of wisdom and compassion—by falling in love with Sheba. I lost all sight of my obligations to my Lord and my people.' Subtly, so slight that Martin wasn't originally conscious of it, the director's voice was rising in volume and power. "My soul has the obligation to open up new fields of inquiry and knowledge, always to advance the concept of a *new world*. I have been paying for *three thousand years* for my unbridled sexuality which took a useless form as mortal love. I shall not make such errors again, Doctor Ruben—never again will I mix my God-given right to sexual expression with my God-given obligation to use *my* ideas, *my* wisdom, to lead a benighted people to the light! It all starts *here,* Martin, on Nommos Island—but it must end in Paradise on earth!"

Ruben stared at her for a moment as self-control and professional detachment quietly suffused him. His knuckles grew white on his stick. If Professor Sinoway was megalomaniacal, Ingrid Solomon was at least egomaniacal—and quite probably schizophrenic, as he had once thought.

There was literally no sense in arguing the points she raised. When one believed herself to be perfect, the psychologist's approach must be noncontradictory, subtle, and gradual.

At that moment he knew that it was his duty to find out what was happening at Solomon Studies and put a stop to it. It was no longer a case of simply taking the next plane home. He could not morally permit such a place to remain in existence under such leadership, but by the same token of principle he had no right to destroy it until he understood all its mysteries. And *solved* them.

He gave her a curt nod. Without uttering a word, he arose from his chair, crossed the richly carpeted floor to the door, and closed it softly behind him. He could still hear the chirping of tiny birds and wind whipping sinuously at her curtains.

Julie Lyle, he thought on impulse; talk to Julie Lyle. See if the neonatologist can be persuaded to open up. Somehow, he thought she wasn't their kind, that when she knew about Jacques, she would talk.

He understood that Dr. Lyle had returned to the children's ward and headed there, quickly, impatient with the elevator and almost running down the corridor. It was nearing ten o'clock at night when he burst into her immaculate office adjacent to the nurses' station.

He stopped short when he found Julie at her desk, but not alone.

Professor Morley Sinoway sat in a plump chair beside the desk. His two muscular aides were nowhere in sight and Ruben wondered what that meant. Sinoway looked annoyed as he lifted his bald head to greet the parapsychologist.

"You're the proverbial bad penny, Ruben," he said in chill greeting. "You spend your day filling youthful minds with claptrap and then turn up in the most unexpected places, hm-m?"

Ruben blurted out the news about Jacques Coquelion. With difficulty, he refrained from charging Sinoway with the death.

The professor stood at once, outwardly shocked. "My dear fellow, I *am* sorry!" he exclaimed. "Awful shame, hm-m? I know the two of you were close."

Was that a threat? "I think we may remain so, Professor, even now," Ruben said flatly.

Julie Lyle's face was a thundercloud of shock and sorrow. "How very dreadful." She put out her hand across the desk to Martin. "Jacques was a very nice man."

"But dangerously emotional," the professor commented. "He was a most difficult, hm-m, patient to treat. Together we made progress but I warned him many times that he should care for himself, to stabilize the advancement."

Ruben stared at him. Then he produced the photograph Jacques had given him and held it before their eyes. "Possibly this was reason enough for Jacques to become emotional."

Julie gasped, made a sound and, pale, turned away. She glanced up once at Ruben and then searched for her handkerchief. It occurred to Martin she might have said more, just then, without the professor's autocratic presence.

"That revolting image was *not* taken on Nommos Island," Sinoway said flatly. His cultivated baritone became almost harsh. "I swear that to you, Ruben, whatever you think. However, sir, it is clear from your little, hm-m, exhibition of horror that you feel I have something to do with it." He bounced off his chair, his bald head level with Ruben. His flat eyes glowed strangely. "Very well, if you wish to know the nature of my experiments, come with me." Instantly he headed for the door, calling over his shoulder like a man summoning his pet. "Come along, Doctor; come, *come!*"

"I want to speak with you," he whispered to Julie fleetingly, "later."

Then he was hurrying after Professor Sinoway, following him through the ward to another hallway. They sped down it and encountered double doors that were locked and bolted. It was dank here. Sinoway stopped; it took three keys before all the locks were apart and the doors swinging open.

Martin shivered. When he followed the man into this new corridor, he had the strange impression that he had stepped into a subterranean shaft. It was clammy here; no, downright cold. The walls seemed sticky, moist. It was also uncarpeted, uncompleted; their footsteps echoed hollowly as the professor continued to lead the way without another word. Suddenly the corridor broke into two sections. Sinoway barely glanced at the one to their right. "Storage," he growled.

Near the end of the tunnel-like corridor it became impossible to see. Ruben, half-expecting attack, remained alert also for spiders and their webs. Ahead of him, however, the professor stepped with confidence into a lake of darkness and his hand moved on the wall. Instantly they were flooded with light and Ruben drew beside Sinoway to look around.

It was scarcely haunted or even the laboratory of a characteristic mad professor, although they stood, indeed, in a large lab room. A door or two led to antechambers. Along the walls were file cabinets, recording equipment, and, in one corner of the laboratory, several compartments that Martin considered nearly cagelike. The usual paraphernalia of the research scientist gleamed sullenly on tables scattered about the center of the room. There were no spiders, no webs. Only modern science.

"What do you know, Dr. Ruben, about cloning, hm-m?"

Ruben appraised the enormous self-assurance of the older man as he folded his arms, smugly awaiting Martin's answer.

"I know the *theory* of cloning, that it's not possible," he replied, fumbling for a Camel and lighting it. "The entire makeup of a man is contained in each cell. Theoretically, it is possible to take a scrap of skin and, from it, build an exact duplicate of that man."

"Ho ho, that's better than most people would do, hm-m?" Sinoway said without amusement. He returned Ruben's appraising glance. "Cloning is made possible by the knowledge we now possess of a cell's most basic components. I assume you've heard of DNA?"

Ruben nodded, already festering from the man's infuriatingly superior attitude. He showed off despite himself. "The discovery of an Englishman named Francis Crick and a young American, James Dewey Watson, back in 1953." He smiled, recalling. "They dropped their incredible bombshell quietly in a magazine, writing, 'This structure has novel features which are of considerable biological interest.' Quite possibly the understatement of history."

Sinoway's eyes reflected their yellowish cast. With the brown, they seemed almost a pair of wary, watchful hornets. "Admirable, my dear Ruben! You have no idea in the world what they were talking about but memorization, here and there, *does* give a surface impression of knowledge."

Ruben reddened. His fists knotted and, to keep from striking the fellow, whirled on his heels.

"Wait, dear fellow—*wait!*" The professor caught him by the shoulder and his mellifluous voice suddenly lightened in amusement. "I'm sorry, doctor, truly *sorry!* I'm alone too much, I suspect. Be a good chap and accept my apology, won't you?"

Instinctively polite, Ruben turned back. It dawned slowly on him that Sinoway was actually anxious to reveal his secrets. At least, *part* of them.

"Very well, Sinoway. But do get on with it, won't you? It grows late."

"Of course, course, course." The professor smiled and edged his way toward the compartments across the floor of the lab speaking as he moved. "DNA is the basic molecule of life, the ultimate in mini-computers. D'you know, Ruben, that all the DNA in a human's cells would stretch from here to the sun and back, four hundred times? Yet, in a single tiny DNA cell, there's enough sheer data to fill two thousand three-hundred-page books!"

"Most interesting, I'm sure. But—"

Sinoway stopped walking so short that Ruben almost ran into him. For the first time Ruben saw that the older man had an athletic, square-shouldered build and powerful, sloping shoulders. He saw Sinoway turn with a frank expression, his deep-set brown eyes sober. But they did not adequately prepare Ruben for the surprise. "I intend *to clone myself*, Doctor Ruben. Not once, hm-m—but *many times!*"

"Now why ever would you do a thing like that?" Ruben drawled slowly.

"The plan is twofold: I shall make myself over one hundred times and also live long enough to initiate an interest in *all* one hundred Morley Sinoways to pursue one hundred different scientific disciplines. None of this wishy-washy PSI phenomena, or the ancient legerdemain of silly kings!" He gestured wildly, happily. "And theoretically, Ruben, it isn't all that *hard!* DNA can be placed in *Escherichia coli,* because that bacteria is well known—so that my *per*sonal DNA can be prepared ahead of time and stored! Isn't that, hm-m, absolutely marvelous?"

"Scientifically," Martin said slowly, "undoubtedly it is. But I know of *E. colio.* What of its dangers?"

"Well, well, there *are* risks, of course."

"Of what nature?" Ruben pressed.

"An entirely tolerable nature, in my professional view," the professor retorted, losing his affability. "There is a possibility, I confess, that the combined DNA cell might, hm-m, prove . . . cancerous. If so, the new life form would produce cancer abundantly." His eyes narrowed. "On a production-like basis, to be blunt about it."

Ruben was utterly shocked. "And if just *one* human being was diseased by it?"

"It would probably wipe out the world." Sinoway shrugged. "But the risk makes it *worth* it, Doctor—surely *you* can see that? No one can be *sure* about such silly hazards. Of course," he added, eyes shining feverishly, "it *is* fascinating to think about . . ."

"What is?" Ruben demanded, unwilling to raise his voice. "*What* is?"

Sinoway smiled. "Fascinating to think of creating

something today, this very week, which would have no instant effect but might cause an epidemic—even a worldwide, culminating plague—*fifty years* from now, a *hundred!* A most distinct and novel kind of immortality, Doctor. *Most* novel!"

"I gather that your tender concern for our programcy isn't original with you, eh, Professor?"

"Hm-m? Oh, no." Sinoway missed the sarcasm. "The symbiosis between genetic engineering and those with social vision was first observed widely, at least, in modern times, back in the, hm-m, Forties."

"Where?"

Ruben snapped at him and the professor frowned. "Actually, in Nazi Germany. But come, *come*, my dear Doctor! Let us not wallow in neurotic concerns when there *is* progress to report."

He had resumed walking and now approached the compartments against the far wall. From the largest, Ruben could hear muffled sounds, like that of something—*rustling,* rubbing against the sides of the compartment.

Something certainly alive.

"You've been experimenting with cloning, then," Ruben observed, feeling a headache developing in the rear of his skull. "Haven't you?"

"It's not an experiment anymore, not when it's *worked!*" Sinoway laughed his delight, almost dancing beside the compartment. "Well, well, I s'pose you think I'm about to show you some, hm-m, monstrously cloned human being. Some, hm-m, horror story Frankenstein with patchwork limbs and electrodes at the temples? Well, not just yet, Ruben, not just yet! Give us research scientists *time!*" His smile was almost affectionate in his self-enthusiasm. "We'll have to make do a while with, hm-m, callers from the past."

The top of the compartment had several rows of air holes, Martin saw when a great, white plastic cloth was thrown back. Sinoway pressed himself close, working. Then the professor was releasing the walls of the compartment from the top and they were slapping, hard, against the floor.

"Oh, my God," Ruben breathed, too weak to shout.

When this creature's terrifying kind last flapped and soared through the pure, thin blue air of God's quiet world, it was eons before the Quaternary, Tertiary, and Cretaceous epochs—deep in the dumb, lush world of the sweltering Jurassic period.

When this creature carved its way through the low skies, it *ruled* them, its powerful curving, shadowed wings clattering like the passage of a mighty night train skittering over an ancient track. *Then*—a "then" Man can only imagine, feebly try to reconstruct—the Atlantic and Indian oceans were only immense, pure lakes, their significant periods of growth still centuries ahead of them. The incredibly fertile Mediterranean, from which civilized Sumer and Mesopotamia would miraculously emerge one distant day, predating incomparable Rome and the ancient genius of Greece and Egypt, was only *starting* to take form beneath a sizzling sun that was nearer, more potent, and more familiar than we know it.

When this creature last lived . . . it was more than one hundred and thirty five million years ago; it had no concept of the frail biped who would someday spring from its trickling Mediterranean, and it had no concept of words, especially one which would, epochs after its frozen death, be applied to it: *Pterodactyl.*

It was nearly Martin Ruben's height and, dressed in perpetual black, struck him—with its shrewd, agate eyes —as a sort of feathered Dracula. He did not know if he was more frightened, ancient fears roiling deep in his remembering belly, or impressed that he stood within mere feet of the world's dimmest past. Its claws—great *heaven*—its *claws* were the length of two of his feet and capable of splitting the skin of his back and picking out the spine as a man might break a chicken breastbone for luck.

"It's only a baby, Ruben, scarcely out of its egg," Morley Sinoway whispered, keeping a respectful distance nonetheless. "Don't worry; it can't fly. Not, hm-m, not *yet*. Besides, the ceiling here is not nearly high enough." His expression was elegiac. "But one day soon I shall take him outside and allow him to, hm-m, soar and to glide above this island. What a sight that shall be, eh?" Now he leaned close to Martin and his perspiration stank. "Note, will you, that it has a small quantity of residual *hair*—a bit of a surprise, right? Think of it man; consider my incomparable, cloned creation in all its prehistoric majesty! This single, marvelous creature has survived pathogenic fungi, geomagnetic reversal, meteors, changes in oxygen concentration, the laramide revolution, racial senescence, and the rise of such mammals as us. Isn't it positively *grand?*"

Ruben saw the beady eyes above the great, talonlike beak, fastened like twin icebergs on his face. The immense bird shivered; it's cold in here for it, Ruben realized with a passing twingle of sympathy. He spoke softly. "How did you accomplish this awful thing?"

"I'm an important fellow, Ruben, remember? Hm-m? A colleague of mine in Paris sent me frozen cells from the bone marrow of its skeleton, when he thought I was dying. I felt it was time to begin practicing what we preach—to produce something concrete, tangible; hm-m?" He waved an arm at the enormous monster and one wing roughly the length of a vampire cape, raised threateningly from its oily and scaly side. "He is the *exact* duplicate of the original—or perhaps he *is* the original, depending upon how one wishes to look at it!" Sinoway giggled and wildly dug at his bald pate. Then he shut his hard eyes as the notion occurred to him. He spoke with awe, respect. "You know, Ruben, to this inordinately ugly chap, I suppose . . . I suppose *I* am God."

Ruben turned on his heel, sickened, grim-faced. "If that pathetic thing comes after me," he said over his shoulder, "I'll get you too, if it's my final act on earth."

"*Stay*, my good fellow, please, *stay!*" Ruben peered back, saw the professor's broad, large face brighten. "There's more!"

Martin sighed but stopped. "Then put the sides of that cage back. I can't converse with you when I feel like an oversized canary's goddamn *lunch!*"

Sinoway laughed. He slapped his foot on a button on the floor. The sides of the compartment slapped together; the pterodactyl vanished with a slight squawk. "He was held in place, Ruben, all along. An electronic device, hm-m? But you were terrified—confess it!"

"What else do you have to say or to show me?" Ruben demanded.

The older man hesitated. "There's no more to, hm-m, show," he said firmly. "But more to be said between us. I don't know *why* you disapprove of my wondrous birdy, but at least there is no way this, hm-m, experiment can be confused—by the late Doctor Coquelion *or anyone*—with monstrous infants. I've simply acted on my theory that DNA carries heredity that does not vanish when the body dies, and I've established the point forever—hm-m? One day, Ruben, we shall have back with us anything from the past we desire—or *anybody.*" He beamed on the younger man but totally without warmth or sincerity. "You see, I have taken the work of Galton, Darwin, Crick and all the others much farther, Ruben. When my friends of the dark past are reborn, they shall become both *superior* and *immortal.* And you know, hm-m, that may literally make me God."

Ruben braced himself. *"Other* appellations are conceivable," he snapped. "For the love of decency, man, *when* do you scientists think of what may *happen* as the consequences of your discoveries? You're talking about a complete *revision* of society throughout the world, a new structure of families, an alteration in the law, the workforce, *everywhere!* If you produced ten thousand cloned human beings, there would be a need for ten thousand more jobs—and that much more food to be consumed, according to you, in perpetuity!"

Sinoway laughed. "There's a Nobel winner named Haldane who suggests we retire when we're young and train our own clones to take over for us. Slavery, Ruben, to which no one can object!"

"I can!"

"But why think *small,* old fellow? With only a scrap of hair, a smidgen of bone to work with, we can restore Lincoln, Jefferson, the Roosevelts, John F. Kennedy— or we can have *ten* of each! Why, the applications are endless, Ruben. We can create *fifty* Einsteins, if we have the will—a *thousand* Beethovens or Shakespeares, cranking out their little ditties and plays throughout eternity! Doctor James Bonner, a distant colleague of mine in biology, says there is nothing to prevent us from making multiple clones of *any* original specimen. He asserts, 'We could grow *any desired number* of genetically identical people from individuals who have desirable characteristics.' We can *grow just whom we wish,* like a human garden, and return mankind to Eden! Ruben, *think* of it!"

Ruben did.

He ran down the corridor from the secret laboratory at his top speed, didn't stop in the ward but kept running past the startled Julie Lyle, ignored the elevator and took the steps, sped through the corridor of the first floor, and flung himself out into the cleansing, cooling rain.

Oh my God, he breathed, lying, panting, on his back on the ground beyond the central building. Oh *dear, forgiving* God.

Ruben wasn't swearing.

Seventeen

The following morning, both sleepless and sexless, gaunt and ill, with his beard shooting in every direction, Ruben told Ingrid Solomon that he was going to seek legal action.

It didn't dent her self-assurance. It didn't even anger her. She admitted to knowing of Sinoway's experiments and said that, while she didn't exactly approve, they kept him happy. And she also wasn't angry with Ruben, who was obviously emotionally out of control.

He insisted, again, that he *would* seek legal action.

And the Director told him, without ire, her violet eyes level and amused by the mere mortal on the other side of her desk, that Nommos Island was *hers*—lock, stock, and barrel. "In a word, Doctor, *I* am the law here. And I'm perfectly satisfied that poor Jacques died from his long-standing critical disease, or, if not that, from forgetting he had just received a life-prolonging injection from Professor Sinoway. Either way, it is a simple little tragedy. Will you accompany me to the prayer room for his funeral?"

Ruben started. "His funeral. Already?"

"What logical reason is there to wait, Martin?" she asked, spreading her hands. He could not answer. "The sooner his sad remains are cremated and properly interred in a vase, the sooner the entire matter will be over and we can all begin adjusting to life without his services."

"Forget him, you mean," Ruben said.

"If you will," she replied coldly.

The services were matter-of-fact and devoid of religion. Martin insisted on saying a few words. He rose to the unmarked lectern and peered out at the handful of faces watching him, all, except Ingrid Solomon, ill at ease.

Some of Jacques' departmental colleagues were there. Morley Sinoway was present with his pair of attendants, checking his watch and trying not to yawn. A few women whom Ruben did not know looked genuinely sad; one had been crying. And Dr. Julie Lyle was on hand, near the lectern, a handkerchief twisted in her fingers. Boldly, she watched and listened to Ruben and he thought, with a rising of hope, that she might well trust him now. Somehow he had to get her alone and speak with her.

"This closed casket behind me," he said with a nod of his bearded head, "is not empty. It contains the remains of a man with all the admirable features, the not-so-admirable foibles, of the human species. He was not an especially good or even extraordinary man, in most ways." Martin's gaze sought Sinoway's and got it. "That is not especially important now. Jacques Coquelion was, simply and very uniquely, Jacques Coquelion. His passing, whatever anyone else may say, is therefore tragic because—in this precise appearance, with this particular personality—he will never walk this way again." He paused and swiveled his head to look at the blond widow, proper and utterly composed. "For those who cared for him, they recognize the tragedy of the loss and it is irreparable, irreplaceable." Ruben bowed his head. "May God have mercy on his soul, and on ours."

The coffin was left behind to be taken to the crematorium, but Ingrid led them outside the building, to the mound. For a moment Ruben thought of refusing to go. But he owed it to Jacques to see what would happen there.

In blazing Indian Summer, that September morning, the usual routine of Solomon Studies was broken. Everyone on the island was allowed to come to the memorial and pay their respects. Ruben was not surprised, in this place, to see no more than a hundred or so people, most of them children.

This day, instead of projecting their customary negative thoughts at the mound, Ingrid briefly asked them to project thoughts of love, for Jacques and all he had stiven to do there. "One day," she said evenly, without a tremor of emotion in her sultry voice, "our fellow man may look to this day, this island, this moment, as having marked the dawn of their finest era."

To his complete astonishment, as he again tried to pray, Ruben felt an enormous sexual passion building in him. He had broken out in perspiration, not alone from the temperature. Three girls who had visited him during "sex activities" sidled closer, each pair of eyes hot and hungry. Despite himself Ruben responded, found himself becoming erect, rebuked himself angrily. My *friend* is in that building, *murdered*, he told himself with another type of passion; *I must not feel* this way!

Ruben succeeded in tearing his gaze away from the beautiful women.

When he did, his eyes darted unintentionally toward the patch of woods separating the major buildings and the mound from the agricultural center.

There, beneath trees turned golden by the lingering

kiss of Autumn, Martin thought he saw *another* woman, in an attitude of waiting—or anticipation. In the quick glimpse he was given of her, Ruben saw a creature with light, silver hair inundating her back and reaching almost to the earth, a face of beguiling loveliness, huge and succulent breasts, and ineffably glorious long legs. She was completely naked. She exuded sexuality in a way that was consuming, enveloping.

His brief gaze was broken by the sobs of Julie Lyle, who burst into tears and ran through the crowd toward the main building.

Had she, too, seen the strange woman? Ruben looked back to the fringe of woods, but there was no one there.

Within twenty-four hours, it was as if Jacques Coquelion had never lived. His psychiatric position was promptly filled by an assistant, Dr. Karl Peabody, who did not, in Ruben's presence, make reference to Jacques. He said almost nothing at all.

What was especially strange, Ruben thought, was that no one came to his room during "sex activities" the previous evening. Not a soul.

And when, a few hours later, he went to meditate by the mound, he found more people than usual gathered at the mysterious hillock.

This time some sixth sense kept Ruben from drawing as close as he generally did. Now he could see the feverish expressions in the eyes of the other adults there. Sometimes they moved next to others, in some cases not those of the same sex, furtively slipping hands into other hands or resting palms on hips or against thighs. They were losing *control*, Ruben saw with shock and concern; whether they were horoscopically compatible or not, those who went to the mound now appeared to be nearly overcome with the need for sex.

Again that night, no woman came to Ruben's suite.

The next day he went to see Ingrid Solomon.

"It isn't that I'm unbearably horny, or anything," he told her, tapping his stick on the floor. "There was a time when I was fortunate to talk to one woman a year into my bed. But after my previous experiences on Nommos, I thought I had a right to ask *why* I'm being left alone?"

For a moment the Director did not reply. She was not herself today, Ruben noted. Her nerves seemed to be on edge and she appeared to find it hard to produce the right words. Even her customary immaculate sense of fashion had gone awry; the colors of her sweater and slacks combination badly clashed. And the little songbirds in their cage were pecking at the bars, obviously hungry.

"I have no idea why my standing orders are being ignored, Doctor," she said finally with a deep breath. "I haven't altered them, I assure you, and you were right in bringing this to my attention. I'll look into it for you, talk with the ladies who share your compatibility."

While Martin believed her, it occurred to him that she probably did have *some* idea what was going wrong. She seemed about to continue her remarks, and finally did.

"I will tell you this much, Doctor Ruben, since you're a qualified department director: You are not alone."

"Oh yes, I *am!*" he exclaimed with a light laugh.

"I mean that you are not the only one with the problem." Ingrid tapped a desk pen nervously. "I've had several reports that the sex activity segment has . . . well, it hasn't been occurring. Not to any extent at all." She sighed, tried to fluff her messy hair. "It began among the men, with numerous absences during the S.A. time on the schedule, then spread to the ladies.

Few of them seem to have left their rooms lately except for working involvements."

Ruben looked at her curiously, hearing not only her startling information but reading its implications as well as the signs of her face and costume. If it didn't sound impossible, he'd say that Ingrid Solomon appeared distinctly *sated*—yet painfully *guilty* about it. And if he was right, Martin mused, what man on this island could Ingrid possibly have slept with who would leave the incisive and dispassionate Director burdened by guilt?

As to what she was describing, it had to seem virtual mutiny or rebellion to Ingrid. Large numbers of men and women refusing to participate in "sex activities" were saying, in effect, that she—the wise Ms. Solomon—was wrong, that they would do what they pleased.

Before he could answer her, Morley Sinoway burst through the door with the monthly progress report in a sealed envelope. His bodyguards trailed after him. How he got it, instead of Ingrid, Martin wasn't sure. Unlike financial progress reports, this form, he knew, evaluated the condition of both staff and sensitive personnel as well as those who were hospitalized.

And the professor could scarcely conceal his eagerness to know the contents of the fat envelope. Ingrid opened it slowly, but, as she scanned it, her face acquired some of its old confidence and beauty.

Before she turned to Ruben and Sinoway, she turned long enough to feed her pair of songbirds. When she addressed them, her face was flushed with pride and happiness. "Final triumph has been achieved," she said simply.

Sinoway, a master of biological complexities, seemed confused. "What are you saying?"

She permitted a smile. "Everyone on the staff, all sensitives, all those who were hospitalized and dying—

gentlemen, we are either *maintaining* our current ages or enabling them actually to *grow younger!* We have done it at last." Restless, she stood and moved to the window, looking out like an empress surveying her kingdom. "Solomon Studies is a genuine Fountain of Youth, my friends. No one here will ever have a sickness again, not the slightest one. While we remain on the program, no dread disease can ever enter Nommos Island." She glanced back at them and licked her full lips. "Not even the disease of old age and death."

"What of the little Australoid, Pigo?" Ruben inquired softly.

She returned to the desk and glanced through the thick packet of data. "He is up and around, apparently quite well." She smiled. "I believe *that* cure, Doctor Ruben, is yours?"

"To what degree am I, hm-m, regaining youth?" Sinoway asked, his voice trembling. "If I may ask, Madame Director?"

She didn't look inside. She already had checked it. "You are a perfectly healthy man according to all signs, Professor," she reported, "and almost a full biological year younger than when you came to us. And by the by, Dr. Ruben, you might like to know that, despite your occasional impulsive forays off the regimen, you are precisely two months, one week, and four days *younger* yourself!"

Jacques Coquelion's replacement, Dr. Karl Peabody, threw the door open so hard that it bounced off the wall. A short, stocky man, his usually impassive face was a cloud of concern and astonishment. "Sorry to burst in," he said, "but there have been—more."

"More *what,* for God's sake?" Ingrid demanded, angered at being disturbed.

"Come, please," he said, turning to return, "see for

yourself."

The Director gave Ruben and Sinoway a what next? shrug and hurried after Peabody. They followed her. Their progress through the corridor was swift, Peabody almost running when he saw that the others were coming. And all six of them burst into a room filled with the ambience of death.

It was one of several lounges provided for the large medical staff, this one earmarked for Coronary Care personnel.

Eight men and four women, the entire department, had gathered in the comfortably appointed lounge. All were seated with dignity, erect and silent in their chairs and couches. And all were quite dead.

For a moment Ruben thought they had blundered into a scene of mass murder.

But Morley Sinoway, white-faced, swiftly performed a series of cursory examinations, and, when he finally returned to Ingrid and him, Ruben's own observant estimate was merely confirmed.

"They've committed suicide." The professor blurted out the news with a helpless motion of his broad shoulders. "*All* of them."

Most had done it with pills. A number of empty vials and an empty glass lay at the end of drooping fingertips. One had died by gunshot to the temple, his hand still gripping the revolver; presumably it was his final noise that brought Dr. Peabody running. An overfed nurse of fifty or so smiled at them absently above a scalpel inserted almost invisibly in her bloody, thick throat.

Each of the people, Ruben could see, had a thin coat of something like dirt on the hands and face. Each of them looked more-or-less at peace.

But what he thought he might never forget, in his first quick survey of the terrible carnage, was the almost beatific smile on every mouth, and over that Mona Lisa smile, a ground-in and distinct imprint of *other* lips. Each of them had received a kiss of farewell. A kiss of death.

Eighteen

Ingrid remained haggard, even seemed deeply upset and concerned by what had happened, but she also remained logical.

Returning to her private office, she asked for a process of possible witnesses to pass through, apparently determined to learn why twelve ultimately healthy, fulfilled staff members would take their own lives. Ruben and Sinoway were asked to stay and to assist; both agreed promptly.

Roused to action, Ingrid fired questions at each interviewee like a particularly alert and dedicated district attorney. When had they last seen so-and-so? What was their mood? What did they say to you? What did you say to them that might have depressed them? Are you *sure* you didn't? Has any patient died in Intensive Care without my knowledge? Are you trying to hide something?

Playing the police game both had seen in films and on television, Ruben and Sinoway acted as the "good guys," smoothing the ruffled feathers of doctors and nurses who were offended by Ingrid's point-blank inquiry, then firing their own demanding inquiries. But while Martin felt that several of those whom they interrogated either had an expression of guilt similar to that in Ingrid's own violet eyes or appeared flushed, as though sexually on edge, no useful data was elicited.

Near noon, results began to filter in from Dr. Karl Peabody, who was in charge of the autopsies being done on the most recent suicides. Unquestionably, they had committed suicide and there were no signs of anyone forcing them to do so. Unless, Peabody noted tightly, with professional care and concern, violence might explain traces of dirt not only on their faces and hands but—in a few cases—in the mouths and on their genitalia as well. He had no idea where the dirt came from other than noting they surely had been outside the central building prior to taking their lives.

By mid-afternoon, most of the staff had been interviewed by Ingrid, Ruben, and Sinoway, with nothing to show for their enormous effort. The latter's guards waited outside protecting the professor.

"I think we must call in someone from outside," Ruben told the Director, crossing his legs and trying to be firm, "investigators who are trained in this sort of thing."

Ingrid didn't even bother to snap at him. She looked sapped of energy. "And try to answer their questions about everything we're doing here? Not just yet, thank you. The public will know when the time is right—astrologically."

Ruben frowned. "We can't just allow something like this to happen and—"

"Oh, indeed we can, Doctor," Sinoway interrupted, humming a little as if to reassure himself. He gave Ruben a cool smile, his bushy brows raised. "I scarcely think that twelve more deaths represent epidemic or even pandemic proportions on an island with our population. Indeed, since we do not know the motives behind these, hm-m, losses, there may be *no* physiological or psychological reasons to concern us. In which case, medical words such as 'epidemic' and 'pandemic' that suggest an outside agent, have no meaning whatever."

"It is precisely because we do not know their motivations that we must learn what they were," Ruben said as patiently as possible. "Morley, it could be the kind of subtle neurotic process that eventually strikes *all* of us!"

Sinoway closed his eyes. "I scarcely think so. Use your imagination, man, hm-m? They may have shared some private matter among themselves that we can't begin to comprehend. An orgiastic argument, possibly, or some shared guilt over, hm-m, a mutual failure in a medical examination that appeared routine and wasn't. There could be a dozen good reasons." He crossed his legs neatly and turned confidently to the Director. "Madame, it's clear to me that our best move is to do nothing else at all!"

Ingrid reddened. Ruben was surprised and pleased to see she was angered, drawing herself erect. "I hand-picked every member of my staff, Professor Sinoway. Brought them here myself, which, in a sense, places them under my protection. That's a heavy responsibility, sir—mine. I do not intend to see people in *my* buildings, in *my* labs, and on *my* island, wasting their God-given gift of life without finding out why!"

Ruben cleared his throat. "Morley, old man, it seems unlikely that there is a shared secret among these twelve members of one department, a nurse in another area, and an old Mexican farmer across the island, and—"

"Your point is well taken, Doctor," Ingrid snapped. "Thank you both for assisting. For now, please return to your respective schedules. Notify me promptly if anything more concrete develops."

Sinoway sighed, piqued because he had been rebuffed, and headed for the nearest men's room. His two bodyguards followed him.

Ruben found Dr. Julie Lyle waiting for him in the corridor outside Ingrid Solomon's office. She touched his hand lightly. "Now, I also think it's time we talked," she said quickly.

"My classroom," he suggested, taking her arm. "There'll be no one there since my classes were canceled while I assisted the Director."

She nodded and, Martin noticed, looked back several times as they walked to make sure they weren't followed.

He closed the classroom door and locked it. There was already a straight wooden chair beside his desk, for students who had something confidential to say, and Ruben held it for her. He took his comfortable chair behind the desk and appraised her in a swift glance. The little redheaded woman was nervous but determined. She looked somewhat peaked and, he thought, out of condition. She was even putting on weight. He still felt drawn to her, by the power of her regular features and sweet modesty of manner, but she was certainly not herself today.

"I've felt, since Jacques' funeral, that you were a person I could trust," she began, picking at her skirt and avoiding his shrewd eyes. "You went out of your way to remember him in a decent way." Now she looked at him and her own eyes were red-rimmed. "I don't know if there's a connection between this awful wave of suicides and what I h-have on my mind, but I *do* know that I must unburden my own soul."

"About what, Julie?" he murmured.

"About—dreadful things, Martin. About Professor Sinoway." She swallowed hard. "I've worked with him, as you know, and he is a master of—of murder. Secret murders which he has gotten away with until now. I've gone to no one because he terrifies me, simply terrifies me."

"Has he threatened you?"

She nodded. "He's told me twice I'll die if I tell anyone of his work. But if th-there's some virus he's concocted and that he's using to m-make people kill themselves, I must *not* die the only one who knows wh-what he's done before."

Ruben saw that she was near tears and ached to hold her. He didn't; he tried to be even more professionally calm and interested. "You have my word that I'll try to help," he said evenly, "and that I won't tell anyone unless your safety is first guaranteed." He paused, then added, almost conversationally: "Why don't you begin with the photograph of that child with the bloated skull?"

Julie averted her gaze once more, clearly ashamed. "It is a scientific fact that a human child's brain size triples during the first year of life. As Dr. Loren Eisley and Dr. Emiliani observed, man has a literally unique capacity for evolving rapidly, both as a race and as an individual." The redhead cleared her throat. "Without that tripling of the brain, a child develops microcephaly —pinheadedness. *With* it, man's amazing intelligence is allowed to develop normally. I needn't add, I guess, that no other creature has such a remarkable brain growth."

"Go on," Ruben said softly.

"Sinoway w-wondered if he might create a superior human being by inducing the brain of a ch-child not only to triple in a few months, instead of a year—but to sextuple."

Ruben was shaken. "Good Lord," he whispered.

"Your friend Jacques, to continue getting his treatments from the Professor, went along—most reluctantly

—with the experiments."

"Who was the child?" he asked.

"It was b-born illegitimately to a woman here." She looked at him with agonized eyes. "I assisted too. The photograph you saw . . . that was the child, a baby boy. He was—undeniably brilliant, in terms of his capacity for intelligence."

For a moment she stopped and stared at the blackboard, unable to continue without weeping. When she continued, it was as though she still saw the outcome of the experiment, perhaps always would.

"The ni-night before your friend died," she went on, "I heard cries from the infant's room. It was the first time, since it was just a few weeks old, that it made the n-normal cries of a little b-baby. A baby in *pain*. Jacques and I—rushed there." Her gaze flicked at him, hot and horrified. "Martin, it didn't even have a name!"

He only nodded, unwilling to try speech just then.

"H-He was holding his enormous head between those t-tiny baby hands, rocking to and fro. There was— blood. And he looked at me, j-just once, with those incredible and terrible *adult* eyes of his, and spoke. Just once, Martin, just once."

Ruben looked toward the window. "What did the child say?"

"'God help me,' it said, very distinctly. 'God help me . . .'"

She burst into tears. It was one of the hardest things Ruben had done merely to put out his hand and lay it lightly on her wrist. "I was afraid it was something like that," he said simply. "What happened to the boy?"

"There's no trace left of Case Number Four-three-three-five," Julie said in a gasp. "Sinoway saw to that with his handy-dandy ch-chemistry set. So there's no proof, Martin, except the photograph."

"From time to time, I've heard women—who shriek in pain. For a while I thought they were merely patients who were ill. They weren't just that, were they?"

Again Julie Lyle looked at her hands, twisting nervously in her lap. "The brain tripling," she said softly. "A woman whom he wanted, but with whom he was not—compatible—became pregnant by another man. The Professor—" she uttered the word with a mixture of abject contempt and a shiver of terror—"*visited* her. Can you imagine, Doctor Ruben, what would happen to a woman if the child in her womb had its brain tripled *before* birth?"

He paled, his composure shaken. He stood, eyes blinking away tears of rage. "The man is monstrous. Diabolical."

"That was *one* screaming woman, Martin," she said, more levelly now, eager to tell it all. "There was also the mother with a pinheaded boy, whom Sinoway determined he could save with the tripling of its brain. Only the size of its skull was tripled and connections between the brain and the nervous system were irreparably torn. If you like that, why, you'll enjoy his experiment with the five-year-old girl suffering from *progeria*—premature aging. He *reduced* its brain pan and—"

"*Please!* Ruben exclaimed. "No more just now, if you don't mind. Tell me, please, Julie—why didn't you go to the Director?"

Her green eyes shone as she peered up at the tall, pale man. "Whose illegitimate child do you think it was whom you *saw* in the photograph? Ingrid's, born just before she married Jacques. She, uhm, *gave* it to Sinoway." She paused to ask for a cigarette and then allowed him to light it, both their hands trembling.

"Jacques made the mistake of telling Sinoway, after the baby died, that he wouldn't tolerate it—that he'd leave the island, if necessary, to stop the Professor. He said he didn't care to live, knowing what he knew. After wh-what happened to your friend, well, Sinoway didn't have to threaten me any longer."

Ruben sat on the edge of his desk and took her hands in his. They were cold, shivering. "Why do you tell me now, Julie? Is it only because of the suicides and because you think Sinoway might be behind them?"

"No." She shook her head, a pretty shimmer of auburn. "No, I don't really believe he's responsible for the suicides. Last night, Morley told me that he plans to *resume,* to *expand,* his experimentation. He—he has found a psychic boy who is terribly bright and who is much older than the infant. One whom Sinoway feels may be able to withstand multiple brain growth, if it's done gradually. The child is part of a minority race and I guess the professor figures nothing's lost if he fails again." Her face fixed in a grimace of passionate determination. "I can't permit that. I cannot."

"Of course, you can't," Ruben said, squeezing her hands. "We'll stop him, somehow. Do you know which one of the sensitives the boy is?"

"Yes, I do." She thought a moment for the name. "It's that little African fellow with the wide, adorable smile. I think his name is—Dhombola."

Ruben's brows shot up. He felt the chill bile of horror rise in his breast and throat. He was so sickened and anxious that he barely heard what else Julie Sarah Lyle said to him.

"There's another r-reason I didn't come to you sooner, Martin," she said in a scarcely audible tone. "A very *sound* reason, I think. It is also why I didn't d-defy the schedule and come to your rooms. You see, I'm pregnant, Martin. It's not far along, but it's definite; I'm pregnant. And the ch-child in my womb—is Morley Sinoway's." She touched Ruben's knee, and her hand was shaking. "His chart and mine were compatible."

PART THREE

Nineteen

They stayed in the classroom into the evening hours. Then Julie persuaded Martin that she would be safe, if no one knew she had been with him. He wanted to escort her to her rooms, but had to satisfy himself by checking out the corridor outside the classroom before she left.

He knew he should really get something to eat, since he'd had nothing all day; but when he went to the cafeteria, even the finest dishes looked nauseating. He took two tall glasses of iced tea to a table as distant from the others as possible.

Across the huge room, he saw Sinoway himself was at a table with a striking young brunette, and Ruben wanted to go to him and smash his face. For the first time he felt that he might be capable of murder. But Sinoway's goon squad waited against the wall.

What else *could* be done? he mused.

He did not dare involve Julie by confronting Sinoway since he, himself, had no authority to stop the professor and when he left, the madman would surely know where Ruben had acquired his information. By the same token, he didn't dare approach Ingrid, who might not know all the details but was well enough aware of Sinoway's experimentation to have given him her unwanted, illegitimate child. When he thought of that,

Martin realized there would be no assistance from the Director. He had always despised the concept of abortion, feeling that it was undeniably murder; but that poor child might have been better off never being born at all.

He couldn't even bear to think what Sinoway might do to the tiny neonatologist if he knew she'd been to him, and he was sure, now, Ingrid wouldn't lift a finger to protect Julie.

Keeping silent, of course, was absolutely unthinkable —especially when Sinoway planned to resume his Hitlerian experiments and had chosen Dhombola as a subject. Ruben could not, would not, stand by and allow the African boy to become a guinea pig, a freak, and—in all likelihood—a dead little boy.

My sweet Lord, he mused, what *have* I gotten myself into? A neurotic sex fiend of a beauty who believed she was King Solomon and a Nazilike genius of a lunatic who'd do anything to save his own skin and indefinitely propagate himself. Ruben was sure that, of all the plans the professor had in mind, one was what fascinated him the most: one hundred carbon copies of Morley Sinoway.

Perhaps a good night's sleep would help. Ignoring the Director's schedule, he went to bed early and was awakened, groaning, with the realization that "sex activities" had come round. Opening the door, he found a languid, probably peroxided blonde of twenty-seven or twenty-eight waiting in nothing but bikini panties. For a long moment he looked at her, feeling himself, incongruously, becoming aroused. "Aren't you going to ask me in?" she asked at last, taking her large, rather low-hanging breasts in her hands and raising them for a kiss. "No," he said with difficulty, shaking his head and slowly closing the door, "not anymore."

The rest of the night was again largely sleepless. The next day he telephoned Ingrid Solomon's office to claim illness and ask to be excused from his classes. Whatever he did, the sooner he did it, the better. There was no way of calculating when Sinoway would decide to go back to work.

The mound, Ruben thought as he dressed for the day in walking shorts and a lightweight pullover—everything somehow seemed to involve the mound.

He left the building and drifted toward it, not without care and a measure of fear for the engrossing, sensual heat he had recently drawn from it. He found little Dhombola was one of the handful of children near the mound, and the boy seemed puzzled. His enormous dark eyes watched the passionate expressions form on the adult faces around him and his own innate sensitivity obviously told him something was wrong.

Martin wanted badly to warn the boy, but it seemed pointless. Where could the child—or he and the child—go to escape Sinoway? No one could swim all the way to neighboring South Bend where it might be safe—especially if they could find a couple of enormous Notre Dame linemen to hide behind!

Dhombola went with Ruben willingly enough for a stroll into the small woods beyond the mound. To him, Ruben was now something of a hero, the man who had saved his Australoid companion from death. Occasionally he would skip ahead to identify some plant they also had in Africa, or point to a skittish animal with a charming folk tale. Once he told Martin a long, rambling tale about Oldannah superstitions concerning "spirits who dwell in forest."

Ruben enjoyed his chatter, even learned a few things from it. But he could tell that Dhombola was disturbed, beneath the level of outer cheerfulness, by some deep-seated anxiety or apprehension. Sometimes the youth paused and stared deep into the wooded area, as if seeing some lurking great cat on the verge of pouncing or a maddened rhino about to charge. Or as if Dhombola, somehow, had some premonition of his own hideous danger.

Something had to be done and Martin shoved possibilities rudely around in his mind, like moving furniture in a room one can no longer tolerate. By the time his idea occurred to him and he was deep in an evaluation of it, the child had ranged far ahead. He was as nimble in the tall, sharp grass as any city boy on cement sidewalks. The man watched the boy another moment or two and then, in a normal tone, called to him: "Dhombola, come back here, please. I want to ask you something."

Ruben realized that, if little Dhombola displayed a psychic talent of value to Ingrid Solomon and in her presence—if he enhanced his own value in her fascinating violet eyes—the Director's interest might well cause Morley Sinoway to look elsewhere for his next victim.

The lad came bounding back to him. He'd taken to wearing shorts now, instead of dashikis, and might at a glance have been a cute black boy from anywhere, except for the sometimes far-off glint in his appealing eyes. It was getting just a little nippy now and Dhombola was breathing heavily, enjoying it, when he stopped before Martin. "What you want, *Docruben?*"

He kept his voice controlled. "Son, your special gifts have always been linked to *touch,* right—except when you helped Pigo? What we parapsychologists call psychometry?" The child nodded. "And you have a splendid knack for picking up things of the past, merely by touching or holding—certain things?" Again Dhombola bobbed his head in assent, not at all impatient with this man. "Does it have to be the *distant past*—months, even years ago? Or can it be the *recent* past, a matter of mere days?"

Dhombola grinned. "Not matter, *Docruben*." He hesitated, trying hard to explain the phenomena. "In vision-things, sir, time isn't same. Not quite real, not way most people see it. Sure, I can touch something just from yesterday. Tell you about it fast."

Ruben studied his serious, honest face. "You've heard about the suicides, haven't you? The ones yesterday?"

"Terrible." His face was sad. "Not make the *important* spirits happy, killing self."

Martin placed his own hands on Dhombola's thin shoulders. "Do you think you could, by touching one of those dead people, learn *why* they killed themselves? What frightened them or made them do it?"

Dhombola frowned, looked grim and unhappy. The prospect of proximity to the dead did not cheer him. "Yes," he said finally, quite simply. "If *you* want me to do it, *Docruben*."

Martin straightened and peered back through the crisp air at the mound, enigmatic and still. Very well, he thought. This may solve two problems at once: It may save this little fellow's life, and it may tell us, at last, *why* so many people on Nommos Island are killing themselves.

"Race you to the Director's office!" Ruben exclaimed, pivoting and sprinting, his walking stick tight in his hand.

The boy hesitated only for a second, displeased.

Then he was hurrying after his friend and mentor, buoyed on the wings of childish trust.

Twenty

They found Ingrid reclining on an ornate, royal-blue sofa in her luxurious office. But Ruben noticed her second. He saw first that the windows were closed tight, that the air was close and vaguely unpleasant to the nose. One of the two little birds appeared ill; both were silent.

She sat up quickly enough with a show of her customary energy, smiling at them, even reaching out to pat Dhombola's head.

But Ruben was appalled. Her bare arms and face were smeared with dirt, as though she hadn't bathed in several days. She had put a coating of makeup over it and her ordinarily lovely face had an unreal, shadowy cast to it, as if she had donned a mask.

In a way, he thought, she had. Beneath the effort she made at a burst of energy he sensed how distracted, even dazed the Director had become. "Preoccupied" would be an understatement. He wondered, given her filthy condition, if she didn't already know more than she was telling.

He explained Dhombola's psychic skills slowly and precisely, unsure if she could follow his train of thought. "I think he can get the information for us," he finished, "tell us what happened to motivate the suicides."

She remained tough-minded, more in control of herself than he'd thought. Obviously enlivened by his remarks, she rose, ready to leave at once. "It's a brilliant idea!" she exclaimed. "But I let the bodies go to the crematorium. We'd extracted all the data we could—or so I thought—and none of them had families. We'd better hurry."

"Wait!" Martin called, stopping her. "I want Sinoway with us."

She stared incredulously at him. "Why? You can't stand the man."

He knew it was essential that the professor witness the new value his Director placed on the boy. "You don't wish me to pry into your private views. Let it suffice that I consider it important for him to be with us."

She sighed. "Very well, then," and reached for the intercom on her desk. "But I don't know whether you're actually very intelligent or merely as emotional and intuitive as the others here." She spoke quickly, told her secretary to locate Sinoway and have him meet them at the crematorium.

The professor must have been nearby. He met them outside the cold, metal door of the room, sweeping Ruben with inquiring and suspicious eyes. Then Sinoway saw little Dhombola and, though he did not speak, his flat brown eyes jerked in recognition. "I hope this is important," he snapped at Ruben. "I was, hm-m, quite busy with my work."

Ingrid spoke instead, explaining rapidly the reasons for their visit to the crematorium. Martin watched him closely, trying to determine if Sinoway grasped the reason why Dhombola was being pushed forward. But the older man simply inclined his bald head and shouldered the door open.

Entering the place was like casually dropping into

Hell. Although the long, narrow room outwardly might have been just another lab, any stranger coming here would look immediately, with something like fear, to the farthest wall.

There, a burly worker, stripped to the waist and his skin glowing a sweaty red, stood beside the actual crematory chamber, poking a human body on a conveyor into a pit of flames so hot it was nearly white. It was Hades-like, to Ruben, ghastly even to the businesslike effort of the muscular worker and the supercilious chief attendant, who drifted toward them with the exacting eye and costume of an accountant.

"Yes?" he asked, bored even though the Director herself had approached him. "I assume I can do *something* for you?"

Suddenly Ruben realized that the bodies being spoonfed to the furnaces were the remaining suicides from the hospital lounge. Only one remained, that corpse stretched on the conveyor at this instant as the half-naked laborer impatiently gave the treadmill a little prod.

Martin dashed with his newfound athletic prowess across the room, leaped, and braced himself to stop the action. But the gears were powerful; he could only slow it and felt, in the inexorable pull, a wince of fear that he might be tugged along. Perspiration had instantly poured from his forehead due to his proximity to the fatal fires and he shouted at them: "Stop this damnable thing! *Stop it!*"

For a fleeting moment Martin thought that the muscular laborer, staring at him with resentful and cold eyes, might actually toss him into the flames.

Then the man's superior was calling languidly to him, "Do what the man says, Joey. We can finish up later."

Joey glared again at Ruben, then turned to obey his

boss. "Fucking nuisance outsider," he muttered over his huge shoulder. "Fucking shrinks oughta stay where they fucking belong."

Ingrid told the crematory manager what they had in mind. He did little more than appear bored, put upon; he motioned Joey to join him at a small records desk beside the door, where they whispered together.

"All right, boy," Ingrid said to Dhombola. "Go ahead. Do it."

He looked up at his tall friend. "Must I?" he asked.

Ruben smiled down. "I'll go along," he said, slipping his arm around the lad's shoulder.

They drew near the corpse, a fair-haired man in his late twenties—the one who had shot himself. The side of his face had been blown away and Ruben turned the head in the other direction, away from the boy. The body wore nothing but a sheet, its pale torso and paler, bare feet indecently protruding from beneath it, and Ruben thought again how strange it was that man left here with no more than he arrived.

"All right, son," he nodded to Dhombola. "Just do the best you can."

The child flicked another glance at the man, then closed his eyes and reached. His small hand rested on the corpse's right shoulder, no more firmly than necessary, and Martin saw the boy's skin pucker in reaction. He shuddered, closed his eyes tighter.

"People, all of a place, at mound." Dhombola had control of himself. His voice was calm enough as he looked deep within, and *saw*. "Hot, they get hot. They —*want* each other. Sexy things." He squinched his eyes in a frown. "But other people not good enough no more. No, they want more—and *more*." Abruptly the boy's eyes shot wide open, gaping at Ruben. "They want—*spirit in mound!* Want it, *sexy* way!"

"Easy, son," Ruben said in soft tones, ready to yank Dhombola away from the informative corpse.

But Dhombola was deeply, mesmerically involved now, and excited in a passionate, disgusted fashion. His face had a look of both revulsion and terror. "*Demon spirit,*" he cried, "come *out* of mound! It—lives there, many, many years. Very, very many! It—get *strong* from all people who come see mound! Oh, it *old,* terrible awful *old!* And now it's . . . freed, *set free, alive!*"

Then Dhombola's small body stiffened, shuddered, yet his beautiful, staring eyes glazed over with a certain youthful fascination. "Ah, Docruben, these people *see* her, *want* her! She—very, very small but—ah, *beautiful*, sir, *wonderful*-beautiful! But there are *more, Docruben!*" He saw it clearly now, Martin saw; saw it the way the others who killed themselves saw it. "Demon has *all* sexy-beauty on earth—part of it *all!* Has *terrible* secret, though—oh, Docruben, a really *terrible secret* is part of that sexy-beauty! She is—bad love, *ugly* love! Monster of evil, *ancient* evil, *Docruben* —evil and death!" Now the boy's face twisted in something like embarrassment. "Oh, Great Master!" he squealed. "These people, they have *sexy* with demon in mound—men, women, *anybody! All* want her but—but *after* it happen, they *kill self!*" He peered almost hysterically up at Ruben. "Can't *live* after they have her!"

"That's enough, son," Martin said softly, gently. He took the boy by the arms, firmly but carefully, and started to pull him away from the corpse.

"Her *name, Docruben—I know her name!*" Dhombola was happy now, with his news, until he uttered it. "Demon-spirit called . . . *Alouqua!*" He whispered it again, intently, to be sure his friend understood. "Demon-beauty named—*Alouqua!*" Then he blurted out the rest of it: "And *she kill ever'body on Nommos*, very, very *soon!*"

He could stand the contact, the vision of the demon-spirit, no longer.

Ruben hugged the sobbing, upset boy against him comfortingly and tried to sort it out: Whether the fact defied the real world or not, whether it threatened his own logical views, there was a demon of incredible sexual magnetism dwelling in an ancient mound—and clearly able to *come out*. Her beauty, moreover, attracted men and women alike but her eternal powers were clearly quite deadly. Dhombola would not lie. When one engaged in sex with the creature, they found the act marvelous and fulfilling—but they *also* would have to die.

Always? he wondered.

Clinging to the boy, Martin turned to face the Director of Solomon Studies. He had realized the source of her nervousness and appearance of guilt and saw, now, that she was nearly hysterical with both recollections of her experiences and the evil she knew the Alouqua represented. She had retreated, unnoticed until now, to a corner of the morguelike room and though her face seemed open and guileless at a glance, her violet eyes gave her away. The mere mention of the delectable Alouqua clearly left Ingrid totally wanton, *starved* for the touch of the demon-spirit.

"Isn't there something you want to tell us?" he asked her quietly.

"What d'you mean?" she asked, her voice higher than usual. She could not return Ruben's gaze. He could tell that her heart was beating rapidly with guilt and with fright. "I don't understand."

"I think you do." It was dreadful, he thought, to

watch her incisive mind deteriorate beneath an onslaught of uncontrolled lust. "Ingrid, tell us. You've had sex with that monster, haven't you?" He kept his tone mild because he knew it would be enough to break her. She did not have sufficient control of her own thoughts to devise a lie. *"Haven't* you?"

Now she shoved away from the wall, upper body thrust forward defiantly from the waist, her bosom heaving. Flecks of spittle formed on her full lips as she sought a clever lie, failed. "Ruben, I didn't kn-know it would drive people to suicide." Her voice was hoarse. "Honest to God, Martin, I didn't know that!" But her thoughts shifted as she pictured the Alouqua in her mind. "But it—it doesn't really *matter*, you see. It *can't!*"

"It should," he told her softly, and took a step toward her, fearful of what she might do in this state.

"I *love* him, I *need* him," Ingrid insisted in a moan, fingers pressed to her mouth.

"Him? You need *him?*" Ruben asked.

"Him—her—Alouqua is what you *wish,*" Ingrid gasped.

"You must fight this," Ruben told her. "Either the creature doesn't really exist in fact or it's a thing of— of *other* than flesh. Of realities, Ingrid, in which *you* cannot remain."

"I know!" she agreed with a whirling, nervous nod. "Alouqua comes only *once* to each person, and, *Lord,* it's not *enough!* He has to accept me again." She laughed bitterly and tears began to flow. "Don't you *see,* Doctor? After . . . after the Alouqua, *no one else* is any good! Man, not woman—not *dozens* of each!" Her gesture suggested far more than the room, more than the building and the island. "Nothing h-has any meaning unless it's with Alouqua! Martin, there is *only*

Alouqua now—nothing more!"

"We'll help you fight it," he said softly, a few yards away now, reaching out to the trembling woman. "Your own staff can deal with this, I'm sure."

"No!" Suddenly Ingrid seemed to fill with some powerful emotional fact, to be inundated by the incredible force of her ardor. "You'll *never* understand until it happens to *you! Nothing* can keep me from Alouqua!"

And before anyone could stop her, Ingrid Solomon dashed with manic speed to the flaming opening in the crematory wall. Gaping at her in shock, they saw her vault—headfirst—through the white-hot aperture leading to the tormenting flames of perdition and eternity.

There was no final scream; not a word. Only the sound of monstrous yellow-orange-and-white flames that *hissed,* in greeting, and coughed obscenely back on the concrete floor a show of dancing, new sparks.

For seconds Ruben and the others stared, immobilized by shock. Then, no one else moving, Martin carefully closed and bolted the furnace doors.

Twenty-one

Martin Ruben pressed his fingers against his throbbing temples and rocked back against the wall, not knowing whether to laugh or cry. *Oh dear Lord,* he thought, *that monstrosity out there is* a real sex object, *genuinely made for nothing except sex! Women's liberation revenge carried to the ultimate degree!* The philosophical and social ramifications of the Alouqua seemed suddenly more funny than deadly, hysterically funny. A true sex object, turned at last upon its sensuous and selfish users—male and female alike—and driving the user *so* mad with lust, with guilt, that suicide became the only answer! Ingrid Solomon with her absolutely careless views on sexuality, her care never to fall in love, had to be its *ultimate* victim, the one culminating the countless hundreds or even thousands who'd been destroyed through the years! And again a demon had discredited and destroyed Solomon.

Dhombola's touch at his upper arm was electric. He jerked away and, in doing so, recovered his poise, shakily. He realized that the sensitive had done it intentionally, caringly. "You okay, *Docruben?* H' okay now, sir?"

Ruben knelt, hugging the little fellow. "I'll be fine, son, fine. I'm sorry you had to see—" he inclined his head to the crematory door—"that."

"S'all right, *Docruben,*" Dhombola replied in complete seriousness. "*Already* saw it—and more—in mind!"

"Let's get back to the, hm-m, Director's office," Morley Sinoway suggested, moving toward the outer door. "I think we'd be more comfortable there."

"For once we're in full agreement," Ruben said passionately.

When they had taken chairs in Ingrid's office, ignoring the wondering stares of her secretary, Martin Ruben turned to the bald genius. "My dear Professor Sinoway," he began, "I will tell you frankly that I have not been approached by the Alouqua. I must ask: *Have you?*"

Sinoway, who had been perched on Ingrid's desk, moved around behind the desk and sank into her chair. "Certainly not. I've never seen the thing."

"Excellent. Then both you and I still have hope and much work to do." He clasped his hands in front of him, consciously trying to marshal his thoughts and energies. "I think we must immediately block off the mound, preferably by having some workmen build an unclimbable fence around it. We may even require lead. And follow that with alternating shifts of guards. In short, we must stop the creature from getting *out* again while we keep everyone from going *to* it. We must not underestimate its long-range hypnotic abilities. And our next task, in my opinion, will be to weed out those who have already had contact with Alouqua and confine them. For their own good."

Sinoway finally found his voice, and, in a sense, his faith. He tapped Ingrid's pen on the desk. "Nonsense!" he said tartly, his hum now a deep, nervous throbbing sound in his throat. "This is ridiculous, Ruben. It is the most completely *un*scientific thing I've ever heard in my whole life. One may as well believe in vampires, werewolves, or fairies!"

"You can't be serious," Ruben answered disbelievingly. "You saw with your own eyes what happened to Ingrid Solomon."

"I saw an hysteric neurotic commit suicide," the professor amended, folding his rather powerful arms across his chest. "She was correct in her own approach to Jacques Coquelion. Life is for the living; life is ongoing. We only saw an irrational, self-destructive act, Doctor —nothing more!"

"By George, you're a special hypocrite, aren't you, Professor?" Ruben's gray eyes gleamed. "You claim to be a scientist but refute the evidence of your own senses. How could you *ever* have been part of the open-minded, questing people who, even if they did it partly to remain alive, came here to seek knowledge?"

Sinoway's bodyguards sensed trouble. They edged forward now, the larger of the two uniformed men clenching and unclenching his fists. Sinoway lifted a palm, restraining them. "I tell you, Ruben, demons and spirits are unreal. Nonexistent. Heaven knows what Ms. Solomon or the other suicides *believed,* but such things run counter to everything science *can* accept. They make a complete travesty of the scientific principle! There is no hard data!"

"Professor, there are *hundreds* of monstrous creatures of nature about which you and your fellow scientists still know nothing, but whose records go back thousands upon thousands of years." Ruben spoke calmly, soothingly, trying to reach the man. "Now I will grant you that a great many of these myths and legends are hard to swallow in the way they have come to us. What you must realize is that there have been problems with language. People thousands of years ago had to use their own feeble tools of reference to describe a phenomenon, so that we're obliged to *interpret* what they meant. And *some* of these ancient legends and myths go back so far that they were handed down by word of mouth, since there was no written language available to them. Naturally, exaggeration or distortion is evinced. But none of that means that the *hard-core nucleus* of *truth* doesn't exist. Chances are," he finished with a smile, "when something endures by reputation for centuries, it actually *does* have a basis in fact."

The professor only grunted. "I s'pose you've already heard of the legend of the, hm-m, Alouqua?"

Ruben nodded, glanced at Dhombola, who sat wide-eyed in a chair far too large for him. "I have. Its legend goes back quite deep in the fixture of time. It was said to be a female demon who sometimes took the form of a succubus, sometimes a vampire, in order to experience a variety of earthly sex and drive its envied victims to suicide."

"What, hm-m, is a succubus?"

"A female incubus. The Latin word from nightmare —*incubo*—comes from *incubare*, which means 'to lie upon,' as in sexual acts. The incubus was often said to show up first as a considerable weight lying on the chest, stifling breath; some people of the past lie in their graves of heart attacks while the records show that incubi killed them. Both succubus and incubus are traced to ancient civilizations and had other names, at times, such as the Assyrian *lili* and the Hebrew *Lilith,* similarly insatiable female demons. Actually, Sinoway, wood nymphs, satyrs, and fauns are sort of pre-Christian incubi, as are the Greek Sirens and the Teutonic Lorelei—even the Arabian *Jinn.*"

"Scarcely enough to give the story credence," Sinoway scoffed.

"I tried to suggest that 'where there's smoke, there might well be some old ashes,'" Ruben replied. "Try this: In the respected history of Scotland, by Hector Boece, he routinely discusses a handsome young Scot pursued by a female demon—merely one of many ostensibly truthful anecdotes." Ruben had an idea, and smiled. "Want to *see* one?"

"My dear fellow! Of course not!"

"Well, Professor, if you change your mind, look up Auguste Rodin's famous sculptures. That great nineteenth-century Frenchman created *Le succube,* which shows a beautiful black figure, nude, kneeling with its lips raised for a kiss. The fact is, old man," Ruben concluded, "there is probably as much historical evidence for the succubus as there is for King Arthur's factual existence! And the Alouqua is the most dangerous kind of all with her knack for conveying *immense* sensual and sexual attractiveness. She is the ultimate vamp, the ultimate temptress. It's clear to me, sir, that our continual efforts to project our frustrations and angers to the mound registered strongly with the sleeping demon, awakening her, more love- and sex-starved than ever."

Sinoway tapped his fingers. "If I can believe such twaddle even for a moment, Doctor, you are then saying this thing is *genuine*—someone can experience it with *all* his senses, film or record it—or that it is a psychic construct of man's beliefs, dredged from the collective unconscious and materialized as an energy form? Or are you saying it is pure thought form, so that those who refuse to believe in it *cannot* be harmed?"

Martin lit a Camel thoughtfully. It seemed he might be winning Sinoway over, at least to the extent of cooperating about stopping the creature. "That kind of thought form is called, in Tibet, a *tulpa*. The anthropologist and author Alexandra David-Neal spoke not only of seeing them but of *making* one, herself, some fifty or sixty years ago. Now if I thought Alouqua was merely a *tulpa*, I would try somehow to psychoanalyze or hypnotize it and disperse its energy through a type of exorcism." Ruben paused. "But I doubt it. We've seen that it certainly has a mind of its own, however narrowly directed—one that can *convince* humans to do the, hm-m, lurid things it wishes."

"Show it to me," Sinoway said flatly.

"I beg your pardon?"

"I said, '*Show* it to me.' Bring it here. Let me record it with my *own* senses. That's the only way a scientist can accept such folderol."

Ruben leaned forward intensely. "With Ingrid and Jacques both gone, we are the only ones who can *do* something about that damnable thing. If you don't agree with my proposal to fence it in, perhaps we should just get the plane here and begin flying all of us off the island."

Sinoway's smile was cold. "Be frightened away by a neurotic notion, hm-m, a whimsical historical tidbit? You ask me what I plan to do about it and that, Ruben, is the *only* thing you've said that makes sense. Because all the decisions concerning Solomon Studies are now mine to make."

Ruben frowned. "How do you arrive at that conclusion?"

Sinoway sighed. "Ms. Solomon was so very anxious to, hm-m, get me here that even in my illness I had the presence of mind to ask somewhat . . . *more* . . . than the others received. She fully appreciated my unique value and, hm-m, granted me that which business types call 'a piece of the action.'" He smiled happily, his thick, bushy brows lifting high into his naked forehead.

"You *own* part of S.S.?" Ruben demanded

incredulously.

"I have, all along," Sinoway shrugged. "Ingrid could do nothing about my experiments. Now, with the Director and her hyperemotional husband dead, mine becomes the *only* controlling interest—both in Solomon Studies and Nommos Island. It is *all mine,* and I have the papers—concealed safely, when I must produce them—to prove it."

Ruben took from his jacket the photograph of the professor's victim, the pathetic infant whose brain had tripled. "What will you do when I show this picture to the authorities in South Bend or Indianapolis? Just how would you explain this poor child, Doctor, hm-m, Hitler? Or is it Eichmann?"

The older man merely smiled. "Your unprofessional viewpoint appalls me, Dr. Ruben. The only individuals who don't know how cheap life is are those who are ordered to give it up. Why, war itself proves the point. People with nothing to offer a dominant society almost *fight* to throw their sad little lives away on drugs, alcohol, in automobiles, in ugly little family squabbles." He laughed. "I can make life in a Petry dish, my dear man, like a saucer of cow's milk. But with my work accomplished, there will be those among us who are giants, who are *worthy* of the magic that is life."

Before Martin could react, one of the professor's guards moved swiftly, tugging the incriminating photograph from his hands. He put it in a large ceramic ashtray and held his burning lighter against a corner.

"That," said the professor, "takes care of that."

"These bully boys of yours won't stop the Alouqua, Sinoway," Ruben told him. Dhombola had run to him and he hugged the boy protectively against his side. "When that rare beauty comes for them—or *you*—your miserable adult playground will be torn apart in moments." He smiled. "You still haven't told me what you plan to do about her?"

"Do?" he repeated. "I do not believe a *syllable* of what you told me, Ruben. I plan to do nothing whatever. Except maintain and propagate the organization left me by your beautiful blond bedmate. And, hm-m, continue my own experimentation on a somewhat more substantial and accelerated basis." He stared directly at little Dhombola, and his ghastly smiles confessed his intent.

"You cannot have the boy," Ruben said bluntly, rising and edging toward the door.

"*I* can have what I please." Sinoway raised both heavy brows pointedly. "Whenever I want it. Not only today, or this year, but for—hm-m, who knows?—for perhaps the next thousand years! All thanks to the dear departed Ingrid Solomon. But run along, both of you. I have work to do." Ruben moved swiftly but the professor's voice stopped him and Dhombola at the door. "Go where you wish on the island. Of course, you cannot leave Nommos in the foreseeable future, hm-m? You will simply resume your regular duties, maintain your schedule, and we shall all get along famously!"

"You expect me to go back to teaching my classes as if nothing had happened?" Ruben marveled.

"Of course!" Sinoway met him at the door, patting his shoulder. "By all means, sir, maintain your little regimen. We must think of your health, mustn't we?" He paused. "Besides, your contract is with Solomon Studies, not the late Madame Coquelion. If you think about all this in a mature way, you'll enjoy continuing to earn your handsome salary and, one day, you'll come around to my way of looking at things, hm-m?"

Ruben didn't reply. For a long while he stared into the flat brown eyes of the new director, not quite able to accept the fact that this madman could ignore the coldest of facts: nearly twenty bodies by suicide, including one observed by his own eyes.

Then Martin took Dhombola's small hand firmly, stepped between Sinoway's muscular, silent guards, and quietly walked into the busy corridor of Solomon Studies.

Twenty-two

To offer them as much safety as possible, Ruben brought Julie Lyle and the boy Dhombola to his own quarters to stay. He felt that the professor's frigid glance at the child meant he still intended to experiment on Dhombola, and it was only a matter of time until he discovered Julie's role in informing Ruben.

While he was preparing his bed for their use—he would sleep on the sofa in the front room of the suite—Martin wondered how long they would be there. Would Sinoway prefer a cat-and-mouse game or would he strike quickly, simply decide tomorrow morning, or the next, to punish Julie and begin working with Dhombola? Somehow he ruled out any possibility that Sinoway, now that he was fully in charge, would change his mind about either of his chosen victims. The man had no spirit of grace; he put his diabolical science first.

But he had brought the pregnant woman and the little boy here to protect them against a force more powerful, by far, than Morley Sinoway: The Alouqua. He doubted that she could strike against a child Dhombola's age, but Julie's impending motherhood did not seem likely to deter the eternal earthen force.

That night, they spoke for some time, filling in each other on details they alone knew. Ruben discovered that room service was still being permitted and the three of them, having done without food for some time, ate surprisingly heartily. He learned that Pigo, the strange little Australoid, was up and around; according to the African, Pigo was almost painfully grateful to Ruben and determined to repay him.

Finally, well after dining, Dhombola fell asleep in a chair and Martin covered the child with a blanket from his bedroom. Julie herself, he saw, had spent so much time in pursuit of her career that she—who worked professionally with tiny infants—had little idea how to treat a child. He mused about the way that modern careers tended to cheat many people of the natural pleasures of life; and he thought, with a wince, how fond he remained of the little redheaded woman.

"Surely there's some way to escape," she said after Dhombola was comfortable. She had taken the other chair with Ruben sitting beside her on the floor. "After all, this island isn't an armed camp."

"I'm inclined to agree with the sentiment," he replied, realizing how tired he was and resting his head against her calf. "But I can't see any way out. There are no boats here; we're dependent on the plane and it's not due for three weeks."

"Then we must prepare for a way to get on it when it comes," she said earnestly, flushing.

Ruben shook his head. "I doubt that Sinoway is so mad he's forgotten the schedule. When it comes, I'm sure he'll do his best to have us locked up somewhere. As to swimming away, Lake Triton is no ocean but quite adequate to prevent our escape—unless you're a female Mark Spitz." He smiled. "A *pregnant* female Mark Spitz."

"It sounds so hopeless," she sighed.

"Well, I think we're all right for the moment," Ruben half-lied, doubting that he meant it. "Presumably Sinoway is happily experimenting away in his laboratory, ruining the life of some other innocent person. If we avoid confronting him, he may well let us alone."

"What about a revolt?"

Martin turned to peer up at her, smiling. "You've read some bad novels in your time, Julie," he remarked. "A *revolt*, for the love of Heaven!"

"Well, why not?" she demanded, coloring. "Why can't we get a few hundred people on our side and simply overwhelm him and his trained apes?"

Ruben laughed at the novel term. "Everybody on Nommos knows, by now, that astrocosmology works. They know that so long as they stay here and no one literally attacks them, they stand an excellent chance of living longer than any human beings in history. As you noted yourself, Julie, that kind of thing tends to generate a dash of gratitude."

"It was Ingrid's work, not Morley's," she argued.

"That's our word against his. I'm sure he'd claim the credit." Martin Ruben stretched, tried to clear his head. "Julie, we're all under far worse danger from the Alouqua than Sinoway in any case. If nothing is done to stop her, she'll eventually kill every human being on this island. The fact that you only mention the professor as our primary threat shows me how dangerous she is. You weren't with us in the crematorium; you're depending on my word, and the boy's. And you don't really *believe*, down deep inside, that she exists, do you?"

Julie shifted her weight and avoided his eyes. "Of course I do!"

Ruben sighed. "Of course, you don't. There's too much scientific training in you, my girl—far too much. Which means that I'm the only one who can defend a couple of thousand people against the damned thing."

He shook his head. "It's the kind of situation in which a large number of people are within a breath of a killer plague and won't even close the doors and windows to protect themselves. Because they don't think the virus exists."

"If it *does,* Martin," Julie began anew, her hand on his shoulder, "what is it? I mean, aside from what you've told me about its history. Unless it is a creature of sheer shadow, it has substance—and substance is *something.* Do you think it's composed of human tissue?"

He lit a Camel and peered thoughtfully at the glowing tip. "I have no way of knowing, and that's what's beginning to bother me. I'm no military authority, but I'm sensible enough to know that you don't defeat the enemy without knowing something about it." He squeezed his lips between his thumb and index finger. "I have the distinct impression you've said something of value—*something* that gives me a clue—but I can't quite put my finger on it."

"You said that Ingrid, and the boy, claim Alouqua is extraordinarily beautiful," the neonatologist recalled. "Very small, but beautiful."

He nodded. "And that troubles me, too, since the one glimpse I had of her, I had the impression that she was tall."

When he had finished the cigarette, Ruben stood. He looked down at the pretty redhead and spoke softly: "I'm going out a while."

"Don't, please!" she exclaimed, worried for him. "It's dark out there and the Alouqua may be waiting for you."

"I thought you didn't believe in her?" he asked, joshing. "I must get a better look at her, Julie. It seems to me that all the suicides happened during the day. And legend told us never to go to the mound at night. Since the ground rules were doubtlessly laid out by that ancient demon herself, I have to think that this means that Alouqua is *harmless* after nightfall—perhaps even vulnerable."

"That's sheer guesswork, Martin," she argued. "Nothing more. Please, stay."

"I have nothing else to go on, and I have to develop *some* understanding of the creature if we're to have a chance of stopping her." He leaned down to kiss her cheek, but Julie shifted her face and kissed him full on the lips. He almost lost track of thought. "Do not leave this place, you or the boy. Keep your eye on Dhombola. Lock the door after I've left, and don't open it to *anyone* but me." He grinned almost boyishly. "You should love this, Julie—it comes right out of those penny-dreadfuls you read!"

"Martin, please—be careful!"

He laughed. "And so does that line. Maybe we *all* say them when we're up against dark enigmas. Look, my dear: You have to care for your child. It may be part-Sinoway, but it's also partly *you*—and that should be enough to defeat a madman's terrible genes. Children make enough mistakes on their own without having to tote along their parents' burden of guilt."

She stood now, arms around Ruben's neck, strangely passionate and close to his face. "I wish I wasn't pregnant, just for a few hours when you get back," she cried softly. "I'd give you such a welcome!"

Rubin sighed. "Well, you won't always be in this condition, Julie. I understand it isn't permanent." He patted her cheek. "Do as I say. Lock the door after me."

Then, armed only with his walking stick, Martin

opened the door and started down the corridor to the elevator.

Twenty-three

The September night was like wearing another garment, humidity-heavy and clinging like a diver's suit. Ruben wondered how much of it was the real hanging-on of desperate summer, and how much the desperate sweat of frightened Martin Ruben. He crept cautiously away from the main building and then darted into the shadows in a single leap, stopping beneath a spreading tree whose name he did not know. He stared into the darkness where he'd been, looking for motion. Nothing. Nothing he could see, anyway.

Who all, Martin wondered, was he running from? In a way, it was Solomon Studies itself and a lifestyle composed in a Byzantine fashion of that which was very old and that which was new, impulsive, and deadly. Principally, of course, he tried to avoid the Alouqua, even while he was here to see her. Not Sinoway himself; alone, he was like most bullies, a threat only to women and small children. Sinoway's two bodyguards—certainly. Ruben could only recall one real fight in his adulthood and that was with a drunk who used foul language in the presence of ladies. No, he wasn't a fighter, physically; and the jarring likelihood was that the professor probably enlisted others in his service by now. Ruben simply had no way of knowing *how* many people might be waiting for him in the open.

Nor could he know for sure if—this particular moment—it mattered to anyone. Except, he felt sure, the demon from the mound, who craved her victims: It occurred to him that the Alouqua was a special kind of adversary since she would take her love objects once, and once only, then leave them for dead. The creature was working herself into a *cul-de-sac* by every victim whose life she ruined—especially on this island.

Martin stayed in the fringe of trees as much as possible, running low, glad now for his recent physical conditioning. He didn't plan to venture near the mound, but to watch it, in the hope of seeing *her* emerge, and—

Shouts, a scream! Ruben stopped, froze in motion; his head shot fearfully toward the long main building. A commotion had broken out near the outer entrance to the cafeteria, the last door of the structure; several men, one or two women and children were rushing toward the entrance. As they arrived they turned quickly away in terror or disgust to call out to others: "God, they're *all* dead!" and "Jesus, it's Bill and his people!" and "How many of them *are* there?" and "Can't tell; m'god they're packed on top of each other like sardines" and "Might be ten or twelve of 'em" and, finally, "Yeah, it's struck again! They've all knocked themselves off!"

For a moment Martin couldn't have budged an inch if his life depended on it. His sharp, aquiline face with its new fringing stub of beard stared toward the death scene; he listened to the marveling and horrified voices, and to intermittent sobbing from those who cared. But for the moment he could not think about the latest tragic loss of life.

He could only think that, of all the men still on Nommos, Martin Ruben was the only one who *knew* about the Alouqua and that she truly stalked the island

—and the only one obliged to know that she had taken the lives of dozens, by now, and was very probably *headed in the same direction—to return to the mound.*

She might be right behind him now! When a leaf touched the back of his neck, he ran again, not caring about the sound he made because he was too panicky to worry about mere human things.

There, the merry-go-round! Still running close to the ground, he spurted to it—the moon chose that instant to disappear behind clouds—and lay panting on the floor of the giant toy, watching.

The silence in the immediate area was made even more nerve-rackingly still by the contrasting sounds of anxious, confused life from the cafeteria entrance. He stared at the mound, not blinking, not daring to look away even for a moment. He decided that, if she saw him and moved toward him, he would spin across the merry-go-round, vaulting the animals until he could head toward the remainder of the woods and work his way through them to the agricultural community. They would probably protect him there.

If it was possible, he thought in mute fright, to be protected from a creature which did not actually *live*. Death and taxes, Ruben thought, and now the Alouqua.

But death and taxes are *insubstantial*, abstract concepts, he mused, remembering dully what Julie Lyle had said, and starting to piece it together. What was this monstrous entity made from? Somehow he knew the answer was close, that it involved Julie's remarks back in the suite, and his own thought about death and taxes being insubstantial; if he could just get some real rest, put a little distance between the recent horrors of Solomon Studies and the plaguing Alouqua—

And again the feeling that he almost *had* it, almost *knew* the Alouqua's secret.

But then, suddenly, *she had arrived*.

She was trapped for a brief second by rays of moonlight and Ruben forgot everything else in the fear that his heart's violent thumping might give him away.

At this distance, with little good light, he could not really see her face nor even make out in a meaningful way her wondrous body and silver hair. But even *this* far off, the musklike, mystic power she wielded over humans was evident. Perspiration leaped out anew on his face and drenched the back of his shirt until he felt like he was lying half-underwater. Lying prone on the merry-go-round, he felt himself—almost painfully—start to grow erect and had to muster all his self-discipline to avoid going to her, seizing her in his arms, throwing her to the ground and—

For a moment he thought she sensed him, looked his way. If so, he realized with shock, it was his fault; his own lust for the creature probably acted as an animal's pheremones, *beckoned* her. He shut his eyes in desperation and thought of *anything* else—the Indiana Pacers; the delicious Morrow Nut House on Monument Circle; Watergate; the new head coach, Bobby Knight, at I.U.; how much he enjoyed Shearing and Les Paul and the *1812* and Sinatra and—

He opened his eyes again and she wasn't looking at him, she was reaching down, almost childlike, to get a handful of dirt and raise it high over her head. She wore nothing whatever. The dirt, instead of falling, drifted with microscopic slowness down the Alouqua's beautiful body in a series of tiny puffs. It was, he supposed, her way of bathing. He was surprised to see she wasn't "very small," the way Dhombola had described her, but quite tall, as he remembered himself from the glimpse he'd had of her at Jacques' memorial. All children generally think of adults who are even average height as "big" people.

Could that mean there are *two* of the Alouqua? Ruben wondered, staring in a mixture of desire and blood-rushing fright. She was at the lower end of the mound now, one bare foot atop it, and she was incredibly well-proportioned. Never, he thought, had there *been* such a female—and when he found himself about to call out to her, even *run* toward her from his hiding place, Ruben finally saw that what he'd thought was absolutely true: There *never had been* such a woman; she was not real, but a sex object somehow comprised of many diverse and dirty dreams, lurid imaginations, and insane beliefs. She was all things sexual to all, male or female; chances were, the Alouqua was not literally feminine or, for that matter, masculine, at all—

But *Oh Lord*, he wanted to have her then! Oh, to *see* that exquisite face up close, to caress and kiss something so *mysterious!* Her tug on him was immense now; it seemed to be growing, even as part of Ruben's body seemed to him to be enlarging.

But then the miracle happened:

She knelt, lowering her knees until—as Martin stared in fascinated longing—her legs vanished into the mound; then her hips, and her waist, merging, blending, consuming and consumed by the mound. He watched in pained perplexity as the gorgeous creature was slowly enveloped. In another moment, along with his rutting drive and the pounding of his troubled heart, she was gone from view.

Ruben waited there for at least another two full minutes, getting his breath. When he stood, at last, he found his own knees trembling; he felt lightheaded, ineffectual, and confused. He felt . . . unfulfilled.

But the Alouqua, he knew then, wasn't. She had

returned home to her earthen grave because of the precise fact that she had "scored," that she copulated in some evil manner he hoped he'd never see with several other men or women and, sated by watching them take their lives one by one, quietly gone back to her immemorial home in the ground.

Every cell of hers, he thought as he circled around the mound and walked back to the main building, merged with the planet Earth. As he was making his slow, discreet way back up the steps to his suite, he again had the impression of drawing near the *truth* about the Alouqua, and what she really was.

But then he could only stare, in consternation, fright, and outrage.

The door was wide open, lock and bolt smashed. The woman and the boy whom he had asked there, to protect them, were gone. Taken in his absence. It could not be the Alouqua; he had seen where *she* went; the traces she left behind were bloody and fatal.

And that left only a human monster with whom he would have to deal in order to save Julie and little Dhombola: Professor Morley Sinoway.

Twenty-four

It was not necessary to leave the main building to reach Professor Sinoway's private laboratories. It would simply be necessary to get past the man's hulking bodyguards and, as Martin Ruben hurried purposively down the carpeted corridor to the hospital ward, he began to wonder for the first time how he would deal with them. Physically, at least in theory, he thought that he might be able to handle one of them. With—he admitted wryly to himself—luck and surprise. But with all the goodwill in the world, he doubted that he could take both men—who were probably well-armed beneath their attendant's white coats—out of the picture.

The hospital ward lay just ahead and, as he knew from earlier visits, the private labs were on the other side. Through the windows, Ruben could see that a storm was building and the lean parapsychologist found himself fantasizing briefly along theatrical lines: It would be a tropical storm from a film of the Forties, the kind of menacing typhoon one used to see on the screen; and while Sinoway frantically tried to salvage his primary experiments, the Bad Guys would run helter-skelter into a trap Ruben sprang for them.

You're really a silly man, Martin, he told himself with a grin, and felt better for it. By now it was quite late and the ward lights were lowered in order to help the patients sleep. *Sleep,* he mused, *while a madman may decide any moment to use your flesh for a lampshade!*

Taking a better grip on his walking stick, Ruben passed the nurses' station as nonchalantly as possible. A grumpy old hoyden merely glanced at him, instinctively fussed with her hair. He doubted that she'd buzz Sinoway to warn him; she looked, in her two hundred pounds and practiced grim expression, virtually able to handle the professor herself.

Would dear, old Morley realize Martin would come after Dhombola and Julie? If he *thought* of it, if it *mattered* to him, he was certainly intelligent enough to know Ruben would. But he became so wrapped up in his work that he might merely have told his guards to stand watch and let it go at that.

Nothing ventured . . .

He crossed the corridor separating the rooms of the ward and there, ahead of him, lay the hallway to Sinoway's lab. At night it was, Martin found, even less illuminated and he was troubled by the fact that, if he got through the double doors halfway down the hall, it would be darker still. Gripping his stick, Ruben began tiptoeing toward the doors.

Locked, of course. He remembered now that Sinoway had used three keys to unlock the doors and stared helplessly at them, hands on hips, quite confounded.

But then the doors were opening . . .

For a frightening moment Martin thought they had opened by themselves; he saw no one there. Then his glance shot downward and, barely visible in the aperture, he saw the tiny figure of Pigo, the Australoid. A broad, toothy grin reached from one ear to the other —he was markedly healthier, and uglier, than before—and Ruben was delighted to see him.

"What are you *doing* here?" he asked the little man,

noticing he had something—perhaps a weapon of some kind—behind his back.

Pigo shrugged frail, bare shoulders and Ruben was surprised to see that he had soft, almost feminine eyes. "Knew doctor-man come. Pick it up from boy Dhombola." His seamed face was serious. "He back *there*, deep troubled. We get 'em *out!*"

Ruben considered. Pigo had picked up considerable English recently, doubtlessly the little African's good work. He bent slightly so that Pigo could hear him: "It's dangerous. You could get hurt; be sick again."

Pigo's gesture was eloquent. "You, boy, helped Pigo; now Pigo's turn." His fingers continued to fly in habitual gesturing; then he remembered Ruben couldn't read finger-language. "You magic, *my* magic—together, *powerful* magic!"

With that, the Australoid produced what he had concealed by tucking it in the waist of his loincloth: Quite obviously, Ruben thought coolly, *that* is a *kundela*—the type of mystical bone whose magic almost killed little Pigo.

And now, reborn as a good guy because he felt his witch doctor had exonerated him, Pigo planned to use it to get an American woman and an African boy to freedom. How do I tell him, when he wants to help—Martin mused, stalling—that this magic-charged stick isn't going to work on two thick-skulled American hoodlums? At last he sighed. Two were still better than one.

Pigo seemed to have read his mind. "Me first," he insisted and immediately began leading them into the darkness of the interior tunnel.

Again Ruben felt how clammy and dungeonlike it was here. Neither sunshine nor the heat from Nommos' generators could reach this awful place. He had the eerie sensation, with the crouching, pygmylike, half-naked savage ahead of him, of having blundered into some old movie or novel. Ahead of them might lay the imprisoned Sydney Carton or the Count of Monte Cristo, even d'Artagnan. Awaiting rescue in a cold prison might be O. Henry, weaving his ironic tales to while away a jail term; or the youthful Adolf Hitler, spewing hatred in *Mein Kamp*.

But Ruben came to a complete halt when he saw what *actually* awaited them: Standing in the corridor leading left, to the portion of Sinoway's labs Ruben had seen before, were the professor's powerful guards. The door leading to Julie Lyle and Dhombola was behind them; clearly, they said, you must get through us to get to them.

Pigo paid no attention! While Ruben, just beyond the curve in the tunnel, had remained unseen, the tiny Australoid headed *directly toward* them! Great Scott, Ruben mused in anguish, did he think he'd had immortality conveyed on him through hypnosis?

He couldn't stay there and do nothing. Casting his eyes about, Martin saw a chance of pressing against the distant wall and, in the near darkness, circle around behind the bullyboys. They would, if he knew pyschology at all, be busy gaping at the incredible and defiant figure of little Pigo!

Ruben crept forward, his body shoved against the wall. He watched the first of the guards step forward a curious foot and lift a broad palm.

"What the hell do you want?" the man asked Pigo. "Who *are* you, anyway?"

Pigo didn't answer. He also didn't stop. He went on covering great chunks of distance in his unveering, steady pace even as Ruben edged closer to the men, unseen.

When Pigo dropped to one knee and brought the *kundela* to an aiming position, the second bodyguard reached into his lab jacket pocket and produced a chunky revolver. "Just hold it right there, Sitting Bull!" he cried hoarsely.

But Pigo began to chant: "You *die,* you *die,* you *die,*" over and over. He was absolutely immobile in the center of the ill-lit corridor, utterly sure of himself.

Before Ruben could get there the first shot rang out. Martin lifted the walking stick high above his head and jumped toward them, flailing with the improvised weapon and feeling it collide, hard, with the skull of the larger guard. To Ruben's astonishment and delight, the man went down like a shot.

"Hold it right there!" the other guard exclaimed, leveling the revolver at Ruben's head, inches away. There was no doubt in Ruben's mind that he would pull the trigger with the slightest provocation.

That provocation was provided by Pigo, who had been nicked in one arm by the first bullet and now vaulted directly before the armed man. Clearly, he was surprised that they hadn't both dropped dead from his *pointing* and, just as clearly, he still expected the armed man to do so. *"You die,"* he cried, then as loud as he could "YOU DIE!"

The gun went off just as Ruben hit the man in the side of the neck with his walking stick. He saw little Pigo recoil, driven back several feet where he collapsed to the ground; but he was too busy to go to the Australoid. The thug was getting to his feet, looking around for the revolver he'd dropped.

Ruben didn't wait. He used the pointed end of the stick, jabbing *up* from the floor, catching the guard flush on the point of his broad jaw. When the man toppled, Ruben paused with exquisite thoughtfulness and then methodically hit him another five times on the top of the head. He stopped when the stick broke.

Panting, perspiring, and terrified by his release of fury, Martin ran to the Australoid's side and knelt.

Pigo made no sound of pain despite the fact that the bullet had gone clear through his left thigh and he lay, now, in a gathering pool of blood. What was *really* disturbing him, Pigo's expression clearly informed Martin, was why the lethal death-pointing had failed him. He seemed mystified, probably in part by the weapon that had been used on him. Undoubtedly, he'd never seen white man's military might any more than he'd seen his magic before.

Martin ripped his shirt off and tore it into long strips, then bandaged Pigo's leg as well as possible. "Wait here," he whispered. "We'll be back for you."

"Vere dangerous, doctor-man," Pigo observed, his impossibly pretty eyes beseeching Ruben from the ugly, leatherlike face. "Be careful. But—get boy out!"

"I will." Ruben stood, then looked down again in afterthought. "You were very brave, Pigo," he said, man to man.

Pigo simply looked more surprised. "Not know 'brave' word," he said. "Just what right or wrong."

I'll have to make note of that one, Ruben thought appreciatively, turning back to the waiting door.

At the last second he paused. Morley Sinoway was mad but he was also incredibly clever. It would be true to his type to let Ruben think he'd gone with Julie and Dhombola to the lab room Ruben had already seen. A trap might well await him there. Instead of entering the door to the left, therefore, Martin approached the one to the right—the one he hadn't seen before, which Sinoway labeled "Storage," and cautiously pushed it open.

Pitch dark. An ominous, end-of-the-world kind of pitch darkness, enveloping and somehow felt by the skin itself.

A match would make him a better target than regular illumination, Ruben decided, and felt around the doorframe until he was able to snap a lightswitch on.

There were no pterodactyls here.

But there were cages, cages of many sizes, some covered with white dropcloths and some not. The ones that were not drew Ruben's eyes first, and almost took from him the courage to face a man as evil and inhumane as Professor Morley Sinoway.

When he was able to, with difficulty, Ruben read the explanatory legends neatly typed and affixed to each cage. One indicated that the "Subject" had been given heavy quantities of protein fed directly into the brain to aid the cells to counter the aging process. The University of Göteborg was also experimenting with it.

The Subject in case was a woman who might have been sixty, her head and face covered with a thicket of massing hair—hair of a dozen colors, streaming not only from her scalp but the pores of her face. She was, in a manner of speaking, still alive—and caged in her own filth.

At another cage the printed information told Ruben that 2-mercaptoethylamine had been injected in massive amounts, a substance known for years as a possible agent to enhance longevity but without knowing any possible harm it might do. Now Sinoway, and Ruben, knew the harm. A girl in her late teens, who might once have been fresh-faced and lovely, had had the reaction of her fatty tissues growing and multiplying. Comatose, she was unable to push herself up from the floor of the cage because of the incredible weight of her gigantic breasts and hips. The rest of the girl might have weighed ninety pounds; the attached chart showed that she weighed 339 pounds.

Ruben staggered to the next uncovered cage, this one in a dimly lit corner, and almost retched. He learned from the label on the cage that it was Sinoway's stepfather, old Harry Pfeiff. He wouldn't have known by looking at the man.

Harry's age had been decreased, all right. Once aged, senile, he was now—at a quick glimpse of the face—a man of thirty-one, thirty-two. Harry's back had been to Martin as he read one of a dozen books scattered on the littered floor of the cage, so engrossed in his study that he did not notice Ruben. The parapsychologist crept around to confront him and then could only gape.

Harry's skin was utterly, terribly translucent. It was possible to see the red blood move weirdly beneath the skin, almost to count the corpuscles. Ruben guessed that the fellow might burn beneath the direct light from a 60-watt bulb. Worse, far worse, was the unbelievable fat bulge at the forefront of old Harry's specially constructed trousers: They dragged on the floor, spread like a raised tree trunk for several feet in circumference. Harry's reaction to his treatment had been a form of elephantiasis affecting the penis and testicles.

It seemed unlikely, to Ruben, that Harry could rise either. And from the passionate way he studied the advanced nuclear physics book clutched in his tissue-thin hands, it was likely that Harry's mentality had entered a refined realm of intelligence, which removed him from the social norm just as senility—at the opposite polarity—had done.

Ruben lifted and looked beneath one cloth only.

A dead infant swam in formaldehyde, with tubes extruding from its pea-like head. When Martin saw that the other, covered cages were of a similar size, he put a hand over his mouth and turned to run—run past a cryogenic freezing compartment in which *things* shine, things that might have once contained the throb of life —ran past several exact duplications of *items* nobody normal would *want* duplicated or cloned—ran past hirsute animal hybrids, prickly plants that breathed, bloated human organs that pumped blood along with silent pain.

In the chamber beyond the lab room Ruben paused, stifling the urge to vomit—"Storage," Sinoway had said about the place—breathing deeply of stale air that tasted marvelous in his lungs after exposure to scientific hell. What Sinoway did was spread cancer, surely; he was a man who played "Can you top this?" in ways to die hideously. Clearly, Ruben hadn't adequately gauged Morley Sinoway's insanity—or his fervent intention to play God.

No. *No,* Ruben said, shaking his head; it was *not* God whom Sinoway was imitating. *Never.*

His jaw set, willing now to do anything whatever to halt the professor, Martin headed directly into the laboratory leading to the left. Because the light here was dazzlingly bright after the dark corridor, and ill-lit alternate lab, Ruben blinked against it, focusing his eyes and thinking, suddenly, that he had *again* almost realized the *nature of the Alouqua*—that he had *again,* unconsciously verged on identifying the creature.

Then he could see properly and forgot about Alouqua.

Julie Sarah Lyle and Dhombola were strapped to examining tables, unable to move a muscle. Ruben saw their eyes strain to see his entrance; he could *sense* the instant welling up of hope, of priceless belief that he could somehow save them. Julie's lips framed his name.

Between the two tables, Professor Sinoway stood in

waiting, brilliant light glinting off his bald head. His bushy brows were curved in a frown of absolute hatred but his yellowish teeth were revealed in a broad, absurdly confident and quite ghastly smile of greeting.

"You are tardy, Doctor Ruben, hm-m?" he said in his rolling, cultivated baritone. "I honestly expected a man of your intelligence—the shrewd, canny, desperate intelligence of your despised race—to get past two dimwits such as my guards in much better time than this."

Ruben, remembering the approach of tiny Pigo to the bodyguards, had not stopped walking directly toward Sinoway. "I won't waste words with such a lunatic killer," he said offhandedly. "I've come for my friends and we're leaving this fiendish island within the hour."

"One moment, sir!"

The cry was so ultimately autocratic and commanding, so much like the you'd-never-dare-to-cross-me orders of potent professors in Ruben's youth, that he stopped—just for a moment.

With a sinuous hiss, the great, sharp scalpels rose from their concealment like miniature missiles from an atomic silo, then poised, glistening directly above Dhombola and Julie Lyle.

Dhombola, to Martin's left, tried to shrink away from the piercing point, his eyes shut tightly. If the machine arm holding the scalpel descended without correction, it would describe an arc in his temple or forehead. To Ruben's right, Julie simply opened her lips helplessly to gasp as the metallic arm hovered, its razor-sharp scalpel over the slight swelling of her abdomen.

"Now, Doctor, I think you will find this, hm-m, a pretty puzzle." Sinoway was at his most peremptory, his most unbalanced, and a nerve throbbed perilously beside a bushy brow. "I enjoy telling the truth when it serves me so richly as this and I always, hm-m, gather all the facts before taking action. Consider: While you are obliged to watch, I am *definitely going to begin* my experimentation on one of these two people." His large hand gripped the control to the machine, a single thumb raised above one of two shiny buttons. "Everything is quite well-time, calibrated, Ruben. And I know my machinery like my face. Before you can get to me, or to either of my guinea pigs, I will have squeezed *one* button and begun the doom of the individual. I might remark that I am quite strong and it is not impossible that I will defeat you and, hm-m, squeeze the other button as well!"

Ruben's eyes darted from one helpless friend to the other. "If I leave, will you call it off—if I agree to be cooperative from here on out?"

"Good heavens, *no!*" the older man exclaimed with amusement. "If you leave, why I shall simply proceed with my plans as they were originally conceived."

Ruben couldn't remember when he'd ever felt so tired or helpless. "Then what, precisely *is* it you are offering me?" he asked in exasperation. "I can't see that you're doing any real negotiating at all!"

"Negotiating?" Sinoway roared, lips parted in astonished amusement. "I'm merely being *sporting* about this, Ruben, nothing more."

"You don't know the meaning of the word," Martin snarled, taking a step forward.

Sinoway held up the device in his hand. "Careful!" he warned. "Well, I confess that I am primarily curious about your opinion in the matter. You're absurdly slow on occasion, Ruben. I'm not offering you, hm-m, a chance to save them both. I'm telling you that I *shall kill* one of these two, that nothing you can do will stop me, and that I certainly shall try to kill *you* when you charge me. But here is where the sporting element enters the picture." His flat brown eyes shone. "It is conceivable that you *will* stop a second death by overpowering me. No matter, since you don't have the stomach for murdering me and an hour later I'll have you properly caged for, hm-m, further work."

"Then—"

"Don't you *see* it? It's so *beautiful!* I'm allowing you to make—the *choice:* My faithless little playmate, Doctor Julie Lyle, or this representative of a, hm-m, second-rate race. Is the romantic or sexual drive stronger than the urge to paternalism?" He raised the control button aloft, beaming. "We shall find out! Which will it be who dies, sir? Do I punish the woman for turning to you, an outsider with whom she did not share the same compatibility—or the boy?"

"You can't be serious," Ruben whispered, horrified.

"But I am!" Sinoway assured him, impatient for his entertainment now. "Come, sir, come! The choice is *yours*. Which one lives . . . and which one dies?"

Twenty-five

"Are you, at all, *human?*" Ruben asked in a quiet voice, consciously stalling now.

"Once, perhaps, before I knew I was to die," the professor replied, "but no longer. A man cannot live for an extended amount of time on the brink of a hereafter, hm-m, in which he has little confidence, without being, ah-m, modified. I am somewhat better than merely human now, Ruben. With all the time in the world before me, I am enabled to suspend the time-wasting considerations of emotion, compassion, and the like."

"There is no guarantee of your literal immortality, Sinoway," Martin responded. He wanted to be informative without being unpleasant enough to make the man push a button. "For one thing, when any of us *leaves* here, it may be similar to the climax of Hilton's *Lost Horizon.* We may immediately recollect all the time we've shed, or worse. And for another, although you cannot grow ill, there's no way you can be sure to avoid accidents. *Any* might kill you."

The professor smiled coldly. A single heavy brow lifted. "Your first point is ludicrous. It suggests how desperately you stall your decision."

"*Why* is it ludicrous?" Martin asked, sounding intellectually piqued.

"Because I never intend to leave Nommos Island or the regimen Ms. Solomon conceived. Why *should* I depart? I have, hm, everything I require here."

"My second point, then," Ruben grasped at straws. "You're made of flesh and blood. An attack by another person, by an animal from the woods—a serious fall, an accident through your machinery . . . who knows?"

Sinoway sighed, idly picked at a tooth. "You're tiresome, Ruben. What 'might' happen does *not* happen to a man who orders his own affairs, who plans properly."

"Ah! You can't answer me, can you?" cried Martin, his glee artificial and tantalizing. "You *know* you might be injured!"

"The *choice*, Martin Ruben!" He'd gone too far. Again the hand, the device—in the air. Sinoway lost the remnant of mad amusement. "I want your selection *now* or I shall make it for you!"

Before Ruben could think of how to respond, his heart thumping frantically, he was startled to see a change coming over the professor's face.

It began as a faint parting of the fleshy lips, moved to a staring of the dead brown eyes, finally included the entire face in an expression of consternation—and, Ruben saw, more.

Much more.

By the time Ruben was slowly, fearfully turning, he already knew that *the Alouqua had entered the laboratory*.

Then she brushed past him, mere feet away, and he could not see her face or eyes. Instead he was left to stare at the long, graceful line of her bare back, the nipped-in tiny waist, the swelling, pearlike hips. Her silken, silver hair switched almost like a creature's tail below the split of her buttocks. Even from behind, her extraordinarily long legs were the most gorgeous he had ever seen and, just at this swift glance, he yearned to lie between them. She was tall, at least as tall as Ingrid Solomon had been; she was Ruben's version of the perfect woman.

Little Dhombola, too young to be absorbed by the creature, seemed hypnotized instead. In his blank face Ruben saw the boy had forgotten the dangers of Sinoway, even of the mechanized sharp scalpel inches from his head.

Julie Lyle was locked in some bizarre tussle for control of her emotions. The Alouqua was passing her now, headed toward Sinoway; Julie's auburn head was thrown from side to side, as if her mind was saying "No" while her body shrieked "Yes!" Perspiration stood out on her forehead and, as she licked her lips, Ruben realized that Julie, too, had forgotten her other hazards. *Does* she see the succubus as *I* see her, Martin wondered, making himself think—or does she see, instead, the wonder man of her dreams? Or is the Alouqua's ancient magic, her palpable magnetism, so great it can arouse lesbian urges in a normal woman?

It was clear what Morley Sinoway saw, Martin realized. Looking at him, Martin knew Sinoway saw *his* version of the perfect woman. His eyes glinted strangely; his mouth worked hungrily.

But *no*, this wouldn't be quite the same as his own ideal, Ruben thought. He knew men well enough to know that each of his kind had his own unique preferences—a dimpled buttock, an inward bowing of the knee, nipples that were either smaller or larger— the range of perfection virtually as great as the number of men alive on earth at a given moment.

Yet Sinoway, clearly, had met his penis' desire.

Ruben realized then that Dhombola had seen her as small because, even without an adult male's capacity for lust, his simple, childish fantasies would quite naturally yearn for someone closer to *his* own size.

Which meant that the Alouqua was not what she seemed to be, Ruben decided wildly, daring to push himself away from the table and stare at her still-retreating, curvaceous back—*So what the bloody hell was she?*

Sinoway had shown a loss of emotional control only once, in Martin's company—when he wept with joy over the news that he would live. Anyone would do that. It was the only human quality Martin had ever seen in the man. Now he saw more, more emotions—with enormous distaste.

The Alouqua was within a foot or two of Morley Sinoway, her hips undulating more deliciously, more enticingly, than any millionaire go-go girl—and, although Ruben could not see her from in front, Sinoway could. Martin yearned despite himself, but *made* himself think: Since Sinoway saw a *different* beautiful woman, this was doubtless the way the monster made sure that others in a room waited until she was through with her *first* victim.

She was diabolical; she remembered to mesmerize the others, entrap them. So why did he care so much that she had chosen Sinoway first, instead of him. Panting, Ruben fought back a burst of insane jealousy, ran a sweating hand over his dripping face.

Sinoway tore out of his clothing, ripping it asunder in a completely mad urge to mate with this creature of anger, hatred, frustration, and longing—this mutable monster of man's darkest fears, beliefs, and needs. Man's *and* woman's: From the corner of his eye Martin could see Julie moistening her lips hungrily, her hips starting to writhe.

The professor was single-minded as always. Forgotten was his devilish career, all that he had worked and tortured and murdered to get; forgotten was the device controlling the mechanized scalpels, which he now dropped numbly to the floor. Forgotten was everything in the world except the need to experience—*now!*—the most fabulous sexual encounter of this life. His penis was engorged with blood, purpling, almost elephantine with rarefied desire as he wobbled like a man toting a flag toward the creature, his eager arms outstretched.

She came into his arms then and, for a moment, all Ruben could see was the spreading cover of her wonderful sleek hair.

Then the two of them—fantasy with mortal needs; mortal with everyman's fantasy—sank to the floor of the laboratory in frenetic copulation.

Ruben blinked. He had to shake his own head frantically to clear it, and to seize the opportunity for which he had waited. Unbuckling Dhombola and Julie from the examining tables, he had to shove them to seated positions, then put his palms on Julie's cheeks and quite literally *turn* her face from the scene on the floor. Sinoway's noises were animal-like—ragged surges of gasped energy, sudden chortles, agonized groans, and enraptured sighs. When Julie again tried to look back, Ruben threw her over his shoulder and, tugging at the boy's brown hand, made for the door.

The bloodcurdling scream behind them made even Ruben turn.

Professor Morley Sinoway, bleeding gouts of fleshy gore from his genitals, was staggering to his bare feet, in immense pain but so suffused with other feelings that little but beginning shame, or revulsion, showed on his face. The man's eyes, Martin saw, had moved over the brink; they were hopelessly insane. Ruben turned, shouting. "Get her out of here!" he told Dhombola, setting the awestruck Julie Lyle on her feet. *"Drag her away,* if you have to! Move!" The boy obeyed; in a second Ruben saw them disappear through the entranceway.

Sinoway was tottering toward his desk, shuffling like an old man looking with aimless determination for his favorite pipe. Ruben saw with disgust that the professor's hard body was coated with dirt, a grayish-brown, filthy, moldlike. Even his pursed lips dribbled globules of dirt and blood, mingling with saliva for a dark stain. "Hm-m?" he asked absently, of nobody in particular, then pawed with spastic hands through things on his desk. Papers fell off. Then, laughing briefly, "Hm-mm!"

The scalpel he'd located wasn't hooked to a machine. Sinoway seized it happily and, in one fiercely direct, wholly mad whip motion of plunging briskness, Sinoway drew it across his throat, from left to right. Blood was prompt; geyser-like. He had driven the scalpel in so deeply that, before his body slumped segmentially to the floor in death, it seemed for an instant that his head would surely topple away from the main trunk of his body.

But as horrible as Sinoway's death was, it was the Alouqua that captured Martin's attention then.

Stunningly.

For he had seen her face, at last, and become immediately faint with consuming heat.

Comparing this face to a dozen motion picture stars or models would not suffice. In a way it was like she had, in shimmering and magical alteration, the face of *every* beautiful woman who'd lived. Certainly they were the glorious features of every woman Martin had ever, seriously, craved.

But about her face it was actually the personal confrontation and near-bludgeoning, eager lust that threatened to leave his mind in shock. Something in the indescribably beautiful features seemed to pledge to Martin: "*You* were the one I sought, all along; only you. *You* are the one who shall make me forget the others, set me free. Just by *touching* me, Martin, they do not exist anymore; they *never* existed; I am new, *for you*—for *no other*." And even that wasn't the end of her potent message as she approached him.

But there were no words possible for the rest of what Alouqua projected then to Martin. No words have ever been sufficiently salacious or wanting, adequately descriptive of the all-giving lust that beckoned from her lovely, strange eyes. She seemed to promise with the sacred honor of a god from the Valley of the Kings or from an Olympus an experience that would be timeless, beginningless, endless, a sexual encounter of which *only* gods were even capable—and she alone could, *would*, make Martin a god too. She seemed to swear with little-girl sadness and some incredible innocence, I cannot *function*—I cannot *live a second more*—without *yours* in me; *you* of all men in history will bring me genuinely alive, will fulfill my every internal hope, will make me your willing, obedient sexual slave whose only task *throughout eternity* to make *you,* Martin Ruben, as delectably, satisfyingly *MAN* as I shall be WOMAN for you. Yes, yes; she knew his name, his every feeling, every nuance of desire, and precisely what he wanted and how to deliver it.

She was only a foot or two away when he even remembered to stare down at her body. *That* was the Alouqua's facial beauty, the magic of her always-eyes.

But when Martin *did* look down, he saw that he was almost gone now, that he was beyond recall, or human redemption. Her throat was melody, her wide shoulders a song. Her breasts lifted at the tops in rising, creamy mounds, swelled to thrusting pneumatic torpedoes nearly touching and firing his chest even from this distance, the nipples—*how could this be; I'm already mad!*—first tiny brown dots high in the centers of mouthwatering flesh and then more massive than bottle bottoms, Playboy-pink and hardening just because he looked at them. Despite his iron resolve, he felt his electrified fingertips rising toward those breasts. She had nearly no waist at all; the navel was a sweet dwarf star deep in a universe of concave yieldingness; her lower belly was soft, perfectly rounded, and gave way to a sumptuous thicket of short, almost prepubescent silver hair that bristled warlike, magnificently, curling for him, even while its width and depth covered an impossible triangle of her lowest woman's body and left its magical center a secret. Below, the long legs were generous as Ruben liked them, almost heavy in the thighs; the knees were lineless and small; the calves curved glisteningly down into almost invisible, small ankles and tiny feet Martin saw instantly as adorable.

Viewing Alouqua's body was, in a way, like staring through the finest telescope of the thirtieth century and spying on a magic world of countless, rich surprises of life finally having fulfilled its promise; for the Alouqua also managed to convey somehow the impression that he was seeing something he *shouldn't* be seeing, that he was being given carte blanche in the fantasy of a women's locker room or ballerina's dressing room, or any of the other, unreachably *secret* places known until now to the opposite sex alone. He was allowed—no, *encouraged!*—to become a voyeur; he was given license to rape, and be loved for it.

Ruben's dumbfounded, sweeping gaze reversed its direction and when his eyes locked at last with hers, he found them absolutely magnetic: They gripped his innermost being, and would not let go. They said, *Now we are one; now,* Martin, we shall *be* one.

For *your always.*

No!—Ruben moaned deep inside, battling even as his twitching, perspiring fingers groped for his belt, for eventual release—*no-o-o!*

Yes . . . the siren voice cooed, inside him; but he knew it was not his own voice, it was the soul of complete femininity moving in, a teasing, wise, yearning, childlike, mature or maternal, yielding, giving/taking syrup of liquid fire that rolled turbulently in his soul, squeezing, making it hunger starvingly for every sybaritic, sibilant, succulent nuance: *Yes-s-s-s* . . .*s* . . .

At that moment *something happened* to Martin that he would never forget or even *want* to forget—except in those elongated and weary hours of the reminiscent midnight when one longed for that which one had relinquished. It was what Martin had *almost* remembered and realized, about the Alouqua, several times—what he had *nearly* come to, on his own. But now the words were clear as crystal in his ears and he never knew if they actually occurred to him on his own or if, as it seemed, they were *spoken* to him by someone no longer on, or of, the planet Earth.

It was what Ruben had heard so long ago, locked in conversation with his dear, late friend Jacques Coquelion: A human being's cells divide some fifty times during his lifespan. And the *only* cells with the capacity to double indefinitely by division, if kept in a proper culture—

Ruben threw up his hands in horror, and *struck* the

Alouqua, knocked her back several feet—and then looked at his hands, revolted even by that touch: *The only such cells were cancer cells. And this monster— this ineffably gorgeous, ideally sensual, magnificent female giantess of desire, of the richest carnal promise he knew he would ever encounter in his life—oh God! the Alouqua was composed entirely of cancer cells!*

In a way, he supposed as he turned, tried to run, she —perhaps *all* evil spirits and demons—was like a *reversal* of death, the negative to life's brightly shining light—the curse of eternal blackness in contrast to the color pictures, the glorious Cinemascope of sun-kissed, God-blessed *living*.

He went down hard, tripping over the dead Sinoway's naked foot.

And his own ankle pinned beneath him, pain scalding his leg. Ruben groaned in agony and tried to sit up.

If the Alouqua had been perfectly *willing* to see humans take their lives before, in tribute to her female glory, she was *eager* for it now, a woman-thing scorned. Or perhaps, Ruben wondered, she'd simply find the supernatural strength now to do the job herself. He shrank away from her loathesome touch as she again filled him with incredible desire. Stooping toward him, her breasts swung deliciously, almost edibly; *I know what fruits Eve offered Adam,* Ruben thought inanely. Her lips were parted, looking down at him; they seemed to cry, *I'll love you to death, Martin dearest!*

But now the monster's actuality was hopelessly marred for him. He was unable to rise and get away, but, as he caught a glimpse of her emerald eyes, he also saw her face fade sharply—give way, disconcertingly and frighteningly before his knowledge—to reveal dimly some . . . *other* . . . face that no man or woman had ever been permitted to see. Or, if they had, they'd not lived to speak of it.

And in that fleeting instant his stomach was rocked by the glimpse of an evil, corrupt ugliness that surely seeped and crawled in excretion from the filthier compartments of Hell. Surely nothing *real* could live, with such a secret face of despicable and lunatic foulness.

He moaned, shrank away, as she reached out for him with fingers-become-claws—

And he saw her stop, frozen, to peer toward the door *behind* him.

Was it Julie, or Dhombola, come to save him? They couldn't, Martin knew *they couldn't possibly!* He strove to turn to the door, but could not.

Alouqua left him entirely, now, left him discarded; she stepped over his aching body as if he did not exist.

Ruben twisted painfully, threw himself flat on his side to stare at the door.

It was tiny Pigo, the Australoid, dragging himself into the room, blood soaking through the rude bandage on his thigh, struggling somehow to get to one knee. In his hand, Ruben saw with dismay, he still gripped the ludicrous *kundela* bone that he had uselessly "shot" at Sinoway's men. Ruben groaned, despairing; the brave little fool would be destroyed along with him, to no good purpose whatever.

She began walking deliberately, toward Pigo; she was unhurried; she knew her power. As she left him, Ruben realized it had been like proximity to an exploding furnace. Instantly it became thirty degrees cooler; his teeth even chattered. He gaped. The Alouqua was near Pigo, now, and Ruben sought to gather his legs beneath him to leap at her.

He absolutely could not; his ankle wouldn't permit it. He was left, helpless, to stare at Pigo's demise.

What, he wondered with dull curiosity, was miniature

Pigo's heart's desire in a woman? What was she like for the Australoid, to the tiny fellow with the soft, feminine eyes?

Pigo had himself firmly positioned on a knee, the *kundela* bone aimed just as he wished it to be. As Martin looked at him, he seemed entirely prepossessed; controlled. Calm, even unbothered. What fantastic will power was Pigo *using* to withstand the Alouqua's power?

Her arms were already reaching out now, aching to enfold the small figure before her, then return to Ruben; *still* Pigo did not flinch, even appear to crave her delectable form.

Instead, a chant began; murmurous, keening, persuasive. It was what Ruben had heard before in the outer corridors of this place, a statement (to *whom?* his gods?) to the effect that She was evil and Unwelcome; that Others wished her Dead, All of them, that She *should be* Dead, and that She *would Die* when he finished his chant and fired the tribal, mystic missile into her outer softness.

Ruben blinked. Alouqua did hesitate, then; just for a moment. As if disconcerted by the reception she was getting.

But then she suddenly groped beneath the little fellow's waist, undoing his loincloth. Her hot breasts were lowered against his head, resting there. Now, Ruben saw as her fingers worked on Pigo, she did seem . . . *confused*. And then Martin was certain about it; she *was* confused! With her back to Ruben, he could not see why.

Stoically, despite the intimacy, Pigo finished his ancient chant. *"You die!"* he shouted, a businesslike proclamation, his voice high and shrill as he altered the message. "You *die! YOU DIE!*"

And at that instant the Alouqua yanked away Pigo's loincloth completely, her own cancer-laden body moving a step back with her yank, and Ruben understood with a sickening surge of reality *why* Pigo had not responded to the demon:

The little Australoid clearly had been convicted by his tribe of *not being a man! He was a hermaphrodite—half-male, half female*.

In certain tribes, he might have been a god. But in Pigo's it had been unpopular, too much; and it was too much for the Alouqua now. She could never reach him with her immortal, fertile magic; she could be one or the other, not both; she was only an historical, evil sex object, and there simply *could be no such thing*, not for poor, impotent little Pigo.

But—as Ruben stared in amazement—Pigo's own magic proved potent, indeed. The following events were so swift it was difficult to follow them, like one of Martin's dreamlike premonitions of old coming to bizarre, ghastly life.

As though a genuine explosion had fired from the *kundela*, Alouqua's deadly body was propelled, tumbling head over heels through the laboratory, caught seemingly by some gusting great wind—the wind, perhaps, said to sweep true, and clean. Ruben, tugged to a seated position on the floor, stared as sharply as he could; and, with her body spinning round and round, he observed flitting visions of possibly a *dozen* other women and a *dozen* impossibly handsome men flickering on her mutable face. Martin's own idealized woman had been swept away and was no more.

The plummeting, hurricane-swept form struck the cages at the far wall of the vast laboratory room and, to Ruben's awestruck horror, he saw another dark miracle of All-Time beckoned to action. Professor Sinoway's animal clones had been released by the force of Alouqua's body. A bearlike entity emerged, shuffling threateningly forward a few feet, then found the oxygen of the lab insupportable and fell writhing to the ground. A huge lizard with speedy, darting tongue crawled clammily, eerily on the floor, and stopped. A monstrous serpent with scales like tank treads scarcely advanced from its cage.

Finally Sinoway's masterpiece of history's long-lost early seconds appeared, spreading its massive wings and beginning to rise, ominously, from the modern lab floor. The pterodactyl seemed aroused to ire, maddened by intrustion; its shrewd eyes blazed with hatred of this new world that dared beckon it from sleep. Its great talons, which Martin had feared might rend him asunder, locked like meathooks into the cancerous flesh of the Alouqua. Lifting like a great plane slowly becoming airborne, the clone issued a screaming, cackling call of defiant outrage from its fierce beak and its evil gaze focused then on Martin Ruben.

It was coming for him! Desperate, Martin hurled himself back to the floor as the pterodactyl's great wingspread seemed to fill the room, its infernal call rattling Martin's eardrums. The screeching was hideous as it cut the air in mighty swaths, soaring almost languidly around the lab but seeking escape, and ready to kill anything to have it.

Finally it discovered the wide picture window across the way and, its sound of joy almost human in its triumph, swept toward it. Ruben peeped between the fingers pressing against his face in terror and saw the immense bird—that furious harridan of Hell still squirming in its talons—crash thunderously through the window as if it did not exist. Glass, shattering, flew everywhere; it narrowly missed Ruben.

He opened his eyes. Somehow Julie and Dhombola were beside him, stooped in concern. Numbly Martin realized they'd returned at the sound of the breaking window and the cries of the great bird of antiquity. Hobbled, helped between them but realizing slowly that they might survive this nightmare, he allowed himself to be led toward the vastness of night revealed by the pterodactyl's exit.

For a moment the three of them could see nothing but winking stars.

Then—*"Look, Docruben!"*—and the little boy was pointing with excitement.

Through the splintered frame of the wide window they could just make out the incredible, distant bird of yore rising higher into the ebon sky, its huge wings beating the air—and *something* still held, and gored, by its enormous talons. There was a final, trailing-away screech of mindless fury and then both were gone from sight.

And Ruben, glancing over at Pigo, who had fainted from loss of blood, understood. At last. When he looked down at the smiling Dhombola, he saw that the African child understood as well.

A creature of flesh and blood cannot be killed by a primitive bone unless it has tasted the isolated wonderment of the lonely tribesman. But another kind of creature, devised and revivified by the hatred and fear, the longings and passions of man's frustrated sojourn on the planet, is *itself* a creature of infinite magic and lurking shadows. The Alouqua *knew* it could be halted, even slain, by the sacred powers of a belief nearly as ancient as itself had been.

Julie Lyle tugged gently at his sleeve and Martin, realizing how much he hurt all over, looked down at the small redhead. Her trembling finger was pointed at the depthless skies.

"Where will they *go?*" she asked, her whispered tone redolent of awe. "Martin, what will they do *next?*"

He hugged her, as well as the boy, against him and mustered a weary smile. "Somewhere that they can be . . . accepted," he replied softly. "Where fear of stygian nightmares of the earth and respect for the sleeping rights of antiquity still exist. If such a place exists on the planet, and hasn't taken, instead, the horrors of manmade weaponry. The modern tools that rend the soul instead of the flesh alone."

"And if they cannot find such a place?" Julie asked wonderingly.

"Why, then, Julie," Martin Ruben said quietly, "they'll do what evil things always do in such circumstances. They'll *wait.*" He paused before finishing, grimly, "With a measure, I think, of wholly justified confidence."

THE TULPA
By J.N. Williamson

PRICE: $1.95   LB799
CATEGORY: Occult

Charlie Kavanagh felt all of his 73 years. He was worried about his aging mind, and his "spells," his dreams—or visions? No one would listen. No one except his son-in-law, who saw things coming, building, promising unheard of horror. Then it came. It rose from within, slowly at first, shuffling through shadows, learning of violence, developing a special hunger. Then it struck—and again. It grew, not quite quenching its thirst on blood and fear. And only one thing could hope to destroy the terrorizing appetite of... THE TULPA!